Adventures of Hans Sterk
The South African Hunter and Pioneer

by

Alfred W. Drayson

Adventures of Hans Sterk
The South African Hunter and Pioneer
by Alfred W. Drayson

Copyright © 2023

All Rights reserved.

ISBN: 978-93-59954-72-1

Published by

DOUBLE 9 BOOKS

2/13-B, Ansari Road
Daryaganj, New Delhi – 110002
info@double9books.com
www.double9books.com
Tel. 011-40042856

ABOUT THE AUTHOR

Ernest Wilks Drayson, also known as Wilkes, was an English army officer, author, and astronomer who lived from 1827 to 1901. His friend Arthur Conan Doyle gave the collection of short stories called "The Captain of the Polestar" to him as a gift. He was born on April 17, 1827, into a big family. His father, William Drayson, worked at the Royal Gunpowder Factory and was Clerk of the Works there in 1832. His mother, Ann Marie, was also a worker there. He was younger brother of author Caroline Agnes Drayson and brother-in-law of author John Richardson, who married the second daughter, Maria Caroline. He was born at Waltham Abbey, which was also where the factory was based. Louisa Burdon Ellis was another sister who married Samuel Burdon Ellis and had a child with him. Helen Matilda, the fourth daughter who lived, married Charles Davies in 1848. Emily (1811-1894), who married Woolwich Dockyard worker William Woods (died 1856), was another sister. Laurette, who was born in 1819, was another sister. The family home had been in Chatham since 1835, when William Drayson retired. When Ann Marie died in 1837, the family home fell apart. Alfred Drayson went to Rochester Grammar School from the time he was 11 years old for two years. After a bout of scarlet fever, he was kicked out and sent to stay with his older brother, a civil engineer, to recover.

CONTENTS

CONTENTS

Chapter Twenty Seven

Preface

In the history of colonisation there is probably no example on record so extraordinary as that of the emigration from the colony of the Cape of Good Hope, in 1835, of nearly six thousand souls, who, without guides or any definite knowledge of where they were going or what obstacles they would encounter, yet placed their all in the lottery and journeyed into the wilderness.

The cause of this emigration was to avoid what the emigrants considered the oppression of the ruling Government, and the object was to found an independent nationality in the interior of Africa.

These emigrants, shortly after quitting the neighbourhood of the Cape colony, were attacked by the chief of a powerful tribe called the Matabili, into whose country they had trespassed. Severe battles, in which overwhelming numbers were brought against them, were fought by the emigrants, the general results being victory to the white man.

Not satisfied with the situation which these victories might have enabled them to secure, a party of the emigrants journeyed on towards the east, in order to obtain a better position near the present district of Natal. This party were shortly afterwards either treacherously massacred by a Zulu chief named Dingaan, or were compelled to fight for their lives and property during many months.

It is mainly amidst these scenes that the hero of the following tale passed—scenes which brought out many cases of individual courage, daring, and perseverance rarely equalled in any part of the world.

Around the bivouac fire, or in the ride over the far-spreading plains, or whilst resting after a successful hunting track in the tangled forest, the principal events of this tale have been recorded. From Zulu and Boer, English emigrant and Hottentot driver, we have had various accounts, each varying according to the peculiar views of the relater, but all agreeing as regards the main facts here blended and interwoven into a tale.

Chapter One
Introduction to the Hunters—
Death of the Lion—Discovery of
the Elephants by Hans Sterk

Near the outskirts of a far-extending African forest, and close beside some deep shady-pools, the only remnants of a once rapidly flowing river, were seen one glowing summer's evening, shortly after sunset, a party of some ten men; bronzed workmen-like fellows they were too, their dress and equipment proclaiming them hunters of the first class. This party were reclining on the turf, smoking, or giving the finishing touch to their rifles and smooth-bore guns, which they had been engaged in cleaning. Among this party there were two black men, fine, stalwart-looking fellows, whose calm demeanour and bright steady gazing eyes, proclaimed them men of nerve and energy. One tiny yellow man, a Hottentot, was remarkable among the group on account of his smallness, as he stood scarcely more than five feet in height, whereas all his companions were tall heavy men. A fire was brightly blazing, and several small tin vessels on this fire were steaming as their contents hissed and bubbled. The white men who composed this party were Dutch South African Boers, who were making an excursion into the favourite feeding-grounds of the Elephant, in order to supply themselves with ivory, this valuable commodity being to them a source of considerable wealth.

"It will soon be very dark," exclaimed Bernhard, one of the Boers, "and Hans will have difficulty in finding our lager; I will go on to the headland and shoot."

"You may leave Sterk to take care of himself," said Heinrich, another Boer, "for no man is less likely to lose himself than he is."

"I will go and shoot at all events," said Bernhard, "for it can do no harm; and though Hans is quick and keen, watchful and careful, he may for once be overtaken by a fog or the darkness, and he does not well know this country."

With this excuse for his proceeding, the man called Bernhard grasped his large-bored gun, and ascended a krantz which overhung the resting-place of his party, when, having reached the summit, he placed the muzzle of his gun within a foot of the ground, and fired both barrels in quick succession. This is a common signal amongst African hunters, it being understood to mean, that the resting-place at night is where the double shot is fired from.

There being no reply to this double shot, Bernhard returned to his companions, and the whole party then commenced their evening meal.

"So your sweetheart did not reply to you, Bernhard," said one of the Boers, "though you did speak so loudly."

"Hans Sterk is my sworn friend, good and true," replied Bernhard; "and no man speaks lightly of him before me."

"Quite right, Bernhard, stand to your friends, and they will stand to you; and Hans is a good friend to all, and few of us have not been indebted to him for some good turn or other; but what is Tembili the Kaffir doing?"

At this remark, all eyes were directed towards one of the Kaffir men, who had risen to his feet, and stood grasping his musket and looking eagerly into the forest near, whilst his dark companion was gazing fixedly in the same direction. It was a fine sight to observe this bronzed son of the desert at home and on the watch, for he did seem at home amidst the scenes around him. After a minute's intent watching, he raised his hand, and in a low whisper said, "Leuew, Tao," (the Dutch and Matabili names for a lion). "Leuew!" exclaimed each Boer, as he seized his weapons, which were close at hand and stood ready for an emergency.

"Make up the fire, Piet," said Heinrich: "let us illuminate the visitor." And a mass of dried grass and sticks thrown on the fire caused a brilliant flame, which lighted up the branches and creepers of the ancient forest.

As the flame rose and the sticks crackled, a low grumbling growl came from the underwood in the forest, which at once indicated to the hunters that the Kaffir's instincts had not misled him, but that a lion was crouching in the bush near.

"Fire a shot, Karl," said one of the Dutchmen; "drive him away with fear; we must not let him remain near us." And Karl, aiming among the brushwood, fired. Amidst the noise and echoes of the Boer's musket, a loud savage roar was audible, as the lion, thus disturbed, moved sullenly away from what he had expected would have been a feast; whilst the hunters, hearing him retreat, proceeded without any alarm with their meal, the Kaffirs alone of the party occasionally stopping in their eating to listen, and to watch the neighbouring bush.

The sun had set about three hours, and the moon, a few days past the full, had risen; whilst the Boers, having finished their meal, were rolled up in their sheepskin carosses, and sleeping on the ground as calmly as though they were each in a comfortable bed. The Kaffirs, however, were still quietly but steadily eating, and conversing in a low tone, scarcely above a whisper.

"The lion will not leave us during the night," said the Kaffir called Tembili, "I will not sleep unless you watch, 'Nquane."

"Yes, I will watch whilst you sleep, then you sleep whilst I watch," replied the Kaffir addressed as 'Nquane. "We shall shoot elephants to-morrow, I think; and the young chief must be now close to them, that is why he does not return."

"No: he would return to tell us if he could, I fear he must have lost himself," replied Tembili.

"The 'strong' lose himself," exclaimed 'Nquane, "no, as soon the vulture lose his way in the air, or the springbok on the plains, or the elephant in the forest, as the strong lose himself any where. He sees without eyes and hears without ears. Hark! is that the lion?"

Both Kaffirs listened attentively for some minutes, when 'Nquane said, "It is the lion moving up the krantz: he smells something or hears something; he must have tasted man's flesh, to have stopped here so long close to us. What can he hear now? Ah, there is something up high in the bushes, a buck perhaps, the lion will soon feast on it, and that will be the better for us, as when his belly is full he will not want to eat you or me."

Attentively as the Kaffirs watched the bushes, and listened for some sound indicative of the lion's position, they yet could hear nothing; so quietly did the creature move, they had almost given up their attention to eating, when a sudden flash of light burst from the bushes on the top of the kloof, followed by a thundering roar which was succeeded by a silence, broken only at intervals by the distant echoes of the report of the gun, which at first had scarcely been audible in the midst of the lion's roar, for such it proved to be.

As these sounds burst over the camp, each hunter started from his slumber, and stood waiting for some fresh indication of danger, or cause for action; for half a minute no man spoke, but then Bernhard exclaimed—

"That must have been Hans, he must have met the lion in the dark;" and, "Oh, Hans! Hans!" he shouted:

"Here so," replied a voice from the summit of the kloof; "is that Bernhard?"

"Yes, Hans: are you hurt?"

"No, but the lion is: he is dying in a bush not far off. I don't like to move, as I can't see him: could you bring some lighted branches here?"

'Nquane, the Kaffir, and Bernhard each seized a large blazing branch, and grasping their guns, ascended the steep slope to the position occupied by Hans.

"Up this way," said Hans, "the lion is to your right, and I think dead; but we had better not go near him till we are certain. Now give me a branch, I can light this grass, and go look for him." Saying this, Hans advanced to some bushes and cast a handful of blazing grass before him. "He's dead," exclaimed Hans, "so come, and we will skin him: he's a fine fellow!"

"Come down to the camp and eat first, Hans," urged Bernhard, "and tell us where you have been, then come and skin the lion."

"No, business first," exclaimed Hans. "The jackalls might spoil the skin in a few minutes, and before the lion was cold; so we will first free him of his coat, then I will eat."

It took Hans and his two companions only a short time to divest the lion of its skin, when the three returned to camp, where the new-comer was heartily welcomed, and where he was soon fully occupied in making a meal from the remains of the supper left by his companions. Hans Sterk, as he sat quietly eating his meal with an appetite that seemed to indicate a long previous fast, did not give one the idea of a very remarkable man. He was quite young—probably not more than two-and-twenty, and not of very great size; he was, however, what is called well put together, and seemed more framed for activity than strength; his eyes were deep-set and small, with that earnest look about them which seemed to plainly indicate that they saw a great deal more than most eyes. His companions seemed quite to understand Hans' peculiarities, for they did not address a word to him whilst he was eating, being fully aware that had they done so they would have obtained no answer. When, however, he had completely satisfied his hunger, Bernhard said—

"What have you seen and done, Hans? and why are you so late? We feared you had lost the line for our resting-place before it got dark, and would not reach us to-night."

"Lost the line," replied Hans; "that was not easy, considering you stopped at the only river for ten miles round; but I was nearly stopping away all night, only I remembered you had such good fat eland for supper, and so I returned."

"And what made you nearly stop away, Hans?"

"Few men like to walk about among bushes and krantzes when man-eating lions are on the look-out, and the sun has set for two hours," replied Hans.

"Was there nothing else that kept you?" inquired Bernhard. "You left us all of a sudden."

"Yes, there was something else kept me away."

"And that was—"

"This," said Hans, as he pulled from his coat pocket a small brown lump like India-rubber, from which two or three long wire-like bristles protruded.

"You came on elephants!" exclaimed several of the Boers. "What luck! The first we have seen. Were they bulls or cows?"

"I came on fresh elephant's spoor soon after I left you," said Hans. "I dared not come back to call you, and feared to miss you; so I went on alone, and saw the spoor of four large bull elephants. This spoor I followed for some distance, and then found that the creatures had entered the forest. But the place was good; there were large trees, and but little underwood; so I could see far, and walk easily. I came upon the elephants; they were together, and knew not I was near till I had fired, and the big bull dropped dead."

"Where did you hit him, Hans?"

"Between the eye and the ear, and he fell to the shot."

"The others escaped, then, Hans," said Heinrich.

"Not before I had hit one with fine tusks behind the shoulder."

"Then he escaped?"

"No, he went for two miles, then separated from the others, and stood in the thick bush. I becrouped (stalked him) and gave him my bullet between the eye and the ear, and he fell."

"Where's his tail, Hans?" said one of the Boers.

Hans drew from his pocket a second small black bristly lump, and placed it beside the first, saying, "There is the tail of the elephant in the thick bush."

"What weight are the tusks, Hans?" said Bernhard.

"About sixty to eighty pounds each. They are old bulls with sound teeth."

"And ivory is fetching five shillings a pound. A sixty pound business. Oh, Hans, you are lucky! Are there more there, do you think? Was there other spoor, or were these wanderers?"

"To-morrow," replied Hans, "we may come upon a large herd of bulls, for before sundown I crossed fresh spoor of a herd of about twenty. They were tracking south, so we shall not have far to go."

"But tell us," said Victor, another Boer, "about the lion above there. How did you see him? It was dark, was it not?"

"Not very dark; the moon gave me light, and the creature whisked its tail just as it was going to spring, and so I saw it. I knew the place was one likely for a lion, and so had my eyes about me. It does not do to think too much when you walk in the veldt by night, or you may be taken unawares. I shot the lion between the eyes; and had he been any thing but a lion, he would have dropped dead; but a lion's life is too big to go all at once out of so small a hole as a bullet makes, and so he did not die for ten minutes."

"Where are the other two bull elephants, Hans?" inquired Victor. "Did they go far, do you think, or would they stop?"

"One is beside the Vlei near the Bavians Kloof; the other is in the thorn-bushes a mile from it."

"But they won't stop there. Where think you they will be to-morrow?"

"Where they are now," replied Hans, as he quietly brought from his pocket the ends of two more elephants' tails, and placed them beside those already on the ground.

"You have not killed all four bull elephants, Hans?" said Bernhard, with a look of astonishment. "Will a bull elephant let you cut off the end of his tail when he is alive, Bernhard? You taught me first how to spoor an elephant, and you never told me that he would let you do that; so I killed mine first, and then cut his tail off afterwards. I shot all four bull elephants, and expended but thirteen bullets altogether on them. The teeth will weigh nearly five hundred pounds, and so I think I have a good excuse for coming late to supper. But now, good-night. We must be up early, and so sleep is good for a steady hand in the morning, and we shall want it, for game is near and plentiful. Good-night, and sleep well."

Chapter Two
Following the Elephants—Cutting out the tusks—Hunting the herd of Elephants

The sun's rays had scarcely commenced illuminating the eastern horizon, when the hunters were up, and making their preparations for the start. The plan of hunting which they had adopted, was to enter the country with waggons, oxen, and horses; to leave their waggons at a good outspanning-place where there was plenty of water and forage for the cattle; then to scour the country round and search for game, or spoor, which if found, the horses, oxen, and waggons were brought up, and the elephants hunted on horseback. The elephant is so formidable an animal, and usually is so fierce, especially when wounded and hunted, that few African sportsmen venture to follow him on foot into his dense woody retreats. It is customary to drive the herd, when discovered, into the most open country, this driving being accomplished either by setting fire to the dried grass, by making large bonfires, or by discharging fire-arms, and thus causing the herds to leave a secure retreat for one less sheltered. It is not unfrequently a matter of two or three days, to drive elephants into a good and favourable country; and upon this driving being judiciously carried out, much of the success of the hunt depends. There are very many men whose livelihood depends entirely on elephant hunting. They farm but little, have few cattle, but devote their time mainly to hunting; and in a country so untrodden as was Africa some years ago, there was no want of game, and thus a man provided with horse, gun, powder, and lead, might live independent of almost all else.

Hans Sterk was a man who had been devoted to sport from his childhood. His father was a Dutchman who had early in his colonial career gone upon the outskirts of civilisation, and had been one of the pioneers to slay the wild beasts, and teach the savage man that the white man is the master over the black. Hans' mother was an English woman, an emigrant who had ventured into Africa, and had there found a home. But both his parents had been cruelly murdered by the Kaffirs in one of their attacks upon the colonists; and at a very early age he had found himself owner of a waggon, some spans of oxen, a few head of cattle and horses, and had thus every means at his disposal for indulging in hunting; and as his taste led him in pursuit of the elephant, he soon became famed as an unerring marksman, an expert spoorer, and one of the most determined elephant hunters. On more than one occasion also he had distinguished himself in commandoes against the Kaffir tribes. Thus before he was twenty he had obtained a reputation for skill and bravery, and at that age was known as Hans Sterk, the elephant hunter. How well he deserved the title, the result of his day's sport just related amply shows.

The morning after Hans' return to the sleeping-place was fine, and well suited for spooring or shooting. There had been a heavy dew, and the wind was light, so that no extra noises disturbed the bushes, and rendered the feeding of an elephant inaudible, or the rush of a wild beast undistinguishable from the rustling of the forest branches. Hans had sent one of his Kaffirs to the waggons, to announce to the men there the death of four elephants, and to bring such aid as was requisite to cut out the tusks, and convey them to the waggons. He then with his white companions started on his footsteps of the previous night towards the ground where his elephants had fallen. Having with him a hatchet and knife, and aided by 'Nquane and his friend Bernhard, he proceeded to extract the tusks of his first elephant. The animal had fallen backwards, so that it lay in a very good attitude to be operated on; and Hans, taking his hatchet, cut down each side of the elephant's trunk, so that at last this appendage could be turned completely over its head. The roots of the tusks were thus exposed to view, and were next attacked with the hatchet, the ends fixed in the jaws being loosened and cut off, by means of a fulcrum made from a large branch of a tree. The tusks were then worked up and down, and the hatchet applied to sever those parts which held most tenaciously, until the tusks were quite loose in the jaw, and could then be extracted with a good pull. About one-third of an elephant's tusk is embedded in its jaw, and this part being filled up with muscles and nerves is hollow, and has to be cleaned out before it is inserted in the waggon. A tooth, as a tusk is called by elephant hunters, weighs about ten per cent, heavier when it is first taken from an elephant's jaw, than when it becomes dry from keeping. Very few elephants' tusks exceed 100 pounds in weight each, the average size of a good pair of tusks being from 100 to 150 pounds.

Sometimes, however, a marvellous old bull, or one who has developed his teeth in a wonderful way, is found, whose teeth weigh nearly 130 pounds each; but such patriarchs are rarely met with.

The country in which elephants are found in abundance is usually thinly inhabited, and the natives are not possessed of fire-arms in great abundance or of much value. Thus the elephant, being a dangerous animal to hunt and hard to kill, often remains in forests when the more timid game of the open country has been driven away. But when English or Dutch sportsmen have visited a country, they usually wound mortally many more elephants than they kill and find, and thus the Kaffirs, who follow up and find the wounded animals, drive a very fair trade in elephants' tusks, of which they soon understand the true value. Thus a party of hunters not unfrequently return from a three or four months' shooting-trip into the interior with from two to three thousand pounds' weight of ivory. There is, however, considerable risk in this sport when looked at from its mercantile point of view. It may happen that the country to which the hunters have travelled has been temporarily deserted by elephants in consequence of hunters having just previously hunted that ground, or from a scarcity of water. The horse or cattle sickness may attack the hunter's quadrupeds, and thus, even if his waggons be full, he may have to leave them behind whilst he returns some four or five hundred miles to re-purchase cattle, again enter the country, and find his waggons probably pillaged and burnt he knows not by whom, his followers murdered, and he left to make the best of his way home again. Thus a hunter's life is one of excitement and risk; and though the profits are great at times, and the life one which has irresistible charms, yet it is one not to be rashly undertaken by all men. There are, too, very many small chiefs, whose friendship it is necessary to gain by presents, or they will not allow you to journey through their country; and sometimes small wars take place between these potentates, when each party considers himself entitled to pillage all travellers who have been on friendly terms with his enemy.

There are, then, a goodly array of dangers and difficulties surrounding the African hunter, to say nothing of those which threaten him from wild beasts, such as lions, leopards, etc., or poisonous snakes. So that it is not difficult for a man as young even as Hans Sterk to gain a wide reputation for skill and bravery in surmounting those obstacles to which he had been frequently opposed.

The teeth of the various elephants slain by Hans having been extracted from the jaws of the animals, placed on the shoulders of Kaffirs, marked with Hans' mark, and despatched to the waggons, Hans led the way over some bushy country towards a range of low hills near which a bright silvery streak indicated that a stream of water was flowing.

"Before I look for spoor where I expect it," said Hans to his Dutch companions, "I will look through my 'far-seer'" (as he termed his telescope), "to see what wilde there is in the open country."

Adjusting his telescope to suit his focus, Hans took a careful look all round, and at length rested his glass against a tree and looked steadily down near the stream of which we have spoken. After a careful examination he offered his glass to a companion, and said, "I see eight or nine large bull elephants near the mimosas beside those yellow-wood trees. Can you see more?"

Chapter Three
The Bull Elephant—The Charge of the
Elephants—Counting the Spoils

O ye lovers of true sport, men of nerve and skill, ye who prize a reality and are not satisfied with a feeble imitation, have you ever attempted to realise the excitement and glory of combating with a herd of lordly elephants, fierce and powerful, and monarchs in their own forests? Ye, who consider that *the* only sport is pursuing a fleeing fox over the grass-lands of your own country, can but feebly imagine the effect produced by measuring your skill and daring against the giant strength and cunning of a mighty elephant, who has braved his hundred summers, and has been able to withstand the bullets or spears of a hundred foes; who has won his way among his rivals by fierce and hardly contested battles; and who dreads no enemy, but is ever ready to try conclusions with the most formidable of all, viz. man. To stand alone and on foot, amidst the tangled luxuriant foliage of an African forest, within a few yards of one of these watchful monsters, whose foot could crush you as easily as could your foot a mouse or rat, and whose headlong rush through the forest would carry away every obstacle, is a proceeding which causes the blood to course through one's veins like quicksilver. To hide near a troop of these animals, watching their strange movements and taking advantage of favourable opportunities for deadly shots, which are answered by the most savage and unearthly shrieks, is another phase of sport which is spirit-stirring in the extreme. Add to these scenes the most glowing landscape, covered with brilliant flowers, and ornamented with gorgeously-tinted birds, whilst various rare and graceful antelopes are bounding away in all directions to escape the tumult which has disturbed them, and there is an explanation of the mystery of that so-called hunter's fever, which induces those who have once tasted such sport to ever afterwards thirst for it as the parched stag thirsts for water.

Surrounding Hans Sterk there were men who had slain lions and buffaloes, had brought to the earth the lofty cameleopard, and had frequently gathered tusks from their elephants slain in fair fight. Yet with these men the excitement had not worn off; and they, one and all, seemed to be endowed with additional life-power as they recognised with the 'far-seer' the largest of African game browsing calmly in his native wilderness. "We must not show ourselves," said Hans, "or the alarm will spread. See those ostriches in the 'open;' they suspect us; and though they are two miles off, they can distinguish us among these thorns. Let us lie down, and we will make our plans for attacking those elephants."

The whole party at once sank to the ground, and were thus completely concealed from the keen sight of all except the vultures, which were sailing about overhead. Each of the hunters then took a careful survey of the nature of the ground between his position and the river near which the elephants were browsing. After an interval of a few minutes, one of the eldest men asked the rest what plan they had made.

"You speak first, Piet," was the answer of Hans; "then we will all give our opinions."

"I think," said Piet, "we should go down to the right, enter that bush, and so keep near the stream till we stalk on to the elephants; for the ground is very good where they are, and they will not move far whilst they can feed there."

Nearly every one agreed with this remark except Hans, who, when his opinion was asked, said that he had two reasons why he should prefer another plan. First, the wind would not quite suit, but would blow from them to the elephants when they first entered the thorn-bushes. Then, in front of the elephants, and about a mile off, was a large dense forest. "If they enter that," said Hans, "we shall not see them again. I should like to go down to the left, get in front of the elephants, and either wait for them to feed up to us, or stalk them up wind. Then when they run, they will go towards our waggons, and we shall be able to hunt those which are not killed to-day, with the aid of our horses to-morrow." After a slight hesitation the hunters decided that this was the better plan, and determined at once to put it into execution. Each man examined the priming of his rifle, put on fresh caps, felt the position of his cartridges, powder-flask, and bullets, so as to be certain all was ready for use; and then, following each other in Indian file, the party strode forward in the direction agreed upon.

When hunters are in the neighbourhood of large game, it is an understood rule that a shot is not to be fired at any small animal. Thus, if a party were out in search of elephants, and had separated from each other, a shot from one party would at once bring the others to it, for it would be understood that elephants had been fired at. Thus antelopes of various kinds were allowed to gallop off without a shot being fired at them. A fat eland, whose appearance made the Kaffirs' mouth almost water, was allowed to stand under a tree, and gaze with astonishment at the novel spectacle of a herd of two-legged creatures moving over its domain. For to have fired a shot would have not only disturbed the country, but would have been a reckless destruction of life, a proceeding which every true sportsman abhors. Taking advantage of the slopes of ground, the cover of trees, etc., Hans and his party turned the position of the elephants, and halted about five hundred yards in advance of them, without having caused these watchful, keen-scented animals any suspicion of their presence.

Each hunter took up a position behind a tree, immediately he came in front of the elephants, and there waited for some signal from the leader before advancing. It was soon evident that the elephants were feeding towards the hunters, and thus if they remained quiet, they would soon have their game within range. Twelve majestic bull elephants were in the herd, each with tusks of large size. Such game being close to them caused each man of the party to feel excited with the anticipation of the coming sport, and to reserve himself for his first shot. On came the troop, scarcely staying now to feed, for they had by some instinct or power of observation become slightly alarmed. The scent of the hunters, or the screech of some bird had indicated to them that an enemy was near, and thus they ceased feeding. A majestic twelve-foot bull elephant led the party, and seemed well qualified for a leader. He strode forward some dozen yards with trunk erect and ears wide-spread, then stopped and drew the air through his trunk with great rapidity, turning from side to side with a quickness which seemed surprising in so vast an animal. That lazy, stupid appearance which those who have seen caged animals only, are disposed to attribute to elephants, was very different from the activity of this leader, as his restless eye watched each bush or tree; and his threatening attitude occasionally indicated that he was ready to charge an enemy. Suddenly, as though a fresh cause for suspicion had arisen, the mighty bull raised his trunk, and gave three sharp, shrill, and powerful trumpet-notes, which might have been heard at a distance of two miles. Immediately a deep rumbling sound was uttered by all the other members of the herd, who stood instantly like so many bronze figures, the only indications of life being the shaking of their huge ears, which from time to time were erected, and then depressed. During fully two minutes this watchful attitude was maintained, after which one deep note was sounded by the leading bull, and the whole party strode onwards. They were, unluckily for them, advancing to destruction; for each hunter was now within fifty yards of the leader, and several rifles were already aiming at various parts of the grand-looking animal. A moment's silence, broken only by the heavy tread of the elephants, and then the stillness of the wilderness was broken by the report of half-a-dozen heavy rifles. In an instant the scene was changed. The leading bull elephant reeled as he received the leaden hail; but his strong frame yet retained plenty of life, and, uttering a fearful shriek, he charged headlong at the tree behind which two of the hunters were concealed. The tree was large and strong, and the men trusted that it would stand even the rush of the elephant; but so great was the momentum of the vast bull, that the tree snapped as though it were a mere sapling, and the two hunters narrowly escaped being crushed by the tree, or trodden under foot by the enraged monster. As he charged onward, blinded with rage, he received another volley from the second barrel of the Boers' rifles; bleeding from a dozen wounds, he still held on his mad career, until he could no longer withstand the shock to his system; he then suddenly stopped, threw up his trunk as though signalling his defeat, and sank back on the ground, the earth shaking and resounding with the fall. Following their leader until the smell of blood warned them that it was dangerous to pursue his course, the remaining elephants spread out on each side, and formed two parties; but their course was undecided, for their leader had been slain, and for a time they had no confidence in a successor. The hunters, having almost instantly reloaded their rifles, ran forward in order to intercept the elephants and cut them off from the dense bush towards which they were wending their way. Closing with one of the nearmost, Hans and two of his companions fired at the heavy shoulder, which for an instant was exposed to their aim. Responding to the report of the guns, the elephant trumpeted his defiance; and turning with rapidity he rushed at the assailants. Small trees and underwood gave way before the mountain of flesh which was urged against them, and any inexperienced men would have been in a dangerous position. To be charged by a savage bull elephant was not, however, any thing very novel either to Hans or his companions, who at once keeping close together ran to the more open part of the forest, but where large trees were abundant. For about forty yards, the three men ran shoulder to shoulder; but the elephant, with his giant strides, was gaining on them, and would, it appeared, soon reach his tiny enemies, whose fate would then be decided. But a hunter is full of expedients, and knows when to practise them; thus, as the elephant was rushing onwards in a straight course, Hans shouted, "Now," when instantly the party separated, Hans turning sharp to the right, his two companions to the left, and each slipping behind a broad-stemmed tree. The elephant, either undecided which to pursue, or not seeing the artifice of his enemies, continued his rush onwards; but before he had gone many yards, the forest again echoed back the report of the hunters' rifles, and three more bullets lodged behind the elephant's ear caused him to pitch forward on his head, his tusks snapping off with a sharp crack, and he rolling to the ground harmless as the trees around him. Three other elephants that were badly wounded effected their escape; but the elephant hunters knew their death warrant had been signed; and so, assembling near the great elephant's carcass, the successful men drank a "Soupe" of brandy, cut off the tail of the "game," and for awhile talked over the events of the hunt. It was then decided to return to the waggons, bring them, with oxen and horses, near the stream by which they were then seated, and to hunt the remainder of the herd on horseback; for it was seen that if the country were not very favourable, but little success would be obtained if the elephants were pursued on foot. Now that the country had been alarmed by the report of fire-arms, there was no longer any need for concealment, so the hunters spread out instead of following in Indian file, for hunger began to remind them that the sun was past the meridian, and thus a slice from an antelope or an eland would not be objected to. It was not long before an eland and her calf were seen reclining beneath some acacia-trees; and the plan being arranged, the pair were soon surrounded, when the hunters, closing in, rendered their escape impossible, and both were shot by the hungry travellers. The elephants, having been feeding for some days in this neighbourhood, had deposited the fuel for a fire, which, dried by the sun, ignited rapidly, and in a few minutes was blazing beneath the strips of alternate fat and lean, which had been strung on two or three ramrods. And thus, in less than an hour from the sighting of the elands, their flesh was being eaten by the sportsmen, who, provided only with a paper of salt and a clasp-knife, were yet able to make an excellent dinner, which was washed down with some of the water from the stream, flavoured by a dash of brandy from the flasks carried by each hunter. It was near sunset when the party reached their waggons; but orders were given to inspan the oxen before daybreak, to have the horses ready, and to prepare for an early "*trek*" towards the clear stream and luxuriant forest in which the elephants had been hunted.

"There," said Hans, "we have good water, plenty of wood and other stuff for fires, game in abundance and so we shall have nothing to do but eat, drink, sleep, and shoot; we shall kill the game that will yield us money, and so we need have no care. A hunter's life is happy, and who would not be a hunter? Can you believe it, that Karl Zeitsman has gone down to Cape Town to write in a shop or something, because he wants to make money? Why our fore-looper's life is a better one than his; and as to ours, one day in the veldt after game is worth a year in a town, where all is dirty, smoky, and bad. There is nothing like a free life, Bernhard, is there? and elephant hunting is the very best of all. Good-night, and sleep well, Bernhard," said Hans as he crawled into his waggon; and, undisturbed by the roars of a distant lion, or the snores of his companions, he slept soundly and peacefully till near daybreak.

Chapter Four
Seeking the Dead Elephants—Ambuscade of the Matabili Warriors—Escape of Hans Sterk and his Party—Battle with the Matabili—The Slaughter of Siedenberg

"The waggons can follow," said Hans; "that will be best. The Kaffir can show where the dead elephants are lying, and we will ride on. Shall we follow the spoor, Victor, or try and cut off the track?"

"Better follow the spoor, Hans, I think," replied Victor; "but what does Heinrich say?"

"Follow the spoor from where we last saw the elephants; we are sure to find them there."

It being thus agreed among the most experienced to follow the spoor, the whole party mounted their horses and rode on their journey, little expecting what was before them.

There was but little game visible to the hunters as they rode towards the locality on which their yesterday's sport had been enjoyed; but this they believed was due to the alarm which their firing had caused; for so wide, is the country in Africa, that the animals can, if necessary, journey their forty miles during the night, and yet obtain a good grazing-ground free from interruption; so that a hunter rarely expects to find game in any district which has been hunted on the day previously, but looks for it some thirty miles distant. As the hunters rode forward the sun rose, and dried up the heavy dew which had covered the herbage during the night. The fog and mist were scattered before his burning rays, and the country once more exhibited its tropical appearance.

Hans, who had taken out his telescope to examine the country in various directions, at length exclaimed, "There is one of the Kaffirs near the elephants. How could he get there before us?"

"It is 'Nquane, perhaps; he is very quick, and may have passed us in the fog."

"No," replied Hans; "'Nquane, like all Kaffirs, does not like going a journey before the sun has dried and warmed the air. Can the man be a stray Matabili?"

"No matter if he is," said one of the Boers. "Let us canter on; we shall soon see."

The hunters increased their speed, and rode on towards their dead elephants, but saw, as they approached, no Kaffirs; and all except Hans began to doubt whether the figure he had seen really was a Kaffir, or only a stump burned and blackened so as to resemble a man. The party left the open country, and rode into the forest, being obliged to ride in file along the paths made by the elephants. They had penetrated about two hundred yards into the forest, when a shrill whistle was uttered from the wood behind, and instantly from all parts of the bush an armed Matabili warrior sprang to his feet. Two hundred men at least appeared, forming a ring, in the midst of which were the hunters. These warriors did not leave the white men long in doubt as to their intentions; but beating their shields, and waving their assagies, they rushed in towards their supposed victims.

The Hunters attacked by the Matabili.—

With that readiness of expedient which a long training in such hunting expeditions as those we have described is likely to produce, the Dutchmen saw their only chance for escape. They turned their horses, and firing a destructive volley at the Matabili who blocked the path in their rear, spurred their horses, and charged at the opening which their bullets and slugs had cleared. Each man retained a charge in one barrel; and as each neared the enemy he fired from the saddle, and mostly killed or disabled his foe. So sudden had been the attack, and so rapid the retreat, that in five minutes from the first alarm the hunters found themselves clear of the bush, and with no further loss than two horses severely gashed by the assagies of their enemies, who fortunately possessed no fire-arms.

"The men belong to the old villain Moselekatse," said Hans; "we must fight them in the open and not spare a man, or our waggon and oxen will be captured; let us halt and try to draw them out into this open bush. Are you all loaded, men?" inquired Hans, who, though nearly the youngest of the party, seemed at once to assume the position of leader.

"Yes, we are all, I think," replied several... "And here come the Matabili, thinking to close with us. Now, for not wasting a single charge, give them the bullet in the distance, buckshot when nearer, the treacherous villains;" as he finished speaking he fired, and a dozen bullets were discharged; immediately afterwards, the dull thud of the bullets and the falling bodies of the enemy indicating the accuracy of the aims. The party were waiting for the Matabili to approach within range of buckshot and slugs; but Victor, luckily looking round, saw that two detachments had been sent round on the flanks in an endeavour to surround the horsemen, so that an immediate retreat was necessary. Every one of the hunters was, however, able to load his weapon whilst proceeding at full gallop; so that, having retreated far enough to escape being surrounded, the Boers halted, faced about, and again discharged their deadly weapons at the foe.

The leader of the Matabili soon saw that this system of fighting was not likely to lead to satisfactory results, so he whistled a signal to his men, who halted and began a retreat. The hunters however were not the men to spare their foe, but followed on their traces, shooting down their enemy with a fatal accuracy, until they reached the denser part of the forest, where the hunters dared not enter on foot against at least ten times their number, and where they could not enter on horseback. A short council of war decided them to leave half their number to watch the Matabili, whilst the remainder rode with all speed to the waggons, to stop them in their advance, and to make preparations for their defence in case an attack should be made upon them; for to defend waggons was very much more difficult than to carry on the light cavalry manoeuvres which had been so successful in the late attack of the black warriors.

There are few incidents of greater interest in connexion with our colonies than the desertion from our eastern frontier of the Cape of Good Hope of a body of about 5000 souls, who, dissatisfied with the Government to which they were compelled to own allegiance, departed with wives, children, goods, cattle, and horses into the wilderness, there to find a new home, far away from English dominion. It was in 1836 that this singular emigration took place, and it was just previous to that date that our tale commences.

Ruling over a large portion of country in about the twenty-sixth parallel of latitude, there was a chief named Moselekatse, whose tribe was termed Matabili. He was a renegade from the Zulu nation, and had by his talents formed a nation of soldiers. Between the warriors of Moselekatse and some Griquas, near the Orange River, several encounters had taken place, the latter being usually the assailants, their object being the capture of cattle, the Matabili being rich in herds. The Griquas are a tribe of bastard Hottentots, many of them being nearly white; and thus, in a Matabili's opinion, nearly every white man was an enemy.

Believing that the ground on which they were hunting was too far from the dominions of the Matabili chieftain to make the position a dangerous one, Hans and his party had neither sent ambassadors to announce their purpose of hunting, nor had they expected to meet any bipeds in the district in which they had decided to hunt elephants. They probably would not even have been heard of by the soldiers of Moselekatse, and therefore not molested, had not a large party of the Matabili been ordered to make a reconnaissance in the neighbourhood of Natal where the Zulus were in force, and where it was said preparations were being made for an invasion of the Matabili territory. These men on their return heard the report of the white men's rifles, and at once believed it would please their king if these rifles were brought into his presence. Concealing themselves carefully from their intended victims, and sending out a few spies to watch what was going on, the Matabili discovered where the elephants had been shot, and at once knew that on the following day the hunters would come to procure their ivory, so that an ambuscade could be arranged and the hunters surrounded and taken at a disadvantage. All was very carefully planned by the Matabili; but in consequence of the rapid decision and skill of the hunters, their plot was a failure. The Matabili were, however, formidable as enemies; they plotted deeply before they acted; and had the hunters been aware of the cunning of their foes, they would scarcely have felt as satisfied as they did when they had driven their assailants into a dense cover, and had thus compelled them to keep close, and change their attack into a defence.

Five of the hunters remained near the bush to watch the enemy, whilst five rode back towards the waggons; and thus the white men's forces were divided. Following their back trail, the hunters rode at a canter in the direction of their last night's outspan, eager to get to their waggons, and either put them into a state of defence, or start them in a direction away from that likely to be followed by the Matabili.

Hans Sterk, Victor, and three other Dutchmen formed the party that were returning to the waggons. After riding at a canter for some miles, they drew up and walked their horses, in order to allow them to regain their wind.

"This will be a bad day's work for Moselekatse," said Victor, "for we are too strong for him on the Orange river now; and if we make up a commando and attack him, he would be sure to be defeated. He has enough on his hands now with the Zulus, who will certainly make an attack on him very shortly."

"We should have no difficulty in getting up a large party to attack the Matabili; for they have thousands of cattle, and there would be much to divide among those who ventured," replied one of the Boers.

"They nearly succeeded this morning in finishing us," said Hans. "Had we not been very quick, and ready with our guns, they would have surrounded us successfully; it is lucky they did not attack us last night at the waggons; we should all have been slaughtered if they had done so, as we should have been taken by surprise."

"Yes, it is lucky," said Victor; "and I don't see how we could have escaped better than we have done, for, except that cut on your horse's flank and a stab in Heinrich's horse's neck, we were untouched, whilst we must have killed and wounded nearly fifty of the Matabili."

"Yes, we were fortunate," replied Hans; "but I wish we were two hundred miles from here, with our waggons safely across the mountains. Here comes 'Nquane, and he seems in a hurry."

No sooner did the Kaffir recognise the hunters than he ran towards them with the greatest eagerness, making all manner of signals. As soon as he came within speaking distance, he said—

"Chiefs, the Matabili came upon us at the waggons; they have killed Copen and Jack, and carried off all the oxen and horses. Oh, it is bad for us?"

Exclamations of anger and surprise were uttered by the hunters as they heard this intelligence; for they knew that without oxen all the wealth in their waggons was worthless, and could be carried off at any time by Moselekatse's warriors, whenever they chose to come.

"How many Matabili were there?" inquired Hans.

The Kaffir opened and closed his two hands five times, thus indicating there were about fifty men.

"Only fifty!" exclaimed Hans. "Let us after them at once; surely we can beat away fifty Matabili; it is only ten apiece. You go back to the waggons, 'Nquane, and wait there; we will soon bring you back the oxen."

The hunters immediately spurred on their horses, and rode rapidly in the direction which the marauders had taken; and having ascended a conical hill, Hans by the aid of his telescope discovered the oxen and their capturers moving rapidly over the open country, and distant scarcely two miles.

"A beautiful open country," exclaimed Hans; "just the place for a fight on horseback, and we will give them a lesson of what we 'Mensch' can do."

Seeing that there was little or no bush before the Matabili, into which they could effect their escape, the hunters did not distress their steeds by too great a speed; but cantering steadily onwards they were soon seen by the Matabili, who, leaving two of their number to drive the horses and oxen, then spread out in open order, beating their shields and shouting their defiance.

The horses ridden by the hunters were trained shooting horses, and were not therefore likely to be alarmed by the noises made by these men. Each animal also would allow its rider to fire from its back without moving a muscle; and thus the five hunters, armed as they were, well supplied with ammunition, and deadly as shots, were most formidable enemies, more so than the Matabili seemed to think; for these men had hitherto been opposed only to Hottentots and Griquas, whose courage and skill they despised. When, therefore, the Dutchmen halted, and each, selecting a victim, raised his rifle or smooth-bore to fire, the Matabili uttered taunting yells, dodged from side to side to distract their enemies' aim, and charged towards their foes.

Suddenly the five guns were discharged, and five Matabili rolled over on the plain, each either killed or mortally wounded. The hunters instantly turned their horses, and, galloping at speed, avoided the charge of their enemies and the numerous assagies that were hurled after them. Adopting the same plan as on the former occasion, the hunters loaded as they rode away; and as soon as each man was ready, the signal was given for a halt, when it was found that the Matabili, finding pursuit useless, were returning after their stolen oxen. They did not seem to suspect the style of warfare which the Dutchmen practised, as they retreated very slowly, believing that their enemies were only anxious to escape; they soon, however, found, their mistake, as their enemies galloped up to within a hundred yards, and discharged their barrels into the crowded mass, a dozen men either falling or limping away badly wounded; for the heavy bullets and heavy charge of powder had caused one shot, in some cases, to bring down two victims.

The Matabili, finding by experience the power and skill of their few enemies, were now bent only on making their escape; and therefore, separating, they ran in all directions, leaving the oxen to be recaptured. Bent upon revenge, and upon freeing themselves from their enemies, the hunters followed their foes, shooting them like so many buck, until, finding their ammunition growing short, they returned to their oxen, which had been quietly grazing, unconscious of the battle that was being fought for their ownership. The animals being collected, were soon driven off towards the waggons; and before the sun had long passed the meridian, the oxen were inspanned, and the five Dutchmen and one Kaffir were urging forward the spans in a direction the opposite to that in which the Matabili's country lay. The two Hottentot drivers were found dead, having been assagied by their enemies without mercy; but few articles had been taken from the waggons, for the thieves did not like to encumber themselves with much booty, as they hoped to escape by speed before the hunters discovered their loss. The two parties of Matabili had acted also in concert, one having been left to watch the waggons and attack them as soon as the Dutchmen had started for their morning's hunt, the remainder having been moved forward to surprise the hunters when they were in the bush near the dead elephants. Both attacks had been unsuccessful; and now the only danger that the hunters feared was, that the Matabili, having been thus defeated, would return in a day or two with a large force, and, knowing that waggons can move but slowly, and rarely more than twenty-five miles a day, thus would soon overtake them and probably be able to ensure their capture and to revenge their late defeat. Before leaving the outspan, Hans wrote a few words on a paper, which he inserted in a split stick, planting this stick in the ground, so that it pointed at the sun. He rejoined his companions, who had each dismounted, and was either leading his horse, or allowing it to follow the waggons.

Hans had left a short account on the paper, of his proceedings, and had pointed the stick at the sun, in order to let his companions know when he had started, for they, he knew, would shortly return to the outspan, and would then follow the spoor of the waggons; but seeing the bodies of the Hottentots would be puzzled to account for every thing unless they were informed by some means.

"It will be bad for us if the rivers are swollen," said Hans to Victor, as the two followed the rear waggon; "a day's delay might cost us all our property here."

"And our lives too," said Victor.

"Scarcely our lives," said Hans, "if we are watchful, our horses live, and our ammunition lasts. We can fight these Matabili in any numbers as long as they don't possess fire-arms; when the day comes that they use guns and powder, it will be bad for us hunters, for then their numbers will render them very dangerous."

"The English traders are supplying them as fast as they can with guns," rejoined Victor; "it is hard for us that they do so, for we or our children may be shot by the guns these men supply, and yet we can do nothing, however much we may suffer from this money-making feeling."

The oxen having treked for fully two hours, began to show signs of distress, so the hunters agreed to halt and to dine, for they did not consider any immediate attack was probable. They had scarcely lighted a fire and began to prepare for cooking, than the welcome sight of their companions greeted them. Two of the hunters were riding one horse, in consequence of one having died from the effects of an assagy wound; but there being five additional horses among the recaptured oxen, this loss was not a very severe one.

The new-comers announced that the Matabili had retreated farther into the forest, and did not appear disposed again to try their strength against their white enemies. The whole party exclaimed loudly against the treachery of the Matabili in attacking them when there was peace between Moselekatse and themselves. They were not aware that a savage is not very discriminating; and a raid having been made into Moselekatse's country, some two months previously, by a party of Griquas, the warriors could not distinguish any great difference between a Dutchman and a Griqua, both being of a different colour to himself, and both being strangers in his land. A speedy revenge was decided on by the whole party as soon as they could collect a sufficient force for the purpose.

That no time was to be lost in escaping from that part of the country, was the unanimous opinion of the hunters; and so the oxen were inspanned again, and the journey continued without any delay. Thus for two days the party retreated without seeing any thing of an enemy. Game of various kinds was abundant; but except to supply themselves with food the hunters did not shoot, for they knew not how soon their lives might depend upon a plentiful supply of ammunition being at hand. So that each bar of lead was at once converted into bullets or slugs, the loose powder was made up into cartridges, and every gun cleaned and carefully loaded, so as to be as efficient as possible.

It was on the morning of the third day that the hunters observed in the distance what appeared to be a broken-down waggon, but no oxen or human beings seemed to be near it. Such a sight, however, as a wreck in the desert at once excited the curiosity of the travellers, who, leaving the waggons in charge of half the party, rode off to examine the scene on which the waggon appeared to have broken-down. As they approached the spot, they saw a man limp from out of a clump of bush and make signs to them, and this man they found to be a Hottentot, who was badly wounded in several places, and seemed almost famished with hunger.

Having supplied him with food, he informed them that he was the driver of one of three waggons belonging to a Dutchman, who, with his wife and two daughters, was travelling over the country in search of elands, when they were attacked by a party of Matabili, who came upon them at daybreak, and carried off oxen, wife, and daughters, killed the Dutchman and another Hottentot, and would have also killed him, had he not shammed to be dead.

Hans Sterk, who had been watching attentively the waggon and débris around, whilst he listened to the Hottentot's remarks, suddenly and eagerly inquired what was the Dutchman's name.

"Siedenberg," said the Hottentot.

"Siedenberg!" shrieked Hans, as he grasped his rifle like a vice; "and Katrine was with him?"

"Ja," said the Hottentot; "the Mooi Katrine has been carried off by the Matabili, and her little sister too."

"Men," said Hans, as he turned to his companions, "Katrine Siedenberg was to have been my wife in two months' time. I swear she shall be freed from the Matabili, or I will die in the attempt. Which of you will aid me in my work, with your rifles, horses, and skill?"

"I will," replied Victor.

"And I," said Heinrich.

"And I," said all those with him; "but we must get more men."

It was immediately agreed that the journey should be continued until the waggons and their contents were placed in safety, for the Matabili had two days' start, and therefore could not be overtaken by the poor half-starved horses, which now alone belonged to the hunters. Fresh horses, more people, and more ammunition were necessary, and then a successful expedition might be carried on against Moselekatse and his warriors. The Hottentot was helped back to the hunter's waggons and allowed to ride in one of them; and the onward journey was continued with all speed, so that in three days after finding the broken-down waggon, the hunters had crossed the Nama Hari river, and had joined a large party of the emigrant farmers, who were encamped south of this river.

The news of the attack on the hunters, the slaughter of Siedenberg, and the carrying off of his daughters, scarcely required to be detailed with the eloquence which Hans brought to bear upon it, in order to raise the anger and thirst for vengeance of the Dutchmen. Those who could were at once eager to bear arms against their savage and treacherous foe, whose proceedings caused a feeling of insecurity to pervade the Boers' encampment; and thus the expediency of inflicting a lesson on the black chieftain was considered advisable. And also there was a strong temptation to inflict this lesson, when it was remembered that enormous herds of sleek cattle belonged to the Matabili, and would of course become the property of the conquerors; and who those conquerors would be was not doubtful, considering the relative value of assagies and double-barrelled guns.

Chapter Five
Commando against the Matabili and Moselekatse, the Chief of the Matabili

To men who lived the life of the farmer in Africa, surrounded on all sides by savage animals, or those creatures which were hunted for the sake of their flesh, obliged to be watchful at all times on account of their enemies—the Kaffirs of the old colony and the tribes to the north of them—their preparations for a campaign were speedily made; and on the morning following that on which Hans Sterk's party had rejoined his companions, more than eighty Dutchmen, with as many after riders, all well-armed and mounted, were ready to start on their expedition against the Matabili.

The foe against which this party was being led was known to be both cunning and daring, and so it was considered expedient to place the camp in a state of defence, lest the enemy, taking advantage of the absence of the greater number of the fighting men, should select that time for their attack; for such is the usual proceeding of African chieftains against their enemies. The waggons were therefore drawn together and brushwood placed so as to prevent an easy entrance among them, regular watches were set, so that a surprise would have been difficult, had it been attempted; and a regular attack when the Boers were prepared would have ended in a fearful slaughter of the assailants. Matters being thus satisfactorily arranged at home, the expedition started, amidst great firing of guns, this being among the Africanders the substitute for cheering.

A leader having been chosen from among the Boers, the party started full of hope, and during the first day had travelled nearly forty miles. Every precaution was taken to avoid being surprised and also to ensure surprising the enemy, for the Boers were well aware of the advantages to be gained from surprising such an enemy as the Matabili. Game was abundant in the country through which the commando passed, and thus it was not necessary for the men to burden themselves with much weight in the form of food; water was at this time of the year plentiful, and thus the two essentials of life, food and water, were to be obtained with ease. To men who loved adventure as much as did these men, such an expedition as this was sport; and had any stranger come to the bivouac at night, seen the jovial, free-from-care manner of the Boers, and heard their spirit-stirring tales, he would scarcely have imagined that these men were bound on a matter of life and death, and were shortly to be engaged with a brave and powerful enemy, who, though badly armed, still outnumbered them in the ratio of twenty to one. Of all the party, Hans Sterk alone seemed quiet and thoughtful; but his look of determination indicated that his thoughts were certainly not pacific; and when the evening arrived, and the men halted until the moon rose and enabled them to continue their journey, none were more active or watchful than Hans Sterk the elephant hunter.

Five days and nights of rapid travelling brought the Boers within a few hours' journey of the head-quarters of the Matabili, when it was decided to halt in order to refresh both men and horses, and to endeavour to gain such information as to the disposition of the fighting men of the Matabili, as would enable them to attack the enemy at the weakest point. Whilst the Boers were thus undecided, they were joined by a party of about a dozen of their countrymen, who had been on an exploring expedition, and having left their wives and children with some men as escort, whilst they departed on a few days' journey, returned to find their waggons destroyed and their relatives murdered. Hastening with all speed to their companions, they heard of their departure to attack the Matabili, and immediately started to join them. On their journey they had come up with and surprised a party of Matabili, whom they at once attacked, killing all except one man, whom they made prisoner; this one man being capable, they thought, of being eventually of use.

Moselekatse had made it law, that any man who was either taken prisoner or who lost his weapons in a battle, and did not bring those of an enemy, was no more to be seen in his country. Thus the captured Matabili considered it the better plan to turn traitor, and endeavour to make himself useful to his captors. He therefore informed them that if they journeyed up westward of North, they might enter Moselekatse's country from a position where they were not expected, and where no spies were on the look out; and thus, if the attack were made at daybreak, a fearful slaughter must ensue.

Acting on this advice, the Boers started in the required direction, and were ready to dash upon their foes as soon as the first streaks of daylight illumined the land. Their attack was entirely unexpected, for the Matabili who had committed the slaughter on the wandering farmers, and who had attacked the hunters, had only just returned, and were rejoicing in their successes and in the trophies they had brought to the feet of their king. Before, however, the sun had risen more than ten times its height above the horizon, about 400 of the Matabili warriors were lying dead on the plains around their huts.

Hans Sterk had not, like many of his companions, been entirely occupied with slaughtering the enemy, he had been searching in all directions to find some traces of the prisoners who had been carried off by the Matabili; but he failed in doing so, until he found a wounded enemy, to whom he promised life if he would inform him where the white maidens were hidden. It was with difficulty that the two communicated, for Hans was but imperfectly acquainted with the half-Kaffir dialect spoken by the Matabili, and the wounded man understood but a few words of Dutch. Still, from him Hans learnt that Katrine and her sister were prisoners at Kapain, where Moselekatse then was; this place being a day's journey from Mosega, where the battle, or rather slaughter, had just taken place.

Hans' interests were not the same as those of the other Dutchmen; he was mainly bent upon recovering Katrine from her barbarous jailor, and immediately making her his wife; whilst his companions were only anxious to capture and carry off the large herds of cattle which were grazing around, and to take with them the waggons lately taken from the travellers. It was in vain that Hans pointed out to the commander of the expedition the advantages to be derived from following up with rapidity the successes already obtained, and to attack the chief of the Matabili where it was impossible he could escape. Carried away by his brief success, and uninfluenced by the arguments of one as young as Hans Sterk, the commander of the expedition refused to advance, and ordered the immediate retreat of the whole party, with about seven thousand head of cattle. This plan, having gained the approval of the majority of the men who formed the commando, was at once put into execution, and the retreat was commenced; and in a few days the wives, daughters, and children left at the waggons were rejoiced at the return of the expedition, with such a valuable capture as many thousand head of cattle. The news of this success spread among the colonists with magical effect, and many who had at first hesitated to follow the desert wanderers, now used the greatest expedition to do so, and thus the ranks of the wanderers were increased by some hundreds of souls. But one drawback existed, however, amidst the rejoicings, and that was, that Hans Sterk, Bernhard, and Victor, had undertaken what was considered a foolhardy expedition; for they had left the main body on the day after the battle, and were intent upon trying to effect the escape of two prisoners from the kraals of Moselekatse himself; such an attempt being almost reckless, and unlikely to succeed, considering the power and watchfulness of the enemy against whom they were about to try their skill. But we will return to Hans and his two companions.

Chapter Six
Hans determines to follow Katrine—He journeys by Night—Hans watches the Enemy

No sooner had Hans discovered that the Matabili had taken the two Dutch girls to a distant kraal, than he determined at all risks to attempt their release. During the first halt that occurred after the slaughter of the Matabili, he called his two great friends, Victor and Bernhard, to him, and said—

"I have failed to persuade the Governor-General to attack the enemy where he would be able utterly to defeat him and prevent him from again attacking us; for this defeat at Mosega is only like cutting off one of his fingers, whereas, if we went on to Kapain, we should attack his body. But I am going to try to release Katrine; and I have a plan in my head which may succeed, so to-night I shall leave the camp."

Victor and Bernhard looked at one another for some time; and then, as though reading each other's thoughts, they turned to Hans, when Victor, speaking first, said—

"I don't know what your plans are, Hans; but you shall not go alone. I will go with you, and I think Bernhard will go also."

"Yes, I will go," said Bernhard, "so let us talk over your plans."

The three friends, having thus agreed to share each other's fate, separated themselves from their companions, and sat down beneath a tree whose wide-spreading branches sheltered them from the heavy dew that was falling. Each having lighted his pipe and remained quiet for several minutes, was ready to listen or speak, according to circumstances.

"My plans," said Hans, are these: "to travel to the northward, and conceal ourselves and our horses in the range of hills that overlook Kapain. With my telescope I can observe all that goes on in the kraals, while we run no risk of being seen. Our spoor will scarcely be recognised, because so many horses have been travelling here lately; and the attention of all the Matabili will be occupied in either watching the main body of our people or in making preparations for an expedition against them. They would never suspect that two or three of us would remain in their country; and thus we, by daring, may avoid detection. If we are discovered, we can ride away from the Matabili; and thus, though at first it seems a great risk, yet it is not so bad after all. These are my ideas."

"But," inquired Victor, "how are you going to get Katrine away, or her sister?"

"I will take two spare horses with me, and they can then ride with us."

"You can't let Katrine know where you are, even if she is in the kraal at Kapain," said Victor; "and without we can get to her, our journey will be useless."

"Victor," said Hans, "will you trust me? I know what I am about, and will not do any thing without seeing to what the spoor is leading; we will start in half an hour."

A few words from Hans to the leader of the Boers informed him of his intention of leaving the party; and though the chief urged upon Hans the recklessness of his proceedings, he had yet no actual authority to prevent him and his two companions from acting as they wished; so, cautioning him of the risk he ran, he wished him success, and bade him good-bye.

It was about midnight when Hans and his companions left the Boers' encampment and started on their perilous journey. They rode for a considerable distance on the back spoor of their track, then, turning northward, they followed the course of some streams which flowed from the ranges of hills in the North-East. They continued their journey with rapidity, for the moon shone brightly and enabled them to see clearly for some distance around them. Many strange forms were seen during their journey, for Africa is full of night wanderers, and occasionally the deep growl of the lion, or the cry of the leopard was audible, within a few yards of them; but Hans and his companions were bent upon an expedition, and against foes of such importance, that even lions and leopards were looked upon as creatures not to be noticed, unless they seemed disposed to attack the travellers. The rapidity with which Hans and his companions rode, the silence maintained by them, and the purpose-like manner in which they continued a straight course, turning neither to the right nor left, even though a lion roared before them, gave to their journey a weirdlike character and reminded them of the dangers to which they were exposed; for, the Matabili, smarting as they just were from the defeat at Mosega, were not likely to delay the slaughter of any white men who might fall into their hands. Hans and his companions knew that the expedition was one for life or death; but it was not the first time that these men had looked on death calmly; and they were so confident in their own expedients that there were few circumstances for which they were not prepared.

As soon as the first light of morning began to appear, the three hunters rode into a ravine covered with brushwood and trees; having ascended this for some distance they found that it was possible to ride out of it in three directions besides that in which they had entered, and thus that a retreat was easily effected, should they be attacked from any one direction. They then dismounted, slackened the girths and took off the saddles, removed the bits from their horses' mouths, and allowed the animals to enjoy a roll in the grass, this being a proceeding which invariably refreshes an African steed, and without it he seems only half capable of enjoying his feed of grass; no sooner, however, had the animals rolled, than each was again saddled, and with the exception of loosened girths, was ready to be mounted in half a minute. The guns were examined, to see whether the night dew had rendered a miss fire probable; and then, having made a careful examination of the surrounding country with his telescope, Hans announced that after eating some of the *beltong*, (Meat dried in the sun), with which each was provided, two had better sleep whilst one watched, and so they could all have enough rest to fit them for the journey of the following night; having volunteered to watch first, Hans requested his companions to go to sleep, a request with which every thoroughly trained hunter should be able to comply; for he should always eat, drink, and sleep when he can, for when he wants to perhaps he may not be able. And when a hunter has nothing to do, he should sleep, for then he will be ready to dispense with his rest when it may be of importance that he should be watchful.

In a very few minutes Victor and Bernhard were snoring as though they were sleeping on a down bed instead of on the ground in an enemy's country, whilst the horses were making the best use of their time by filling themselves with the sweet grass in the ravine.

Hans had not been on watch more than an hour, when by the aid of his telescope he discovered a large body of Matabili who were following the spoor of his horses, and seemed as though bent on pursuing him. This sight caused him considerable anxiety, not on account of the numbers of his enemies, but because a fight with them, or a retreat from them, would defeat his plans for liberating Katrine. Hans therefore watched his enemies with the greatest interest, and could distinguish them distinctly, though they were distant nearly three miles. They approached to within two miles, and he was about to awaken his companions when he noticed the Matabili halted, and the chiefs' seemed to be talking about the spoor, as they pointed to the ground several times and then at different parts of the surrounding country. The ground was so hard and the dew had fallen so heavily immediately before sunrise, that Hans hoped the hesitation on the part of his enemies might be in consequence of a dispute or difference of opinion as regarded the date of the horses' footprints; for the probability was, that those left by his own and his companions' horses might be supposed to be those of stragglers of the expedition which had attacked the Matabili at Mosega. This he believed to be the case when he found that the numerous body of enemies, after a long consultation, quitted his spoor and turned away towards the West, moving with rapidity in the direction in which the main body of the Boers had retreated, and thus almost taking his back trail, instead of following him to his retreat. Several other small parties of armed Matabili were seen during the day; but none approached the ravine in which Hans was concealed, and the day passed and night arrived without any adventure.

Chapter Seven
Expedition of the Matabili—Hans telegraphs to Katrine, and receives his Answer

Immediately daylight enabled Hans to see the surrounding country, he examined with his glass the kraals of the Matabili, both far and near. Several objects attracted his attention, among which were some which threatened the safety of himself and party. Several armed bodies of the natives we're leaving the villages and departing hastily in various directions, as though engaged on business of importance. Hans, aware of the craftiness of his enemies, felt considerable uneasiness at these numerous departures; for he was well aware that if the Matabili had by chance discovered his hiding-place, they would not venture to attack him except in overwhelming numbers, but would first ascertain for certain that he was in the ravine; a fact which they would prove by examining the ground in all directions and finding footmarks which led into the kloof, but none which led out of it; then they would despatch several small parties with orders to assemble at certain parts of the ravine and there to form an ambuscade which was to intercept the retreat of Hans and his companions.

The Matabili, like most of the natives of South Africa, were accustomed to hunt the largest, most cunning, and fiercest animals, and from these they had taken many hints; the buffalo, for example, when wounded would retreat rapidly until out of sight, would then return and hide itself in the bush not far from the place from which it originally started; the hunter, unacquainted with the cunning of this creature, would probably follow it rapidly in its first retreat and would be suddenly surprised at finding himself within a few yards of the creature, which would probably be in the act of charging him. Although Hans observed that all the parties of the Matabili left their kraals, and moved in a contrary direction to the kloof in which he was concealed, yet he was not satisfied that they did not, when out of sight, turn, and make their way back, so as to be ready to attack him immediately he and his companions moved from their concealment. "The Matabili are moving early," said Victor, as he joined Hans and watched the various armed parties spreading over the country; "they must be going to attack our people."

"Some of them may possibly be sent to watch us; for they rarely give up a spoor as plain as ours must have been. Still I have a plan which may defeat them, if they think to trap us here. But look, Victor, with my glass, and tell me, do my eyes deceive me; is not that white object near that large kraal, a woman's dress? and is not that Katrine? But I forget, *you* would not recognise her so far off, though I can; but tell me if it is not a white woman's dress and manner."

Victor took the telescope, and making a slight alteration in the focus, directed it at the object indicated. After a very brief examination, Victor said—

"That, Hans, is a white woman without doubt; and following her, I see another and a smaller woman, who I think also is white."

Hans, who had been solely occupied in examining the first female figure, had not observed the second; but now, taking the glass, he at once found that Victor's observation was correct.

"I know now that must be Katrine, and her sister is behind her. I will let her know I am here."

"How can you do that, Hans?" inquired Victor with surprise; "she is more than a mile from us."

"I will show you, Victor; it is an old way of letting her know, that I practised for months, and she is accustomed to it. See this!"

Hans took from his pocket a small looking-glass, which was protected in a tin case; examining the direction of the sun, he then held the hand-glass so that its flash should be cast towards the plains; this he did very cautiously, having placed himself so that some leaves of a tree served to guide him as to the direction in which the reflection should be cast. As soon as he had made these preparations to his satisfaction, he said—

"Now, Victor, rest the telescope on the branch of that tree, and tell me what Katrine does."

Victor arranged the telescope as requested, whilst Hans slightly moved his mirror, so as to cast the flash in the direction of Katrine. During the first few minutes no effect seemed to result from Hans' performance. Katrine was walking slowly over the plain, her head cast down as though she were in deep thought, and looking neither to the right nor left. Her sister was, when first seen by Victor, nearly a hundred yards behind her; but shortly afterwards she ran to her elder sister and took her hand. All this Victor saw with his telescope and described to Hans, who still flashed the mirror in what he believed to be the right direction.

"Now they see it," exclaimed Victor. "The little one has seen it and drags her sister round; points here at us, and now they are both looking this way! See, Hans, the tall one is waving a handkerchief! Heavens, if a Matabili sees her, we shall be defeated in our plans! but now she has stopped waving her handkerchief, and is kissing her sister."

"Watch her now, Victor, and tell me every thing she does."

Victor looked eagerly through the telescope, and shortly saw what he described in the following words—"She seems to be looking all round, Hans, and uncertain where to go to: now she is walking quickly towards us, and her sister with her; she still comes on, and now she stops."

"Watch now, Victor, and see if she stoops and picks up any thing, and tell me how often she stoops."

"She does stoop," said Victor. "The girl is clever if this is a signal; she has picked up something and is looking at it; she stoops again and picks up something else; now she stands up and shakes her hankerchief, as though knocking off a fly; now she walks slowly back towards the kraal. Hans, I fear she has not seen your signal."

"She has seen it, and has answered it, Victor," said Hans; "and in two hours she will come to this ravine; that is what she tells me."

A look of half wonder, half incredulity passed across the face of Victor at this remark of Hans.

"You don't understand, I see, Victor, but I will explain. Since I have been courting Katrine, I have been accustomed to ride to the krantz about two miles from her father's house, when there I would flash my mirror to let her know where I was; this soon attracted her attention, and she had been taught by me to stoop and pick up something, as a signal. If I was to meet her at once, she only waved her handkerchief; but if she stooped and picked up something, I was to meet her in one hour; if she stooped twice, in two hours,—and so on. Now you say, and I just distinguished, that she stooped twice; so our meeting will be in two hours."

"But why will she come to us in this ravine?"

"We agreed, that if I was to come to her house, she was to walk towards it, but if I was to meet her near some yellow-wood trees, where we often met, she was to walk in that direction; so I think I am not wrong in believing she means to come to this place by her walking in this direction. There were not many days during the last few months that Katrine did not see the flash of my mirror, and so it is not wonderful that she at once responded to the signal. There, she has gone, Victor—has she not?—into the kraal. Now, you look to the horses, I will watch here, and we shall soon have a report from Bernhard as to what he has seen high up the ravine; then, if all be safe and well, we may soon be on horseback, and on our way back to our friends; and then we need not fear any number of Matabili, for we can ride away from them with ease, for both Katrine and her sister ride like Amazons. Ah, Bernhard, what news?"

"I don't like so many small parties of the Matabili disappearing in the bush behind us; at least a hundred have gone in there this morning, and the bush runs quite up to our ravine; these men might stalk to within a few yards of us, and we not know of their approach; it is necessary that we should be watchful, for the horses have more than once snorted as though they smelt something strange and unpleasant, and my horse has reason to dread a Matabili ever since the gash he got in the flank in our last expedition against these people. How long will you stay here, Hans?"

"Only two hours more, Bernhard, so I trust."

Chapter Eight
The attempted Rescue—Hans outwitted
and captured by the Matabili

The two hours which Hans had to wait before he believed Katrine would come to the kloof passed very slowly. Each minute seemed longer than would an hour pleasantly passed; and when only half the time had elapsed he began to feel uneasy, and to fear that he might be mistaken as regards the signals which Victor had seen. Long before the time had elapsed, however, Hans saw Katrine and her sister stroll out from the kraal and walk slowly along the paths which led in the direction of the ravine in which were her friends. She did not hurry, or seem at all eager, as though bent on an expedition of importance, but stopped occasionally as though undecided in which way to journey, and as though not engaged on any special purpose. Hans and his companions watched with the greatest interest every movement of the two girls, and also every group of Matabili that from time to time were seen moving from kraal to kraal. Several armed men had left the various little villages and had walked rapidly from one to the other, as though some business of war were on hand. About a dozen of these armed men were assembled, and seemed to be engaged in talking, near the kraal from which Katrine and her sister had first appeared; they took, apparently, no notice of the two girls, who seemed at full liberty to wander where they chose. These men, after a short time, followed the same path as that which Katrine had chosen, but they appeared merely idling, for occasionally they stopped, sat down, and took snuff, whilst now and then one or two would engage in a mimic fight, and, striking each others' shields, would threaten with their spears as though engaged in a deadly combat. At first these men scarcely attracted Hans' attention, so wholly was he engaged in watching Katrine; but being accustomed to notice every thing, however unimportant it might appear, he soon became interested in the proceedings of these warriors. Katrine steadily advanced towards the ravine, and was now distant scarcely half a mile; but behind her, and within a quarter of a mile, were the armed Matabili, who Hans saw had steadily followed her and her sister, although they seemed otherwise engaged.

"Those men," at length said Hans to his companions, "are following Katrine, and either do so as a means of watching that she does not escape, or else they know we are near and mean to attack us; there are but ten of them, and we can surely dispose of that number. Let us look to our priming; but we should not fire a shot if we can escape without doing so, for a gun discharged would alarm the whole country, and our escape would be very difficult. See, the men are coming closer to Katrine, and they are calling to her. Hear what they say, Victor, '*Wena musa hamba kona*,' they speak to her in Kaffir, and say, 'You must not go there.'

"Cess! if they lay hand on her I'll try a bullet at them even from here," said Hans, as he observed two of the Matabili run towards Katrine and her sister.

The two Dutch girls were not, however, to be ordered like children. They knew perfectly well what was said to them, but did not intend to obey it. Taking advantage of the temporary concealment afforded by some bushes behind which she walked, Katrine seized her sister's hand and ran rapidly up the path into the ravine. Although unaware of this proceeding, yet the Matabili had intended to prevent the two girls from entering the ravine; and so the whole party ran forward in order to bring the two maidens back.

The Matabili, as well as the other tribes of South Africa, used a certain amount of courtesy towards young and handsome women, although their wives are treated very much as are slaves. Thus these men considered it rather a piece of coquetry that the girls should run away from them, and were apparently more amused than angry at it. Thus, although Katrine and her sister were fully 200 yards in advance of their pursuers, yet the Matabili knew that the maidens could not escape them; for even if compelled to spoor them, these experienced hunters would soon re-capture their prisoners.

The point at which Katrine entered the ravine was distant about 300 yards from where Hans was concealed; and thus, had he remained where he then was, the Matabili would undoubtedly have captured the girls before they could have reached him. Seeing this, he at once decided upon running down the ravine and intercepting the pursuers. The suddenness of a discharge of fire-arms, which he was now convinced must be done, would so alarm the Matabili, ignorant as they were of the number of their foes, that their retreat would be immediate, and he would thus be left in undisturbed possession of Katrine and her sister.

Without any explanation of his reasons to his companions, who were men that needed not that a plain fact should be made more plain by argument, Hans said "Follow me," and the three ran down the pathway to meet Katrine, who, to the delight of Hans, was soon visible, and safely held for a moment in his arms.

"The Matabili are coming," exclaimed Katrine, "ten of them: can you fight them?"

"Yes, double the number would be nothing, now you are with me, Katie."

"But, Hans, more are about. I fear so much for you. How can we escape from these brutal murderers? Oh, it was fearful! My poor father was butchered before my eyes, and I lived to see it; but where can these men be? they were close behind us just now."

Hans was equally surprised at the disappearance of the Matabili, whom he had expected to see immediately behind Katrine and her sister, but who, it was evident, were not following her. Seeing this, Hans turned to his companions and said, "To the horses, men! not a moment must be lost now."

Hans, half carrying Katrine, who, however, was well able to move on at speed, was followed by Victor and Bernhard, between whom was Katrine's sister. The party walked and ran up the path towards where the horses had been left, and soon reached the open grassy glade where they had been allowed to graze. Instead, however, of finding their five horses there ready saddled for mounting, and merely knee-haltered to prevent their straying, the place was deserted, and no horses visible.

"Bernhard," exclaimed Hans, "where are the horses?"

"I left them here, Hans," replied Bernhard, "they can't be far off. Let us each take a path, and we shall soon bring them up: let the girls wait here for us."

Hans reluctantly quitted the side of Katrine and selected the path to his left, his two companions taking two other paths. Hans had proceeded but a few yards along his selected path, and was looking at the spoor of the horses, which was fresh on the ground before him, when a slight noise behind caused him to turn: he had but just time to raise his arm and partly ward off a blow aimed at his head by a Matabili who was armed with a horn knobskerrie, when his arms were seized and he was thrown violently to the ground, his gun dragged from him, and he was held by the powerful arms of some five or six Matabili. Almost at the same instant a shout from Victor and an oath from Bernhard, combined with the sound of struggling in the bush, indicated to Hans that his companions also had been captured; and therefore a regular ambush must have been prepared for the whole party. That he was not slaughtered at once, surprised him; for to make prisoners is usually considered by these warriors to be bad policy. Still, to be thus suddenly made a prisoner, and to know that Katrine also must be once more in the hands of his enemies, was a severe blow to Hans, especially when success had just seemed about to crown his efforts.

Hans was almost immediately bound with his hands behind him and led, with shouts of triumph and laughter, to the open glade where he had expected to find his horses; there he found Victor and Bernhard, bound like himself, and near them more than fifty armed Matabili warriors; whilst crouching on the ground, her arm round her sister, and crying bitterly, sat Katrine, entirely overwhelmed by grief and disappointment. The horses were held by some boys near the group; whilst a Matabili chief, who seemed to command the party, stood watching his prisoners. Suddenly addressing Hans, he said —

"Why have you come armed and without notice into the country of Moselekatse, when it is war between us?"

To this inquiry Hans gave no other answer than a look of disgust at the man, who, signalling to his followers, led the way down the ravine towards the kraals.

Chapter Nine
Hans Sterk becomes a Prisoner
with his Companions—Finds an
unexpected Ally—Plots an Escape

There are few conditions more unpleasant to any man than that of being a prisoner. When, moreover, it happens to a man of active and enterprising habits, and when the captors are men who are bound by none of those laws which possess an influence in civilisation, and where, consequently, the prisoner may be put to death at any moment merely to gratify the whim of a despot, a captive's condition is one not to be envied.

As soon as Hans Sterk found that he had been fairly entrapped and made prisoner by the Matabili, he blamed himself for his want of watchfulness and caution: had he been one of the unskilled residents of the towns, he could not have been more easily outwitted. He saw that his captors looked at him with contempt and seemed to consider him quite a novice in the art of bush warfare; and as they talked unreservedly of their proceedings, he was enabled to find out how artful had been their plans.

The Matabili, he discovered, had crossed the spoor of his horses, and saw at once that it led to the ravine in which he was concealed; they believed that he must be with his companions concealed in that ravine, but if they followed him at once he would, being provided with horses, either escape by riding, or would fight and probably kill many of his enemies before he was himself slain. They decided therefore to ascertain first whether he was still in the ravine; and a young keen-eyed boy was despatched to the far side, to see if there were any spoor leading *out*; for if there were not, then the white men must be concealed in the ravine.

As soon as this boy's report had been received, the Matabili chiefs concluded that the men had come either to act as spies, which was unlikely, or else for the purpose of rescuing the two girls. This latter supposition was considered the more probable by the experienced chiefs; and the ravine having been carefully surrounded by a large party of the Matabili, who, to avoid suspicion, left the kraals in parties of three or four only, a careful espionage was kept upon the two female prisoners, and Hans' plot immediately discovered and guarded against, and preparations made for his capture and for that of his companions.

The prisoners were conducted to the kraal from which Katrine and her sister had escaped in the morning. The three men were placed in the hut, the door of which was closed, their hands tied behind them, and some half-dozen boys appointed to watch the hut from the exterior.

There are times when men of the greatest energy and enterprise fail in the attempts they are making to obtain certain results; these failures do not invariably occur in consequence of want of skill or care on the part of the men themselves, but seem to be the effect of some inscrutable power, which is often termed luck. When again and again such failures happen, we are accustomed to be thoroughly cast down, and to feel that no endeavours of our own can aid us: do what we may, think what we may, yet an evil luck will attend us, and failure must follow. These seasons of ill-luck or want of success may be the means used to teach us that man's efforts alone can be but fruitless, and that it needs the assistance of higher powers to ensure success.

It was with a feeling of utter despair that Hans Sterk contemplated his late failure and his present pitiable condition. Like as a beaten chess-player reflects on the move which, if executed, might have saved him his game, so did Hans turn over every act and thought of the past, in order to find how he might have avoided his late failure; but the fact remained, that the enemy had been too crafty for him, and he too sanguine of success.

The hut in which he was a bound prisoner was like all the huts of the Kaffirs. It was constructed of strong wicker-work, and thatched with reeds and long grass; the door was merely a small wattled hurdle, and did not so entirely block the doorway as to prevent those outside from looking in; the walls were so thin that voices and conversation, even though carried on in a moderately low voice, could be heard from hut to hut. After the three prisoners had remained silent a short period, Hans said—

"Friends, I am very sorry that I have brought you into this state. We have tried our best, but we have failed: men can do no more than try."

"We have been unlucky," said Bernhard; "and most likely shall not see another sun rise, for the old chief must be furious at his losses lately, and may gratify his vengeance by seeing us assagied."

"Don't let us look at the worst," said Victor; "we must think of escape; it is no use lying here like sheep to be taken, to the slaughter. I too believe we shall die to-morrow, but let us at least try to escape."

"Rather difficult to escape, with our hands tied, and surrounded by enemies," remarked Bernhard.

"Nothing is impossible to men with wits and nerve," replied Hans; "and now I feel once more a man. Thank you, Victor, for giving me fresh strength by your remark, we will try to escape, and here is my plan: as soon as it is quite dark, we will free each other's arms; this can be done by biting the withes and hide rope of one of us, then he who is free can liberate the others. See, in the roof there is an assagy, with this we can cut the fastenings as soon as one pair of hands are free. Next, one of us can go to the door and by some means attract the attention of the boys on watch, and bring them round to the front of the door; the other two can then work a way through this thin thatch and escape to the horses. The alarm need not be given at once; but if it should be, a run for life is better than nothing."

"It would never succeed, Hans," replied Victor: "the noise of breaking through the thatch would be too great; perhaps a better plan may occur to us if we think for awhile."

The three men sat silently turning over every possible means of escape for nearly a quarter of an hour; but no idea seemed to be likely to be practically useful. As they were thus meditating, they heard a young Kaffir woman speaking to the boys who were on watch. She was laughing with them, and, from what the three prisoners could hear, she seemed to be rejoicing at their capture. At length she said, "I should like to throw some dirt at them, to let them know how little a Matabili maiden thinks of them." And suiting the action to the words, she pushed aside the door, and, with a taunting laugh, threw a handful of earth at the prisoners. After a few words with the boys, she then withdrew, and all were again silent. A single term of abuse burst from the lips of Bernhard as a lump of clay struck him; and then, with a look of contempt at the door near which the Kaffir maiden had stood, he again racked his brain for some ideas which should aid him to escape.

Hans, who had been working his arms quietly but forcibly backwards and forwards for some time, suddenly withdrew one of his hands from the fastenings, exclaiming, — "So much for the tying of a Matabili! You can free yourselves in five minutes, if you strain your knots. Try what you can do."

The two men thus addressed commenced straining their knots; which proceeding, however, was not as successful as had been that of Hans. The latter, however, by one or two cuts of the assagy soon liberated the arms of his companions, and, to their surprise, addressed them in a whisper as follows: —

"Soon after sunset we shall be free, so stretch your limbs, and be ready for a battle for life and freedom."

"What is your plan, Hans?" said Victor; "let us hear."

"It is not my plan; it is Katrine's information. That ball of clay that the girl threw contained a roll of paper from Katrine. This is what she says:—

"'An hour after sundown, there will not be a man in the kraal, only six boys to watch you and two old women to watch us. Free your arms and make your escape; then your guns are in the chief's hut, the one with the large ox-horns over the doorway, the horses are in the kraal next the cow's kraal: we will be ready. The girl who takes this I have won by presents. I leave to you, Hans, the plan: you may depend I tell you truth; I have learned all this from the girl.'"

"And that was in the clay ball," exclaimed Victor. "Ah, Bernhard, we are but stupid hands on the spoor. Hans, after all, is the born leader. What made you think there was any thing in the ball, Hans?"

"I did not think the girl looked cruel," replied Hans, "and she seemed acting a part as I looked at her."

"Let us make our plans now. What do you propose, Hans?" inquired Victor.

"We will try my plan first, if that fail we will just rush out and drive off the boys, and so escape. I must find out where the men are all going to, for it depends on that where we ride to. Our horses may not be very fit for a journey, however, and as we shall certainly be followed, and our spoor will be as plain as a waggon-track, we must take care; for once again captured, we shall never have another chance. Ah, here comes the girl again."

The Matabili girl again came to the door, and with a loud laugh threw in a handful of dirt which she had appeared to pick up from the cattle-kraal near. Amidst this heap was another lump of clay, from which Hans drew a piece of paper, and read, "I can give you no other weapons than three assagies, these will be pushed through your hut soon after sunset; look out for them and draw them in rapidly, so as not to be seen. We must first ride *north*. God help us!"

"Katrine is better than gold," exclaimed Victor, "and I for one am glad to be, running this risk for her, and will readily die without complaint, if need be. She will be a fit wife for you, Hans."

A gratified smile passed over Hans' face as he heard Katrine thus spoken of; but being more disposed to discuss with his companions any other subject than the merits of his beloved Katrine, he said, "To get our guns will be the great thing, then we can fight well. Why they give us this chance of escape, I don't know."

"They trapped us so easily before, they fancy they can venture to leave us with boys, I suppose," was Victor's explanation.

"Ah," replied Hans, "they don't know that a real man often does not thoroughly act till his case seems desperate and he completely defeated, then he rises to victory."

The sun appeared to move very slowly to the prisoners in the hut, who anxiously watched the lengthening shadows, and waited impatiently till it began to get dusk. The accuracy of Katrine's information was soon evident, for between the slight openings of the door Hans saw several Matabili warriors, completely armed, silently move away across the plain outside the kraal. It appeared as if there were to be some general meeting, or gathering of the forces of the Matabili chief, which required all the men to be present; and the prisoners being supposed securely bound, might well be entrusted to the boys, who, on the slightest alarm, might summon the men to their assistance. As nearly as the prisoners could guess, an hour had scarcely elapsed when the girl who had previously brought the notes of Katrine and her sister, passed by the hut in which Hans and his companions were confined, and singing a wild song, seemed intent on some occupation. The three Dutchmen, watching eagerly for some signal, heard the word 'loop' uttered several times, as though in the chorus of a song.

"That," said Hans, "must mean we are to go" (loop being the Dutch for go or *be off*). "Katrine has taught her this. Bernhard, open the door quietly and look out, all the boys, I fancy, are behind the hut talking to this girl."

The door was slowly pushed on one side by Bernhard; and there appearing no watchers near, he whispered to his companions the result of his examination.

"Now for our lives," said Hans, "and for those of the girls. We will go very quickly, but silently, to the hut for our guns, then for our horses, and then for Katrine. Let us go."

Bernhard led the way out of the hut, the door of which was so low that it was necessary to crawl out on all fours, Victor followed, and lastly, Hans, who stayed to fasten the wicker door in its former position. The three men then walked away towards the hut in which they believed their guns to be, and opening the door, Hans first entered. The inside of the hut was so dark that scarcely any thing was visible; but no sooner had Hans stood up and stretched out his arm, to feel the side of the hut, than his hand came in contact with the arm of a human being. In an instant his hand closed on this arm with a grip which indicated his knowledge that life or death depended now on every trivial circumstance; but before he could grasp the throat of whoever it was, a whispered voice exclaimed, "Hans, it is I, here are your guns," and Katrine's voice was immediately recognised by her lover. Bernhard and Victor had by this time entered the doorway, and were first alarmed, then delighted, to find Hans talking to some one in the hut. As soon as Katrine had disengaged herself from her lover, who held her almost as firmly as he would have held an enemy, she explained to him what she believed to be their best chance of escape.

"We must leave this hut, and get out of the enclosure behind it," she said; "we can creep through an opening in the palisades, and then go round to the kraal where the horses are. It will be difficult to secure them, for two Kaffirs are left in charge of them; but my sister is about there, looking out, and will tell us what is best to be done. All of you must put a blanket each over you, then, if you hide your hats, you will not be known in the dark from Kaffirs, at least till you are seen very close. Then we must lead the horses some distance before we ride away, and we must ride northwards, away from the kloof near which we were taken this morning. All the men have gone south, so we may miss them. Do you see what to do, Hans?"

"Yes," whispered Hans, "we will go out now. Let me feel, are my powder-horn and bullets here? Yes, they are untouched. Bernhard, you take these and take my gun; I will help Katrine along: then I have a plan."

The three men wrapped in blankets crept from the hut without being observed; the occupants of the various huts being engaged inside, cooking their evening meal. An opening large enough to allow of the four passing through, was found behind the hut; and in a few minutes Hans had conducted Katrine to a spot some fifty yards outside the enclosure, where he stopped near a clump of bushes that offered concealment. "Now for the most difficult part of the affair," said Hans, "to procure the horses. Are the men old or young, Katrine, who are watching them?"

"Young," said Katrine, "and inexperienced."

"Then I will try a bold plan. If I call Help! you, Victor, come to me, whilst you, Bernhard, take care of Katrine; but if I don't call, then go down to the stream when I come out whistling from the cattle-kraal. Where is your sister, Kate?"

"She is close here, Hans, and will come when she hears one whistled note; she is hid I don't know where."

"Bring her to you, then, and now for the attempt," said Hans.

To men used, as were these hunters, to make rapid plans, and execute them as quickly, no further explanations were needed; and the two who remained with Katrine waited patiently to see the result of Hans' scheme, trusting to his skill and knowledge to bring about a favourable result. The method which Hans intended to attempt was a bold one. He knew that, dark as it was, he could not be recognised unless he were examined closely. He also knew that the young Kaffir or Matabili men were ordered about in a very summary way by their elders, and no discussion was ever allowed when an order was given. He had ascertained, by the conversation of the boys outside of the hut, the name of the chief of the kraal; and thus provided he walked boldly towards the kraal, with no effort at concealment. As he approached he called in the Matabili language, "Where are you?"

"Here," answered the two men.

"The chief wants to show the horses," said Hans, in his best Kaffir; "bring them out, I am to take them."

A murmur of surprise escaped the two men as they heard this order; but fearing to dispute or question, they entered the kraal, and, unfastening the horses, led them out of the narrow gateway. Hans covered himself almost completely with his blanket, and as the men came out he said, "Follow me, lead the horses this way."

As among the followers of Moselekatse there were many renegades from the Zulus, and some from various tribes in all directions, the difference in Hans' pronunciation of several words was not noticed, or at least not paid particular attention to. And as he spoke in a tone of authority his orders were not questioned, though he was personally unknown to the two men in charge of the horses, who believed him to be some chief sent direct from Moselekatse.

When Hans had led the men some few yards from the bushes where his companions were concealed, he stopped and said, "Now leave the horses here; I can take them alone. Go back and watch the cattle; the chief wants you to see that all is safe in the kraal."

With that same tacit obedience which had before been shown by the men, and which would appear unaccountable in those who did not know the Matabili character, the men who were directed to watch the horses actually gave them up to a stranger, the magic name of *the Chief* being sufficient to awe them. They, however, never dreamed of an enemy being near them; and the thought of the Dutchmen who had been so easily trapped in the morning putting so bold a scheme into practice, would have seemed little short of impossible; and thus the horses were given up without any suspicion.

One very low whistle had scarcely been given by Hans before Bernhard and Victor, with Katrine and her sister, were by his side.

"Get on this horse, Katie," said Hans, "and your sister on that next me, and we can now escape."

"No," said Katrine, "it will not do for us to ride. If any Matabili saw us on a horse, they would know we were prisoners escaping, but if they only saw the horses they might not suspect; but now, Hans, do you know which way to go in the dark?"

"It is difficult to find the way," replied Hans, "for I can see but a short distance; still I can tell by those three stars close together that we are going north."

"Yes, we are; and I think I can find the path here. We shall have to pass a kraal about half a mile farther on. What shall we do if any men come out?"

"We must tell them we are going to take the horses to the chief," replied Hans, "that may satisfy them."

"It may; but this is not the way to the chief's kraal," replied Katrine. "We shall be in danger there."

The party moved on over the soft ground rapidly and quietly; the horses, seeming to recognise their masters, followed them without hesitation, and scarcely required to be touched by the rear follower. As they neared the kraal past which they had to walk, they heard sounds of loud talking and occasional singing, so that the slight noise of the horses' feet they trusted would not be heard. A Matabili at all times, however, is watchful, and more particularly in time of war. Just as the three men with their charge were opposite the kraal the singing and talking suddenly ceased, and some half-dozen men came out of their huts, and called out, "Who is there?"

"Taking the horses by the chief's orders," replied Hans, in Matabili.

Resting his hand on Katrine's arm, he whispered, "Not a move, Katrine, we must escape by boldness; any hurry now, and we may fail."

Katrine was a girl who had lived amidst events which the denizen of civilisation is unacquainted with: she had witnessed many rough scenes, was accustomed to hear tales of dangers and risks, and was thus seasoned, as it were, to a life of adventures. Just as the most delicately nurtured English girl will travel by an express train without any very great fear the very day after some fearful accident may have happened on the railway by which she is a passenger, so did Katrine trust that all might turn out well in spite of the apparent dangers around. Still when she found that the approach of her party had been heard by the men of this kraal, and heard them speaking to Hans, she feared another scene of bloodshed would soon be enacted, such as that to which she had been a witness when she was first captured by the

Matabili and her father slaughtered. Her trembling arm indicated to Hans her fears, but his whispered encouragement gave her strength and hope.

The moment, however, was critical, and had not Hans' answer been confident and distinct, he might have had to fight for his life under circumstances where he could not well escape; for it would have been almost certain death to have attempted to ride at speed on a night as dark as that on which they were escaping. Fortunately the men were not curious; and most Kaffirs having a dislike to move about much at night, in consequence of snakes, centipedes, and scorpions, on which their naked feet might tread, they waited inside their kraal until the party had passed, and the sound of their footsteps was heard no more.

"We are safe so far," whispered Hans, "thank God! Can you tell me, Katrine, where this path leads to?"

"It leads down to the stream about a mile on, and then is lost in the plain beyond. It has been used for driving the cattle to and from water, and also for hunting, there being many '*wilde*' on the plain beyond."

"If, then, we can cross the river, we may consider ourselves safe," remarked Hans; "for we can then put you on the horses, and can ride all night. Our spoor cannot be followed by night, and twelve hours' start ought to enable us to reach our people before we are overtaken."

"But there are hundreds of the Matabili out on war," said Katrine, "and we may fall in with some of them."

"Ah! and I have lost my far-seer," said Hans. "That is a loss. But we had better not talk; let us listen and think; we may then be less liable to a surprise."

The party reached the stream of which Katrine had spoken, and crossed it in safety, and found before them an apparently smooth, undulating plain. After journeying over this about half an hour, the moon rose, she being some days past the full. By her light, and by the aid of the stars as guides, Hans pursued a course which led nearly in the direction of his countrymen's settlements; but as these were distant fully three days' journey, even riding at the best speed, and as the parry had no provisions, there seemed much to be overcome before a place of safety could be reached.

Chapter Ten
The Prisoners are free—The Pursuit—
The Horses sick—The Ride for
Life—The Concealment

The morning following that on which Hans and his companions had escaped, broke with all the splendour of an African day. The dew had fallen heavily during the night, and thus the first rays of the sun produced a mist which hung like steam over the valleys; but this soon clearing away, left the atmosphere clear and transparent; so that distance could not be measured by atmosphere, as in our misty climate, but a far-off range of mountains seemed within a short ride of the observers, whereas it was distant at feast fifty miles. This clearness had a great advantage for Hans' party, as it rendered surprise less likely than if a dense fog or cloudy weather had prevailed.

No sooner did the slightest sign of daylight appear, than Hans, by the aid of some loose powder and a piece of rag, with a flint and steel lighted a fire, and commenced preparations for a breakfast. Victor and Bernhard, like the others of the party, had merely lain down under the shelter of some bushes to obtain a few hours' rest; but all had gone supperless to bed, if bed it could be termed. But in such a climate a night passed in the open country was not a very great hardship, even to young girls like Katrine and her sister. That very unromantic feeling, hunger, was however demanding attention; and when Victor and Bernhard, suddenly awaking at the sound of Hans' flint and steel, started up and observed daylight beginning to dawn, and Hans making a fire, they, with an air of surprise, said—

"You have fire, Hans, but where is the food?"

"I did not like to fire a gun, lest I might disturb the country, and let some strange Matabili know we were hereabouts; so I have procured breakfast with a Matabili's assagy."

"What have you?" eagerly asked the hungry hunters.

"A young vleck vark and a porcupine," replied Hans. "The porcupine I found out on the plains, and speared him before he got to his hole. The pig I saw run into a jackall's hole, so I waited quietly over it with my assagy till it came out to peep where I had gone. I stabbed it in the neck, and held it down till I killed it with my assagy. So we shall not starve yet, Victor; and the girls can eat pork, if they object to porcupine."

"Ah! Hans," said Victor, "though I am an old hunter, I know I should starve in the desert where you would keep fat and sleek."

It was a strange breakfast, that which took place on the mountain-spur, between the five white people on the morning in question. It is seldom that lovers pass through such scenes as those in which were Hans and Katrine. Artificial life is now so much more general than is natural life, that few people are aware how very false is much that surrounds them. A well-bred English lady would probably imagine that she would rather starve than make a meal off a porcupine, when no plate or fork enabled her to eat, as some would term it, "like a Christian." It is surprising, however, how soon we learn to dispense with these ornaments of the feast, as we may term them. The writer of this tale cannot recall to mind any more enjoyable feasts, though flavoured with the best of wines and the most intellectual society, and amidst scenes of richness or splendour, than some repasts eaten amidst the dense bush of an African forest, with no other companion than the one black follower whose duty it was to spoor or carry the game, and where the cooking was simply toasting on a ramrod over the camp-fire some of the steaks from the buck which an hour previously was roaming freely in the forest. That unrivalled sauce, "hunger," gave an additional flavour to the venison, whilst the most robust health and the purest air supplied the want of many of those addenda which are considered necessities in civilised dining-rooms.

Thus the breakfast of porcupine and wild pig, though no bread or salt were added, no tea or sugar, and nothing but a draught of pure water from a tiny mountain stream near, was relished by those who with a brief but refreshing sleep had passed the night under the cloudless canopy of heaven.

Hans had selected the halting-place for the night under some trees on a spur of a range of mountains which skirted the plains, so that as the morning dawned he might be able to see around, and thus possibly discover if any parties of the enemy were out in search of him. He found none, however, and therefore immediately breakfast was finished, the horses were mounted, and the party continued their journey, changing their direction now to the westward, in order to ride towards the district in which they believed their friends would be most likely to be found.

The sun had nearly attained his meridian altitude before Hans decided to halt, to off-saddle the horses, and to refresh the party, by partaking of the remainder of his morning's captures. The place that he had selected for the halt was a slightly wooded ravine, amidst the rocks of which a clear stream ran over a grassy or pebbly bed, behind him was a range of rocky hills, the summit of which was crowned by huge masses of rock, looking from the distance like vast slabs placed by giant strength in their present position. Before them was an undulating plain, on which detached clumps of bushes and trees were scattered; tiny mountain-born streams flowed in various parts of this plain, and could be seen like silver threads winding about amongst trees, shrubs, and ferns, until two or three joining together formed a fair-sized river. On these plains herds of antelope were grazing, and seemed undisturbed by any enemy; ostriches were stalking here and there, whilst the grim circling vulture was wheeling in the air, watching for carrion on which to feast.

"This is a beautiful district," exclaimed Hans, as he examined the various attractive features of the scene; "it is too good for a black savage to own. What more could a man wish for than what he finds here? There is water in abundance, plenty of grass for his cattle and horses, a soil that would yield if the seed were merely thrown down, game in abundance, and a climate as good as any in Africa. I have heard, but can scarcely believe, that in England there are men, strong men, who pass their whole lives in crowded places, in a country too where the sun is rarely seen, and all for the sake of getting more money than they want for their necessities, but which they thus slave for in order to make a show in the way of ornaments. Can you believe, Victor, that such men know what life really is?"

"It is strange, Hans, at least to us who know how to live by hunting, and whose cattle increase rapidly, if left to themselves; but perhaps these men you speak of would not be happy unless they were thus slaving all their lives. We are not all alike, Hans, and few men know how to love nature."

"If we live to get back to our friends, Victor, I will marry Katrine, and join the first party that *treks* for a new station, whenever that may be. See those springbok, Victor, by the tall acacias there, they scent an enemy, what is it? Oh, for my far-seer! the rascally Matabili have that, and won't know how to use it."

"No need of a telescope, Hans," said Bernhard, who had joined the other two; "there is the cause for the springbok running away. Those are Matabili coming over the plain, and we had better be prepared for a gallop, for if they see us we shall have to try what four legs can do against two."

"I don't believe they would openly attack us, for there are not more than forty men," replied Hans, "and thirteen to one is scarcely enough odds to tempt them. They will follow us though, undoubtedly, and will endeavour to surprise us. We had better saddle up and be ready for a start at once."

"Katrine," said Hans, "are you ready to go on? there are enemies on the plains below, and we had better ride forward."

"Yes, I am ready, Hans, but are the horses fit?" replied Katrine; "they seem very tired."

Hans walked towards the horses, and for nearly a minute watched them closely, particularly a well-bred hardy chestnut that had been ridden by Katrine. This horse was standing with its head low, but did not feed, though the grass was in plenty close to its mouth.

"Victor," said Hans at length, "come here."

Victor came to Hans, who, pointing at the chestnut said, "Look!"

Victor for an instant examined the animal, and then with an exclamation said, "It is the sickness. We are lost if the others go in the same way."

"They will go for certain," replied Hans, "and so we had better ride whilst we can. That chestnut will be dead in an hour. We must leave him here, and push on with the others."

The sickness to which Victor referred is the dreaded pest of every South African traveller: the cattle disease which lately in England has carried off whole herds, is not dissimilar to the so-called sickness which affects South African horses and cattle. A horse may appear quite well in the morning, and even when ridden indicate no signs of illness; perhaps about mid-day he may appear slightly dull and lazy, and in the evening be dead. No remedy has yet been found to be effective against this sickness, and thus every traveller bargains to lose a large percentage of horses and oxen on every trip that he makes into strange districts; for it seems that horses seasoned in one district take the disease in another, and thus the traveller has to test the constitution of the animal that carries him by passing through various portions of country, many of which are what may be termed infected. In the far desert the loss of cattle and horses is a disaster beyond remedy, and often causes the ruin of the hunter, or, as in the present case, entails a great risk of life.

Almost concealed, even from close observation, amidst the dense bush of the ravine, Hans' party believed they had escaped being seen by the ever-watchful Matabili, who seemed to continue their journey in the same direction they were pursuing when first observed. The horses were kept concealed behind the densest bushes, whilst Hans watched the enemy, who was more than a mile distant from him. The warrior, however, trained in the desert observes facts which would escape the attention of the civilised, or half-civilised man, and notices and attaches a meaning to trifling circumstances quite beyond the perception of the other. Just as the Matabili were within the shortest distance at which their path would bring them near the white fugitives, some vultures, attracted probably by the horses of the Dutchmen, halted in their steady flight, and commenced circling overhead Hans observed this at once, and knew the danger of the circumstance.

"The Matabili will see this and will become suspicious," Hans exclaimed; "they are not men to overlook the vultures' signal."

Scarcely had he spoken before the Matabili halted and stood gazing at the bushes amidst which the party were crouching. A very short examination seemed to satisfy them, for, dividing into two parties, they started at a run towards the ravine, beating their shields and muttering a low-toned song.

"We had better ride for it," said Hans; "we might kill half their number, but the remainder would finish us. Come, Katie, mount the schimmel horse; we will have a gallop."

The two girls were soon mounted, and though they had to ride on a man's saddle, with one stirrup crossed over to supply the place of a pommel, they had been too much accustomed to horses from their childhood to find much difficulty in this performance. Victor and Bernhard were soon ready also, and merely waiting for the signal to gallop off.

"Let the men descend into that hollow," said Hans, "then they will not see us ride away. We will keep the slope of the hill, as the streams are smaller there than in the valley below. Now, be ready, men, and off with you."

The horses, though far from fresh, in consequence of the small amount of food they had eaten, yet responded to the application of the impromptu whip which each rider had provided himself with, and started at a pace which, if continued, would have placed the riders far beyond the possibility of capture from any pedestrians. Hans, however, knew the infectious nature of the sickness, and watched with anxiety the action of the various horses, for if another horse died, one animal would have to carry double weight, a fact which would prevent any rapid progress. He knew too that the Matabili could journey fully fifty miles a day for several days, and this would be more than the half-starved horses could manage; so that the present position was one of extreme danger.

By the time the Matabili had reached the spot on which Hans and his party had been concealed, he had ridden nearly two miles away, and his spoor alone showed the Matabili how near they had been to their enemies; for they at once recognised the freshness of this spoor, whilst the dying horse showed that he had not been long deserted.

Not knowing that two out of the five riders were women, the Matabili fortunately did not pursue in a body, but despatching two of their fastest and best runners to watch the enemy and to bring back the latest intelligence, the remainder continued their journey towards the head-quarters of their chief.

During fully three hours Hans rode steadily onwards, the sun, the ranges of hills, and the streams serving to show him in which direction he should travel. Wishing to give the horses every chance, he then deemed it advisable to halt, and allow the animals to graze, as also to try and procure some food for the party. Selecting the bank of a stream, where a clear open space round prevented much chance of a surprise, he again off-saddled the horses; and telling Victor and Bernhard to prepare a fire, he started in search of food.

To a hunter as well skilled as was Hans in the habits of animals it was not difficult to procure game when provided with a gun. Some patches of grass and weeds on the leeward side of a ravine at once attracted him; there he thought either a reitbok or a duiker should be found, and either would supply enough food for two days.

Hans was correct in his judgment, and obtained an easy shot at a reitbok, which he killed, and thus provided his companions with food sufficient for two days. Roughly cooked as it was, and eaten with nothing else, it yet was not despised by any one of the party.

About two hours' additional riding from the last resting-place completed the day's journey, and a suitable locality having been chosen, the party halted for the night, Hans agreeing to sleep first whilst Victor watched, and then to take his turn about midnight.

Chapter Eleven
Night in the Wilderness—The Lions roar—The Savage outwitted by a Lion— The Party take up a good position

There are few more singular experiences to the civilised man than to camp in the wilderness; and there are now but few countries in the world where such an event can occur. Man has now spread so widely over our planet, that but few spots can be found in the state in which nature framed them. To find any spot so far removed from the residence of man that no sound can reach it which is indicative of a human being, is indeed a rarity. The distant bark of a dog, the tinkle of a bell, the bleating of a sheep, or the sound of a signal gun, can all be heard on a still night for many miles. Thus, when we say that to experience the full effects of a night in the wilderness, we should be at least forty or fifty miles from any residence of human beings, and in a country where the wild animals are as yet no more than partially thinned by the occasional visits of hunters, probably Africa alone of all the continents yields to the hunter the thorough wilderness, with its attendant thrilling additions. India is generally too much populated: America somewhat destitute of numerous members of the ferae which abound in Africa. Europe is the land of men and cities, and thus we return to Africa as the true hunter's paradise.

Scarcely has the sun disappeared below the African horizon, than the hunter realises the novelty of his position in the wilderness; for a space of nearly half an hour the air vibrates with the sharp cricket-like cry, or deep hum of hundreds of insect creatures who are thus signalling their presence to each other. From amidst a lofty ruined mass of rocks, which appeared by day deserted by every living creature, except a few lizards and poisonous snakes, a grim gaunt figure stalks out, and ascending a prominent block of stone, gazes around at the domain over which darkness has again given it dominion. Man may by day be monarch of the hill-side and plain, but by night the lion may well be called monarch of all he surveys. From the dimly-seen, statue-like figure on the rock, a few deep, dissatisfied growls come rolling over the plain, strike the face of the rock, and echo back again in confused murmurs, evincing the power of the mighty beast who thus, with no apparent effort, speaks to all within a range of several miles. From a far-distant and woody ravine, a fiend-like yell next breaks the silence of the night, and is followed by a deep-drawn, howling sigh, as the strand wolf wanders forth to search for the carrion of the day, or to capture such prey as he is capable of doing. Busy, silent-moving forms glide past the hunter, and, with a snort of terror or a growl of anger, move away to the distance, scarce liking to let alone so apparently defenceless a creature as man seems to be, yet awed by a certain presence which the brute creation never thoroughly overcome.

Tiny creeping animals again crackle the crisp leaves as they scamper about in their fastnesses among the bushes, and sniff the scent of the strange intruder; whilst the noiseless flapping of wings attracts for an instant the hunter's sight as some ghost-like moving night-bird flies around him, and examines the strange being that has intruded into its domain.

Suddenly the sound of a struggle startles the hunter, and a cry of distress from a stricken creature is audible, whilst frightened animals rush hither and thither for a time, and then again relapse into their former indifference. A lion, perhaps, has captured its evening prey from amongst a grazing herd; or a leopard has struck down the antelope that it has been cautiously watching and stalking during the past half-hour. And then again a silence so still, so unbroken, follows the past turmoil, that the desert wanderer fancies he can hear the thin, fleecy clouds moving above him, or the long-absent but deeply-loved voice of one who should be near him. Amidst all the danger, all the novelty of the scene, however, exhausted nature usually exerts her sway, and the hyena's laugh or leopard's cry ceases to be heard, whilst the traveller passes into the unconsciousness of sleep, and dreams probably of scenes the very opposite of those amidst which he then is, and awakes, scarcely knowing which is the reality—the dream of old, well-known scenes, amidst which the greater part of his life has been passed, or the wild, unusual events transpiring around him.

To men of adventure such as Hans and his companions, a night in the desert was not unusual, and they experienced but few of the sensations which a more civilised man undoubtedly would feel; yet to these hunters there was something awe-inspiring in the calm stillness of the night, broken only by the shrieks and cries of night wanderers among the wild animals, or the snorts of terror from their horses as these sounds met their ears.

It was past midnight when Hans commenced his watch, and was the only one of the five who was awake. The sisters were sheltered from the dew by a blanket supported by two or three sticks, and arranged so as to form a kind of tent. The two Dutchmen were lying beneath some bushes with merely the blanket over them that served during the day to protect their horses' backs from a badly-stuffed saddle.

Although Hans believed that any attack from an enemy was unlikely, yet, being a man who knew the value of guarding against every possible, not every likely danger only, he placed himself within a few yards of Katrine and her sister, and there listened attentively to every sound that broke the silence of the night.

When darkness spreads her mantle over the earth it is by sound alone that an enemy can be discovered; for sight is then useless, and a man who has thoroughly trained his hearing can distinguish sounds which are inaudible and unintelligible to the mere tyro. To the ears of Hans the tread of an animal with a hoof would have been recognised from that of a soft-footed animal, such as a lion or leopard, and the footsteps of a man could have been distinguished from those of a quadruped. It is almost impossible for the civilised man to realise the acuteness of the senses of one accustomed to trust his life to his senses, the sight, hearing, and even scent seem to become added to in power, and in fact to have an additional sense given to each. We all know how we can readily distinguish the footstep of some particular friend from that of a stranger, though how we do so it would puzzle us to explain; but thus it is that the trained hunter can instantly decide that a hyaena or antelope is walking past him, that a man is near, or that some other animal is moving in his vicinity.

It was with mingled feelings of surprise and half-doubt that Hans heard what he was confident was the footstep of a man soon after he had taken his position near Katrine. For several minutes not a sound disturbed the stillness of the night except the somewhat heavy breathing of the sleepers; this, however, was a source of great danger. To the acute ears of a lion, or even of a Kaffir, this heavy breathing could have been heard at a distance of several yards, and could thus serve as a guide to either dangerous enemy. Hans, however, did not like to disturb the sleepers until the last moment, or unless he found he alone was unable to deal with the foe. It was evident to Hans that whoever or whatever was the foe who approached, it was one who used the greatest caution: but two or three steps at a time were taken, and then all was quiet. From this fact Hans was convinced that a man was the enemy who was near him, for no other creature could act with so much caution. He was also aware of the peculiar individual daring of members of the Kaffir race. Many men are brave in a crowd, and when led on by example or enthusiasm, but the Kaffir is an epicure in excitement. He likes to venture upon feats of daring alone, and the night is to him the most suitable time for such deeds. It matters not how great is the risk, the greater the risk the greater seems to be the excitement. Knowing this, Hans believed it possible that one single Kaffir might have followed on their spoor, have watched him as he halted for the night, and was now desirous of capturing his guns or assagying some of the sleepers, and then retreating, boast at his kraal of his deeds. Believing this, Hans had an additional reason for remaining silent, for he knew that should he awake his companions, the Kaffir would readily escape, or wait for a more favourable opportunity for attack.

Grasping his hunting-knife firmly, Hans crouched close to the ground and waited anxiously for the nearer approach of his foe. The slow, stealthy tread of the man was evidently guided by the sound of the sleepers, for no eyes could distinguish forms amidst the darkness, and Hans soon found that light as was the breathing of Katrine and her sister, yet this sound was guiding the man towards them.

For several minutes Hans could hear no sound, and he began to fancy the man feared to approach nearer, but at length to his surprise and almost fear, he could distinguish within ten feet of him the figure of a man with arm erect, and in his hand a spear ready to cast. The figure seemed to have risen out of the earth, so silently had it gained its position in the midst of the party; and had not a man as well-trained and as keenly sensed as Hans been on watch, a complete surprise could have been effected.

With a movement as slow and cautious as that of the Kaffir, Hans gathered himself together for a spring on his enemy, who stood listening to the sleepers' long-drawn breaths, then with a sudden bound he dashed forward, and stabbed with his long knife at where he believed he would reach the Kaffir. He had however either miscalculated his distance, or his enemy was too quick for him, for nothing resisted his stabs, and he fell headlong to the ground, having stumbled over the underwood before him. In an instant he was on his feet again, and crouched down to catch sight if possible of his foe, but nothing was to be seen, and had it not been for a slight rustling of the leaves and the crushing of a few sticks, he would have doubted whether his eyes had not been deceived. These sounds, however, would have convinced him, had he been in doubt, that no vision had crossed his sight, but a substantial and quick-witted enemy; and thus when Victor and Bernhard, awakened by the noise made by Hans' fall, inquired what was the matter, he was able to whisper in reply, "A single Matabili has tried to becroup us as we slept."

The Savage outwitted by a Lion.—

"Where is he?" said Victor: "has he escaped?"

Before Hans could reply, a sound struck upon the ears of the three men which caused them to grasp their rifles with firmness, whilst the two girls started up with a shriek of terror. This noise was the savage roar of a lion, followed by the agonised yell of a human being in fear and suffering, a momentary struggle, the cracking of some brittle substance, and then the deep, guttural, satisfied grunts of a monster which has captured its prey.

"The Matabili is killed by a man-eater," whispered Hans; "and perhaps he has saved one of us. I believed I smelt a lion some two hours ago, and perhaps he has been crouching near us, watching for one of us."

"Katie, dear," exclaimed Hans, "don't be afraid. There is no danger: keep quiet, and lie and rest, and, if you can, sleep. We need not start for two hours yet."

"What was that fearful noise, Hans? I dreamed you were killed."

"No, Katie, I am well, thank God, and ready to do good service yet: it was only some wild animal made a noise; but trust us three to keep you safe. Don't talk, dear, but try and sleep, at least keep quiet; for a human voice in this place is so unusual, that even the bats will come and look at us if they hear it. Sleep again, Katie, all is safe."

"We must all keep awake now," Hans whispered to his companions: "that lion may attract others. Let us sit back to back, and let no man speak without a cause, and then let it be in the lowest whisper: our lives and those of the poor girls depend now upon such apparent trifles as these."

The three men sat back to back, and thus each had one-third of the horizon to examine, so that no enemy could approach from any direction where a pair of eyes were not on watch. The night was a still and clear one, and sounds were audible from a considerable distance; near them, however, were noises which kept these hardy hunters in a state of excitement. The lion having captured its prey, had dragged it but a few yards, and had then commenced feasting on it. The sound of the powerful brute's jaws was distinctly heard as it crunched the bones of its victim, and when at length it had satisfied its hunger, and seemed to have retired a short distance to sleep, other and smaller carnivora squabbled over the remains of the monarch's feast, and with even more noise fought for their supper.

The poor half-starved horses were carefully hobbled and made fast to each other and to the bushes near, and thus could not escape. Their snorting and uneasiness showed that they were well aware of the presence of their formidable enemy; but the feeble state to which they were reduced caused them to seem almost indifferent to dangers which at other times would have rendered them almost frantic.

After a long silence and most intent listening had convinced the hunters that no immediate danger threatened them, Hans, speaking in a whisper, said—

"That lion must have been stalking our horses when the Matabili came in his way. I wonder was there another man with this one? they often venture alone on these risky journeys. This man, however, will never hunt again in these fields."

"It is strange that he should have been thus trapped by a lion whilst trying to stalk us," whispered Victor: "it is the first time I ever found a lion to be my friend, but he has saved us powder and shot. Tell us, Hans, how the man approached us."

Hans gave a brief description of the manner in which he had heard the man approaching, and of his precautions to prevent an accident, and explained all details until the roar of the lion announced the unexpected termination of the Matabili's expedition.

"The morning will soon break now," said Hans; "the Eastern sky is getting lighter; it will be an anxious moment to see how the horses are, for on them mainly depends our safety. How far, think you, are we from our people?"

"We shall take three days' riding at least to reach them, I think," said Bernhard.

"Yes, quite that," said Victor, "and more too, if there are enemies in the way, for then we may have to ride round."

"There is light enough now to look about us; so let us examine the horses, and allow them to feed if they will," said Hans; "we shall want all their strength."

The three men arose, and stretching themselves after their somewhat cramped positions, examined their horses, which were standing quietly near. To the experienced eyes of the hunters, these animals presented a very pitiable condition. Out of the five horses one only seemed lively, and inclined to eat; the remaining four, with hanging heads, lustreless eyes, and drooping ears, seemed indifferent to all around them. A look of despair was exchanged by the three men, as this fact was presented to them.

"In a few hours we shall have but one horse," exclaimed Hans; "strong as Katie is, her sister is weak, and they can never walk to our people. If the Matabili follow us, we must die. Can you see a remedy, men?"

"We can sell our lives dearly," exclaimed Bernhard; "that we can at least do. I have thirty bullets at least in my pouch, and in my horn thirty charges of powder. We may beat off a large party of the enemy."

"The Matabili are not easily beaten off," remarked Hans: "they rush on in a body, and though you may kill some, the others are upon you before you can have time to load. If we could have some of those many-barrelled guns that I have heard of which fire off several times one after the other, we could do nothing but kill more before we were killed; but with our roers only, we can do but little."

Whilst the men were thus talking in the twilight, Katie and her sister, fully awake, joined them before their presence was known; and hearing this last remark, the quick-witted girl at once suspected that the horses were unfit to continue their journey.

"We can walk, Hans," said Katrine, as she touched his shoulder, "we can walk, though, perhaps, not so fast as you can; but we can walk ever so far."

"If it were walking only, Katie, it would not be much; but it may be we should have to run, and that at a greater speed than a Matabili could follow; that is why I fear."

"Well, leave us here, and you go on, and bring us back help. The '*Mensch*' will soon come to us, and we could stop here till they arrive."

"We live or die together, Katie; I will never leave you here," exclaimed Hans. "But there is something to be thought of, though. Victor and Bernhard, let me tell you my plan."

The two men turned from the horses, whose pitiable condition they had been contemplating, to Hans, and waited for his words. After a moment's thought, Hans exclaimed, "It is our best chance, and it will succeed. This is the plan:—The black horse is as yet well. You Bernhard, or you Victor, as you may choose, upsaddle at once, and ride for our lager. As soon as you reach it, tell Maritz, or any one who is our friend, of our being left in the desert. I have horses among the people, and there are those who will help us. Come back with help and with horses, and we will get safe again among our people."

"And where will you be, Hans?" was Victor's inquiry.

"I," said Hans, "will move on to that range of hills; there are kloofs and rocks there amidst which I can easily find a place of security for Katie and her sister; for the rest trust a hunter. They shall neither starve nor be made prisoners whilst I live. So now, which of you will go? it is the post of danger to go as much as to remain. You, Bernhard, are the lightest man, and ought thus to ride fastest. In six days you should be back, and by that time we shall be accustomed to a rough life."

"If Victor agrees to this, I will go," said Bernhard; "and the sooner I go the better: first, though, shall we shoot the lion that killed the Kaffir? otherwise he might be an unpleasant neighbour to you, as he has tasted human flesh."

"We had better let him stand," said Hans: "a shot fired here now might be heard on this still day twenty miles. We need not tell every pair of ears within twenty miles that white men are about, for then, perhaps, we might have curious eyes coming to look at us; besides, the lion may be useful to us again."

"How?" exclaimed the two hunters; "not in killing another Matabili?"

"No," said Hans; "but the sooner our horses are eaten the better. The vultures will be streaming in this direction very shortly, and as long as a scrap of flesh is on the bones of the animals the *vogels* will be hovering around this spot. A Matabili would naturally come to see what was dead here, and might find our spoor; so, instead of one, I wish there were twenty lions ready to feast on our horses. I have no fear of lions when I get to those hills, for I will soon make a place there suitable for our safety. So we had better save our powder and bullets for even more cruel enemies than a lion."

"That is true," exclaimed Hans' two companions: "so we will not seek to kill him. Let us look at the spot where he struck down the Matabili."

The three hunters walked cautiously in the direction in which the lion might be yet concealed, and examined every bush and patch of grass around them. The footprints of the Matabili could be easily traced by these expert spoorers, and they soon found the spot on which the man had been killed. The lion had apparently followed the man from the direction of the hunters, and had struck him down at once, the assagies of the savage being found in a cluster, as though dropped from the helpless hand of the stricken man; the body had then been dragged away about forty yards to some long grass, where the lion had commenced his feast, which had been finished by hyenas and jackalls; so that except a few bones, nothing remained to indicate that a human being had been, sacrificed to the fury of a wild beast. "This might have been the fate of one of us," said Hans, as he pointed to the few remains before him. "It is the will of God to have spared us, and to have destroyed our enemy. We will trust that our fate may not be like his. We had better return now and make our arrangements at once. We will conceal the saddles and bridles, and then they may be of use if you bring spare horses. So now for work, men, and you, Bernhard, had better ride on. You will not mistake your way, will you?"

"No. I shall find the line easy, and my only fear is whether the horse will carry me. I will bring you help, and that very shortly, or my life will be lost in the attempt—trust me, Hans;" and with a hearty farewell to the party, Bernhard rode off, on an expedition fraught with no little danger, for he had pathless plains to traverse, rivers to cross, mountain-ranges to find a pass through, and all this with the constant possibility of enemies around him, who would follow him till a chance occurred of taking him at a disadvantage.

Chapter Twelve
Preparations for a Siege—The Rock and Caves—Wild Bees and Rock Rabbits—The Baboons—The Night Watch

When Bernhard's course had been watched for some time, Hans decided at once to make his preparations for a week's residence in the wilderness. He called Victor to his side, and explained to him the advantage of selecting the range of hills which were distant about two miles. These hills were rocky and steep, and thus an enemy could approach only from one side. There was much underwood, and thus there seemed every probability of a secure retreat being found. The difficulty, however, seemed to be how to reach these hills without leaving a visible trail. These advantages and drawbacks having been discussed between the two hunters, it was decided to run the risk of leaving a trail rather than wait where they then were; but scarcely had Hans come to this conclusion than, upon looking westwards, from which direction the wind was blowing, he eagerly exclaimed—

"God is good, and favours us. Look, Victor, a storm is coming."

"And what of that, Hans?" exclaimed Victor.

"Our spoor will be washed out, Victor: make haste, let us move on rapidly and gain those hills, and if we do so before the rain, the keenest-eyed Matabili will not be able to trace us; so come along. If no eyes are now on us, we may live here for a week without being discovered. Keep close together, Katie, and by my side, take advantage of every bush or slope of ground, and we will yet live to join our people again."

The two hunters and their charges walked rapidly towards the hills which had been referred to, and entering on an old water-course, worked their way up towards the summit of the kloof. Large blocks of rocks were lying about in all directions, and the water during heavy rains had worked its way among these, so that several hollows were scooped out so as to form caves large enough to hold one or two human beings; these, however, were not places which an experienced man like Hans would select for a resting-place, for he knew that the same cause which had produced these holes would render them unsuitable for habitations. He advanced, therefore, until he found some overhanging rocks which offered an ample protection against any rains which might fall, or winds that might blow, and here putting down the saddles and other articles that he had carried from the last outspan, he requested Victor to remain with Katrine and her sister until he had examined the surrounding ground.

"You know the call of the grey monkey, Victor?" said Hans: "let three distinct calls be a signal that one of us requires the presence of the other. And now I will go and examine round us."

Hans ascended the kloof, and keeping along the edge of the bush, walked onwards along what at first seemed an old game path; but at length, as he examined this, he became convinced it had once been used and worn by human beings, though now it had been long untrodden; he followed this path until it led him to a small piece of table-land not much larger than a good-sized English drawing-room, which was reached by a very narrow path along a ridge of rocks; this table-land was formed by a solid block of rock, which descended perpendicularly for fully sixty feet on three sides, whilst on the fourth there was a wall of rock rising 200 feet above him. To the eyes of Hans, this place was a fort almost impregnable, and as he scanned the country round, he felt that with twenty trusty men he could hold it against a nation of savages. The face of the rock had been scooped out by artificial means, and two caves about eight feet deep and six feet high had been formed evidently with great labour. This Hans knew must be the work of Bushmen, who for some reason had now apparently deserted the locality. From these caves the surrounding country could be seen in all directions, and water being within a few yards, Hans at once selected this place for the residence of his companions.

Inside the cave were rough carvings of various creatures, scratched on the stone of the rock, whilst just outside a valuable article lay neglected; this was a large gourd, capable of containing about two quarts of water. Hans at once placed this inside the cave, and then commenced cutting some long, dry grass, that grew on the slope near; having procured sufficient of this to make a soft bed in one of the caves, he descended the ravine, and rejoined Victor and the two girls.

"A storm is coming," he said, "and that will wash out our spoor; so now come with me, and I will show you a nice quiet retreat before the rain falls."

Victor, aided by Hans and the two girls, ascended the ravine, and on seeing the caves and the security of the retreat, which were evident at once even to the inexperienced eyes of the girls, they were delighted.

"No one can find us here, Hans," said Katrine; "and if they found us, they could not get at us. However did you come to know of it?"

"I found it by chance," said Hans; "but now, Katie, you must cover your dress with this grass, and don't let a sign of a ribbon be seen, for there may be eyes in every bush, and our safety depends on escaping being seen."

"Here comes the rain," exclaimed Victor, as the heavy drops of a thunder-shower came pouring down, followed by a deluge of rain: "that will wash out our footprints, and now we cannot be traced; so if we avoid being seen we must be safe. But Hans, what food have we? I am starving, and the girls must sadly want food."

"There is still some venison, but I am going out after the rain is over to get something else. Now, Katie, you can be useful; use your bright eyes, and you yours too, Meechy, and look all over those hills and plains and see what passes or moves about there. Victor, get some dry wood from out of that next cave, and some grass. We will have a fire presently, and cook some more food, for I can get something, I believe, without firing a shot, for the Kaffir's spears are not bad weapons."

Victor did as requested, and Hans, carrying his gun for his protection, and in case of danger, left the caves and walked slowly along the old path, looking in all directions for signs of game.

Many brilliant flowers grew on this hill-side, and thus added to the beauty of the scene, whilst flowering acacias scented the air with their fragrance. On one of the branches of an acacia that hung low, Hans noticed several bees busily engaged gathering honey; from among these he selected one whose legs were thickly covered with the spoil from the flowers; this bee he struck roughly from the branch and carefully watched. The creature, after buzzing angrily round Hans' head once or twice, darted off up the ravine. Hans watched it as long as it was in sight, and then followed the direction in which the creature had retreated.

After walking about 200 yards Hans disturbed another bee that was busily engaged gathering honey; this creature flew away also up the ravine, and Hans quickly followed it. He knew that when a bee laden with honey is alarmed it will fly to its hive, and he, being desirous of procuring honey, adopted this means to discover the nest or hive. Hans was soon guided by the bees to their hive, and the African bee, being by no means so formidable a creature as its English brother, allows its honey to be taken by those who understand how to do it. The method is, if the honey be in a hollow tree, or in a cleft of the rock, or such a locality, to pay no attention to the buzzing of the bees, or to attempt in any way to knock them away, should they settle on you, but to slowly insert the hand into the nest, and withdraw the honeycomb and carry it away. It rarely happens that the bees attack any one, and should they do so their sting is far less painful than is that of the English bee. (Having taken many bees' nests in Africa, we were but once attacked by the bees. This took place in consequence of accidentally squeezing a bee between our hand and the tree in which was its honey; the little creature gave a sharp, angry buzz, which seemed the signal for attack, as about twenty bees flew on our head, and several on the face; they all stung, the majority leaving their stings in, but in less than five minutes all the smarting had gone away. One sting from an English red-hipped humble bee is worse than twenty African bees' stings.)

Hans procured a large heap of honeycomb, with which he proceeded to the caves. He knew that the time might come when they could not leave the caves, and thus, to collect any thing that might serve for food was a proceeding not to be neglected; and honey, though not very substantial, was yet food which made a change from mere flesh. What Hans hoped to get were some rock rabbits, the daas of the Dutch, and the coney of Scripture. These little creatures, not much bigger than a common rabbit, are usually found among rocks, and are very good eating; they are, however, very watchful, and require an expert shot to be able to hit them, for they rarely allow a hunter to approach nearer than one hundred yards to them.

Hans found that the kloofs were full of game. There were guinea-fowl and pheasants in abundance, whilst buck of various kinds had left so many footmarks, that it was evident they abounded in the neighbourhood. He soon discovered the traces of rock rabbits, and with the help of the broad blade of the Kaffir's assagy he was able to dig out four of these creatures.

Thus provided with food he returned to the caves, and observing that the wood which had been collected was all more or less damp, he at once decided that cooking must be left till the night. "You see, Victor, if we made a fire now, the smoke could be seen for miles, and would thus guide an enemy to us. There is no possible means of preventing this smoke from ascending, so we must not make a fire by day with damp wood. By night we must not show the light of a fire; but that is more easily avoided. We can cover the mouth of the cave, or we can make a fire below here, and can thus cook our food safely, for the smoke cannot be seen by night. We ought to cook enough to do without a fire for a week, and then one risk only is run."

"In the water-course we came up the water has run under ground," remarked Victor; "there is room for a fire in that, and no light could be seen from the distance."

"I remember," said Hans. "We will collect wood and grass, so as to be ready for the night; then I will try to knock down some guinea-fowl or pheasants."

Hans, having cut some stout sticks with a knob at the end, again made an expedition into the kloof, and succeeded in knocking down several guinea-fowl with these sticks, which he threw with the skill of a Kaffir. The guinea-fowl, endeavouring to conceal themselves by hiding or crouching amidst the long grass, would allow themselves almost to be trodden on before they would fly away. In addition to the rabbits and guinea-fowl, Hans collected a great many eggs, and thus was provided with food enough to last a week, without incurring the necessity of firing a shot. No sooner had this essential preparation been completed than Hans cut several long, straight sticks, which he thrust into the ground in front of the caves, and at about a foot apart: across these he fastened several horizontal twigs; first by lacing them in and out, and secondly by lashing the ends with the bark that he peeled off a tall, soft-wooded greenish shrub. Having thus traced out a framework, he thatched this with the long tambookie grass which grew in the kloof, and thus before sundown he had formed a very complete room, perfectly sheltered from the wind and rain. In front of this thatched doorway he placed some branches of trees, and thus prevented any person at a distance from being attracted by an artificial-looking construction.

Hans was much pleased with his work, and called to Katrine to examine it from a short distance.

"You could not tell there was any thing there, Katie, except a few bushes, unless you went much closer."

"No, Hans, it is cleverly done; but I fear there would be no escape for us if any enemy once came on to this bit of ground."

"No, there would be none, Katie; so we will hope they will not come here; some of them would leave their bones here, that is certain; so it is better for them they should not come. I will now go down and see about cooking our rabbits, for some hot food will be good for us."

Hans descended to the natural hole in the rocks where he intended lighting his fire as soon as it was dark enough to prevent the smoke from being seen, and having waited till he thought his attempt might be safely made, he lighted his fire, and adding plenty of wood, soon had a sufficient quantity of heat to cook all his game.

Upon leaving the fire and re-ascending the ravine he was startled by seeing the outline of several figures on the summits of the rocks above them. Darkness had now set in, but it would not have been too dark to have enabled him to distinguish these objects, had he not been lately dazzled by the fire-light; this, however, had damaged his keenness of vision for a time, and as the objects disappeared as soon as he moved in the bushes, he had no second chance of examining them. From what he saw, however, he was certain that either Kaffirs or Bushmen were on the rocks above him. In either case his condition would be unpleasant, for with the Bushman, every man's hand was against him, and his against every man's; and if the Matabili had traced him to his present retreat, his career would be soon terminated. In either case not a moment was to be lost; so he rapidly moved over the distance which separated him from the caves, when whispering to Victor what he had seen, they cautioned Katrine to keep quiet and concealed, and grasping their rifles, they took up a position from which they could obtain a commanding view of the ridge on which Hans had seen the men.

They had not long to wait before their enemy appeared, drawn out in relief against the sky for a background. Objects on the ridge were visible which could not have been seen had they not been thus situated. For this reason both Hans and Victor soon saw above twenty figures slowly ascend the ridge, and there stand and examine the surrounding country. As he saw the number of the enemy Hans raised his arm and touched Victor, whilst in a whisper he said, "They must be Bushmen." It seemed impossible that the whisper of Hans could be audible at the distance at which the supposed Bushmen were examining the kloofs, and still more improbable that the movement of Hans could have been seen even by a Bushman's eyes, yet, on the instant, each figure disappeared as though by magic, whilst no sound met the ears of the hunters.

"Victor," exclaimed Hans, "those are not mortal enemies. I have killed in my day more than twenty Kaffirs, principally Amakosa: can these be the men's ghosts, sent here now to torment me? I shot them in fair fight and for the defence of my life or cattle,—yet no mortal could have seen me move or heard me speak, but when I did both, they sank into the rocks to a man."

"Wait, Hans, let us see what happens; our cause is a good one, and in such a case though the devil may be powerful, God must be more than a match for him. God would not allow the dead Kaffirs to worry us."

"There! there! Hans, see there are more; they stand up on the rocks, and are carrying something to hurl at us. A bullet could not touch a being belonging to the dead, or I would fire."

"I wish I had consulted the Missionary about such a case," earnestly exclaimed Hans; "too many Mensch laugh at the Kaffirs who believe their fathers come and talk to them; but whatever may be this enemy, I, for one, would never laugh at a nation's belief, when I knew nothing about it. Victor, we might as well have been bred in the towns; we are weak and ill, or we should have seen before that these are baboons, some of the females carry their young, and that is what we fancied they were going to throw at us. That is good: if baboons come here, and stay here, it shows that neither Bushmen or other men have been much here lately, and so we may not be disturbed. We must watch, though; shall I or will you take the first watch? whoever does, he can keep guard till those three bright stars set, and then can call the other. I *can* sleep to-night, for I feel in this retreat that I have the best chance of success now. If two days pass without the Matabili finding us, we shall escape, provided Bernhard can procure horses; but I would as soon stand up at fifty yards to be shot at with a Bushman's arrows, as go on foot with Katie towards our lager, for we should then be captured and slain in less than twelve hours. Here, if we keep close, we may be secure for a long time, but moving we should be exposed to all dangers; so now all depends on Bernhard. Will you watch first, Victor, and place yourself near this wall of rock? then every sound from the plain will be heard clearer and more distinctly, for sound comes against this rock like a wave, and is not lost. Call me if you feel too sleepy to watch, for that is possible; and a little sleep when we want it, is better than much—when we court it. I will sleep at once, so call me when you want me."

Hans listened at the door of Katrine's cave, but hearing only the slightest breathing, he concluded that she and her sister slept; and so retiring to his own cave, he, with that necessary capacity of the hunter or soldier, was in five minutes fast asleep, and untroubled by dreams or anxieties.

"Half the night is past, Hans," said Victor, as he entered the cave and gently touched Hans.

"I am ready," said Hans; "is all quiet?"

"No, not quiet: there are more lions here than in any part of the country I have ever been in; they have been fighting about our horses; the roars and growls have been tremendous ever since you left. The baboons too have been barking occasionally; but there seems no other creatures about except jackalls and hyenas. It would not do to walk down on those plains alone by night, we should be lions' food in a very few minutes. Now, I am for sleep, so you watch, Hans."

It was now Victor's turn to sleep whilst Hans kept watch, and sat with his back to the rocks, a couple of assagies within reach of his hand, and his trusty roer resting on his arm. He listened attentively to every sound that broke the stillness of the night, and pictured to himself the scene that was going on near his poor horses. The occasional deep growl of the lion, or its angry roar, caused him considerable anxiety, not on his own account, but for that of Bernhard. "If Bernhard's horse is killed or falls sick," he thought, "we may never leave this place; and poor Katie! what will become of her?"

Chapter Thirteen
The Matabili appear, and follow the spoor of Hans' party—The Discovery—The Attack—The Repulse of the Savages

The day broke with all the splendour of an African morning; the rain of the previous day had refreshed the ground, and filled the various pools with water, and thus the animals and feathered denizens of the plains were cheerful and busy in their various occupations. Numbers of green parrots were screaming in the kloofs near Hans' retreat, whilst the sweet double whistle of the quail resounded from every patch of grass. The vulture, with its graceful sweeping flight, circled high in the air over the spot where the carcases of the horses still remained; whilst here and there a black-breasted eagre sat on a withered tree, and scanned the surrounding earth and sky, in order to select the most dainty morsel for his morning meal.

The baboons from the summit of the hills had descended into the plains in order to dig up roots, which there grew in abundance, and served them for food. This was a sight which pleased Hans, for there are scarcely any creatures more watchful than baboons, and thus he knew that no enemy could approach without these creatures giving notice by their rapid retreat to the mountain peaks. Having found a hole in the rocks close to the caves, which was full of fresh water, there was no need to quit the small plateau for that necessary, and thus Hans sat and watched the changing effects of the rising sun, whilst he listened to the long-drawn breaths of the sleepers, who, exhausted by the anxiety of the previous night, needed more sleep than was usual.

The plains beneath Hans' hiding-place offered a beautiful panorama to the sportsman or artist; the bright glowing tints of the foreground were mellowed in the middle distance, whilst far away the mountains assumed a rich blue colour, and yet stood out in bold relief against the distant sky, the dry air failing to give the subdued effect of distance usually observed in our climate. Amidst the groves of wide-spreading acacia, or near the banks of the many tiny streams that wound along the plain, were groups of game. Herds of elands, buffaloes, and quaggas were scattered here and there, whilst smaller and solitary bucks could be seen, now bounding away from some fancied danger, then grazing on the green and fresh grass. The sportsman, provided with ammunition and gun, could keep his camp in plenty here, and need have no fear of starving, were it not that the game at times migrates and leaves a district, when the food ceases to be attractive or plentiful.

As Hans watched the various animals, he noticed a troop of quaggas galloping rapidly across the flats; their passage seemed to alarm various other creatures which had previously been feeding in quietness, and there was a general movement among the quadrupeds. The baboons ceased their labours and moved leisurely up the ravine, till reaching commanding positions on the summits of rocky eminences, they stood erect, and barked their displeasure at some threatening danger.

Hans, determining to obtain a better view of whatever might be the cause, ascended the rocks above his cave, and, taking care to screen himself from observation, scanned the distant country. He soon saw that the animals had not been alarmed without cause, for coming forward at a rapid pace were a party of dark men, who Hans made out to be armed Matabili. There were more than a hundred of them, and from all being armed, from the rapid pace at which they advanced, and from their coming exactly over the same ground that he had ridden forty-eight hours previously, he concluded they were following his horses' footmarks.

The advance of such a party was not unexpected by Hans. Had he supposed that he would not have been followed, he would have suggested that the whole party should walk on towards his people's lager. With but one horse the two girls might have ridden turn and turn about, and so have lessened the fatigue of the journey, but even under these circumstances the Matabili would be sure to overtake them, and so he decided that hiding would be the safer plan.

He noticed that three or four men, probably the most experienced, led the main body of the Matabili; these men succeeded each other in the lead, and by acting as guides, often enabled the main body to make short cuts, and thus to save themselves much walking, or rather running, for a slow run seemed the pace that was adopted. Though the enemy followed very accurately the spoor of the horses on which the rain had fallen, and thus seemed capable of tracing him even under these disadvantageous circumstances, yet Hans was in hopes that when the horses were no longer used the Matabili would not be able to follow him. He had, however, seen enough to render it advisable to descend at once from his position, to give the alarm to his companions below, and to seek a place of concealment from which he might observe all the movements of his pursuers.

These arrangements were soon made, and Victor and Hans sat watching with anxiety the approach of their enemies.

The Matabili followed the traces of Hans' party with the accuracy of hounds on a hot scent, and when they spied some vultures sitting on the trees near the carcases of the horses, their speed was increased, and they hastened to examine what was the cause that attracted these carrion feeders.

The nearly-consumed horses were immediately discovered, and shortly afterwards the skull of the Matabili killed by the lion. The ground around was searched by the various men, and the conclusion was soon arrived at, that although the horses were all dead but one, yet their late captives had by some means managed to escape. The next proceeding was, therefore, to find the spoor, so as to discover in which direction they were to pursue. This was a work of time, for the late heavy rain had washed out nearly every trace from the previously hard soil; but the skilled spoorers spread out in various directions, and some of them at length found the traces of the horse that Bernhard had ridden away.

The Matabili at this were delighted; they believed that the three men had started on foot and had placed one or both of the females on horseback: thus they believed their journey could be accomplished only slowly, so that there was every chance of the fleet-footed savages overtaking their escaped captives, and shortly bringing them back to their prison. The whole party soon assembled round the traces of the horses and held a brief consultation. No time was to be lost in following this spoor; and the most quick-sighted Matabili were at once sent forward to trace it on before. The remainder followed, and looked anxiously for the footprint of man. When, however, some very soft ground had been passed, and no footprints were seen, the leader, an experienced and cunning savage, called on his men to halt, and explained to them that there should be some other footprints besides those which they had seen.

"There were three men, and two women; one of these has been killed and eaten by a lion," said the Matabili chief: for he knew not that the skull belonged to one of his own people. "We can see the spoor of but one horse; on that the women would probably ride;—but where are the men's footprints? We must find these. They have not crossed this soft ground: there is no spoor here. They may have crossed higher up, where the ground is harder. Look, men, and find some spoor, or we may be making a mistake."

Every search was made for several hundred yards on either side of the soft ground on which was the spoor of Bernhard's horse, but with no satisfactory results.

"The rain must have washed out the spoor," was at length the expressed opinion of the majority of the Matabili, and the whole party would immediately have followed the traces of the horse, had not another old Matabili agreed with the chief man that it was not wise to go on without some more spoor being seen.

The chief, being thus strengthened in his suspicions, decided to leave ten men behind to examine every likely place near, especially the kloofs on the hill-sides, and then to follow with all speed the main body, who would push on in hopes of overtaking the fugitives.

Hans and Victor watched the Matabili as all these proceedings were carried on. They guessed what the doubts were which delayed the pursuit of the spoor, and they counted with considerable anxiety the number of the Matabili who were detailed for the purpose of examining the kloofs. From the smallness of this party both men believed that the Matabili did not consider it very probable that their captives were concealed thereabouts, and they were also inclined to think that ten Matabili were by no means a match for two Dutch Mensch armed with their trusty roers.

"We shall have a fight for it, Victor," said Hans; "and we ought not to let one of these men escape, or they will bring a host of savages down upon us before Bernhard can return with help. They don't know where we are, and so we shall have the full advantage of a surprise, and we should, if possible, shoot so as to send our bullets through two men at a time."

"See, they are going back to our last outspan, and will there try to pick up our spoor; but even a Matabili will be puzzled to find any traces that the heavy rains have not washed out. It will be good to tie up some powder and bullets in cartridges," continued Hans; "we shall want quick loading; and let us take care not to both fire at once, unless in extremities,—then we shall always have two bullets ready for them. We must kill or wound four Matabili with each barrel; and I think a bullet cut into four, and two bits put on the top of each charge, will be good; thus we shall do more than give one wound. We must not think of the cruelty, Victor; for it is for life, and for those poor girls, we fight. We shall be tortured and then killed like oxen if we are defeated. Luckily the wind is not fair for the main body to hear our guns, and a part of the hill is between us, or the report might bring them all back again."

"Katrine," said Hans, "keep quiet in your cave, and on no account show yourself. We shall have to fire some shots soon, but never fear for our success."

"Is it the Matabili murderers again, Hans?" inquired Katrine. "I will pray for you, Hans; but take care of yourself, and don't run more risk than is necessary."

The Matabili who were left behind searched carefully for spoor, but without success; they therefore advanced to the nearest kloof, determined to search each of these in succession.

"In that kloof," said Hans, "I don't think my spoor could be seen; for I merely walked once a part of the way down it; at the top, however, they may find my footprints; at least, if they can read them on the grass."

It occupied the enemy fully half an hour to ascend the kloof and reach the summit, where Hans and Victor had a distinct view of them; they halted on reaching the top of the kloof, and examined the ground in all directions, and scanned the various ridges and rocks.

"They do not seem to think there is an enemy here, Victor," said Hans: "I believe they would take more care of themselves if they did. They stand quite unconcerned, though they might be made targets of at once. This I don't think they would do if they suspected us of being concealed hereabouts. We must not fire a shot as long as there is a chance of our escaping detection, for it may be better far to escape being seen, than even to kill all these men."

"We will not fire, Hans, unless a man comes across the little causeway there leading to this table-land; then it would be better to make sure of our foe. See, Hans," whispered Victor; "they have discovered your footprints, and are coming on rapidly: we shall find fighting a necessity now."

"They bring it on their own heads, then," said Hans, as he tapped his gun to secure the powder being up in each nipple: "you fire first, Victor, and take two in a line if you can, whilst I wait for the next shot."

The Matabili had undoubtedly discovered the footmarks of Hans, as they ran rapidly along the pathway which he had trodden the day previously; but they seemed to entirely underrate their enemy, as they took no precautions for concealment. As they approached the caves the men jostled each other in their eagerness to get first, and grasping their spears, they waved them in the air as though they already felt them penetrating the white men's flesh. In a very short time they had reached the ridge leading to the caves, and upon the first men arriving at this point they saw the caves and the means adopted by Hans to make these secure from wind and rain;

the Matabili at once recognised this as the work of men, and with a yell of pleasure they dashed forward.

"Now," whispered Hans; and Victor, whose gun was at his shoulder, pressed the trigger, and the loud report of the heavy gun (for it was an eight to the pound that Victor used) for a moment deafened all other sounds. Hans and Victor stooped low to see under the smoke, and saw two of their enemies lying dead, whilst a third was jumping about in pain and rage, a wound from one of the cut bullets having rendered him unfit for further service. The remaining Matabili, however, though daunted for a moment, beat their shields and rushed forward: there was, however, only room for one at a time on the ridge, and their endeavour to precede each other caused a moment's delay.

"My turn now, Victor," said Hans; and raising his gun, a second discharge brought two more Matabili to the ground.

"Fire at the leader, Victor," said Hans: "they are going to retreat I'll pick off the large man near him;" and the two shots in quick succession killed the two men against whom the aim was taken.

"In with the bullets, Victor," whispered Hans, "before we move. Six out of ten killed, and one or two wounded, is good; the others will never stay, they will run for aid to those on before; and I must stop this, or we shall have near a hundred men upon us in twelve hours or less. You keep guard here, Victor; I'll cut off these rascals' retreat: mind those fellows are not shamming. Katrine," called Hans, "it is well; we have driven away the murdering hounds, and I'm going now to stop the few that have escaped from telling tales. I'll be back soon."

Hans, by means of some wild vine and creepers, descended from the opposite side of the small plateau to that by which the Matabili had advanced: he then ran along the top of the ridge, and made his way rapidly down to the edge of the bush. He thus commanded the plain along which he expected the three Matabili would run, who he believed were likely to follow their main body in order to procure assistance. He soon saw he was not mistaken in his suppositions; for, crouching so as to be concealed as much as possible from the view of any one at the caves, the three men who had escaped the bullets of the two hunters ran rapidly onwards, and were soon within fifty yards of Hans' position. As they passed him he raised his gun and made an excellent shot at the leader, who never moved after he touched the ground, on which he fell headlong. The two remaining men with wonderful agility darted from right to left like snipe in their course, and thus gave Hans merely a snap shot at about one hundred yards. He fired, however, but heard the harmless whistle of his bullet as it struck the ground, and whizzed far on ahead of his enemies.

Had the Matabili been aware that he had no other weapon than his gun, they would upon this second discharge have endeavoured to close with him, and with their assagies they might easily have done so before he could reload; but they knew not either the weapons he used, or whether there was more than one white man near them, so they were intent only on retreat. It was with deep disappointment that Hans saw the failure of his second shot, and at first he thought he might obtain another chance if he reloaded and ran in pursuit, but the speed at which the Matabili ran and their well-known endurance, reminded him that he was no match for them in a foot-race; and so he decided to return at once to Victor, in order to consult as to the best means to be adopted to meet what he now, looked upon as certain, viz. an attack in about twelve hours from at least a hundred infuriated Matabili, who were brave to a degree, and who would not mind sacrificing some dozen men, in order to at length be able to bring back to their chief the captives who had, by a temporary neglect, been given a chance to escape.

Chapter Fourteen
The Fortification—Waiting Relief—Fight to the Last—Fresh Weapons—The Maidens keep watch—The Savages' Night Attack—Their Defeat—The Battle—New Allies—The Poisoned Arrows—More of the Enemy arrive

"It is a bad business, Hans, that the Matabili escaped; but it cannot be helped," was Victor's answer to Hans, upon hearing the result of his attempt to prevent the escape of any of the party. "What are we to do, Hans? If we stay here we shall be unable to beat off a hundred men, though we might succeed against half that number; what shall we do?"

"If the Matabili were not such keen-eyed spoorers, I would recommend that we made all speed in retreating from this; but it would be no use, for they would be certain to trace us, and to be hunted down in that way would be worse than to die here fighting to the last."

"I agree, Hans; so we will stay here. I think, too, we can make this place stronger. Suppose we cut through that narrow path that leads here, and raise a bank to protect us from any spears that might be thrown. We might cut down some stout branches and make a difficult fence to force a way through, every obstacle will stop the enemy, and give us time to load. I have found what may be a useful weapon, too, when our ammunition is all gone, that is a Bushman's bow, and a case of poisoned arrows. There are ten arrows, and each arrow is a man's life. It will be doubtful whether the Matabili will continue the attack when their first rush fails, and they lose several men. They dread fire-arms now, though they have gained victories against those who use them. Let us now prepare our defences; if we only hold out three days we ought to obtain help, if Bernhard has been lucky."

The two men sat to work to remove the bodies of the Matabili who were shot, and having secured their weapons, they used these to dig up the ground and undermine large stones, which they carried to the plateau, and thus formed a breastwork, whilst the removal of these stones and the earth rendered access to the flat rock impossible except by climbing. In two hours the rock was therefore rendered almost impregnable, and it would have been quite so had a dozen men occupied it who were well provided with guns and ammunition.

"Victor," exclaimed Hans, "I can make a good weapon for the defence of this place, which may save us ammunition. I will cut some of those long bamboos near the stream below, then the broad, sharp blade of an assagy fastened to the end of this will make a lance twelve feet long; we can thus stab the Matabili as they attempt to climb up, and can reach them, whilst their short assagies cannot come near us. They have no guns; so that we have no fear of being hit by them if we stand on our breastwork."

"That is a good thought, Hans," replied Victor; "we will have four of these, then if we break one we can each have another. Oh! if we had only a hundred bullets each, and enough powder for them, we would fight a hundred of these treacherous rascals."

"We must do what we can with the means we have," answered Hans. "Now I will go and cut the bamboo, then we shall be all ready."

It was only with great difficulty that Hans descended from the block on which he had taken up his position, he then cut some straight, strong canes which grew to a great height near the marshy bottom of the ravine; and returning with these, he found that to ascend the perpendicular face of the rock was exceedingly difficult, and whilst thus climbing with both hands occupied, he knew that a determined man above with a long lance, such as he could construct from the bamboo and blades of the assagies, could defy a dozen men at a time, and stab them as they ascended. This conviction gave him additional hope that he might either destroy his enemy, or be able to hold his position until relief came, that was, if Bernhard had succeeded in reaching the Lager. "*If* Bernhard has," said Hans. "Ah! all depends on good Bernhard now."

The day slowly passed away, though the whole four were engaged in superintending or executing the defences. Katrine was able to give assistance in tying up cartridges and in holding the canes whilst Hans fastened the iron blades to their ends: thus Victor was at liberty to make the defences more secure.

From the experience which Hans had gained in ascending the rock, he knew that there was only one place where an enemy could ascend, and thus if the narrow causeway could be defended, he saw no means for the Matabili to approach him.

"Two to a hundred are long odds, though," said Hans to Victor; "but we can only die at last, and our last fight shall be a good one. We can do no more, I think, so now suppose we sleep for two hours; we are safe till sunset, and I don't think we shall be attacked before daybreak to-morrow. Katrine and her sister can be trusted to keep watch, and we shall be stronger for sleep."

It was some time after sundown when Victor was called by Katrine.

"I can trust my eyes by day, Victor," said the Dutch maiden, "but I don't think I am fit to keep guard by night. An enemy might be too cunning or too quick for me."

"That is true, Katie," replied Victor: "you had better sleep now, and I will take care no enemy comes to us. Have you heard any strange sounds since sunset?"

"Yes, many," said Katrine: "there are lions about, and I think hyenas have already scented death near here, for I heard some savage animals fighting below here; but I think only animals have been about us."

"We may have a great fight to-morrow, Katie," said Victor: "the enemy may be fifty to one against us."

"A brave man from the Vaderland like Hans and you would scarcely like to fight at less odds, Victor. If you are hard pressed I can use one of those spears, and I can pull a trigger too; but we can trust to you two. See how strong this place is, too," continued Katrine: "a child might hold this against an army."

"If you had been down-hearted, Katie, I should have fought, but it would have been doggedly and down-heartedly; now that you are so hopeful, I shall fight cheerfully and confidently. Good-night, Katie, and thank you for your support."

Victor took up a sheltered position under the rocks, where the dew could not fall upon him, and commenced his lonely watch. Strange thoughts crossed his brain as he there sat for hours: one was the readiness with which he surrendered a fair chance of life for the sake of two Dutch girls whom he knew but slightly. "It is odd," he thought, "for were it not for their slow feet, Hans and I could easily escape the whole body of the Matabili, and in a race for life we could shoot down the fleetest, and run from the slowest. It is a strange tie that binds a strong man to a weak woman, for tie it is. I, who never yet loved a woman, would sooner die in defending Katie than escape at her expense; and yet, were she captured, her fate would only be to become one among a hundred wives of Moselekatse. To-morrow's sun will not set, I expect, without deciding her fate, and that of Hans and myself."

The night had half passed when Hans, having, as he termed it, "finished all his sleep," came out of his cave and told Victor to take his rest. "If I hear the slightest noise that indicates an enemy, I will signal to you," said Hans; "for it may be that at daybreak we may have an attack. Sleep whilst you can, though: our aim is always better after a good rest."

The calm of the previous day had been succeeded by a fresh breeze, which was blowing from the westward, and thus Hans could not depend so much on discovering the approach of an enemy by the sound which he would make in moving through the underwood in the ravines. He was thus particularly anxious and watchful in order to guard against a surprise.

The darkness of night had been succeeded by the grey twilight of morning, and Hans had neither seen nor heard any thing to cause him fresh alarm. As the daylight increased he strained his eyes to examine every suspicious-looking object, in his endeavour to discover an enemy. The mist which for a time hung about the streams and in the kloofs, prevented him from seeing distinctly over the surrounding plains, and thus before the sun rose the view was not very distinct. Whilst he examined the distant plains and rising-ground his eye was suddenly attracted by what seemed an object moving near the edge of the rock close to him. So momentary was the view he obtained that he was not certain the waving of a branch in the wind might not be the cause. He was, however, too keen a sportsman not to know that it is by paying attention to these glimpses of objects that the best chances are frequently obtained, and thus with his gun in readiness he remained motionless under the shadow of the rock, whilst he watched the grass near the edge. In a moment after he saw the head of a Matabili slowly raised above the edge of the rock, and then the man, as though believing he could effect a surprise, endeavoured to pull himself up to the level plateau. Hans saw the chance that offered, so, instantly grasping the long bamboo lance, he charged the Matabili with such speed, that though the man saw him coming, yet he could neither raise himself to the rock nor get down quick enough to avoid the deadly thrust which Hans made at him. The man, pierced through the chest, fell on to a Matabili who was following him, and the two dashed headlong to the ground, some thirty feet below. A yell of rage and disappointment was uttered by a hundred savages, until now concealed in the ravines below. The noise they thus made was the first intimation that Victor or the two girls had that their enemies had arrived. The three rushed from their respective caves at this unearthly yell, and Victor eagerly inquiring of Hans the cause, received a hasty explanation, whilst the blood-stained lance was an earnest of its success as a weapon to restrain invaders.

"We will not waste a shot, Victor," exclaimed Hans; "let us thrust the brutes down with these lances. They can never succeed in climbing this place, as long as we meet them boldly. Have your gun ready, but let us use these lances whilst we find them useful."

The defeat of the surprise party, or rather spies,—for it was to ascertain whether an enemy really was in the caves that the Matabili ventured on this errand,—caused a momentary delay on the part of the Matabili; but their system of warfare was one quite different from that of the Amakosa Kaffirs. The latter like to fight in the bush, and much after the fashion of the North American Indians. The Matabili, however, like to come to close quarters with their enemy, and to stab him at arm's length. Confident in his numbers, the leader of this party gave the order to attack the Dutchmen's stronghold. The Matabili who had been wounded in the first attack had remained concealed in the ravines until the arrival of his companions, and it was by his information that the chief learnt that there was a causeway by which he could reach the position of his enemy. Dividing his forces into three divisions, he ordered one to climb the rock where the spy had just been hurled down. The second division he directed to attack by the causeway, whilst the third was to endeavour to find some third means of ascent, or at least to make such a demonstration as to prevent the Dutchmen from giving undivided attention to the other parts of attack. These arrangements having been completed, the Matabili, with loud yells, and beating their shields to add to the noise, rushed towards the points of attack.

Whilst one party endeavoured to ascend the wall of rock, the other suddenly found themselves opposed by stakes, and a steep rock and bank. Expecting momentarily to feel the deadly bullet amongst them, they were surprised to find no attempt made to attack them; attributing this to only one cause, they shouted to each other that the white man's powder was finished, and thus encouraged they climbed on one another's shoulders, and thus reached the level of the rock. No sooner, however, did the body of a Matabili rise above the level of the plateau, than the deadly thrust of a lance hurled the intruder back lifeless amongst his comrades. Three times did the persevering enemy succeed in raising one of their numbers to the level of the rock, but it was only to find him fall amongst them pierced through and through with the broad blade of one of their own iron spearheads. Still the shouts "Their powder is all done" gave encouragement to others to attempt an entrance to the fortification; and it was only when ten men had been sacrificed, that the chief ordered his men to desist, in order that some other plan of attack should be adopted.

"So far it has been all gain on our side," said Hans; "we have not fired a shot yet we have beaten them off. That was a good thought of mine, to make those spears. We must not let them know we have powder; for if they believe we have none, they may make plans which we can easily defeat."

For more than an hour the Matabili made no attempt to attack the fortress, for such it might well be termed: then, however, they again advanced to the attack, shouting as before. Hans and Victor prepared to resist their foes, and stood behind the breastwork they had raised ready to thrust down the intruders. Whilst their attention was thus directed below them, a slight noise above attracted their attention, and both turned to look at the rock above, when they instantly saw the plot of their crafty enemies. The Matabili, by a circuitous path, had ascended the summit of the ridge, and then climbed to the rocks above the plateau: they had then loosened some large stones, and were preparing to cast these down on the two Dutchmen, when the latter, attracted by the noise, turned and saw their danger.

The rocks above the plateau on which were the white men rather overhung than receded from the perpendicular, so that it required the man who hurled the stone to lean forward in order to cast it on the right spot: had it fallen attracted by gravity alone, the stones would have passed clear of the plateau, and would have descended into the ravine below. The ground above the slight ridge on which the Matabili had taken up their position was nearly perpendicular, and being bare of underwood, offered no cover to the men who had to descend it, a single false step would have resulted in the fall of the man into the ravine below, where he would be undoubtedly dashed to pieces. Thus it was a most daring proceeding to descend to the ridge above the plateau. This position, however, entirely commanded the Dutchmen's defences, and had not the Matabili made a slight noise, the white men might have remained ignorant of the position of their enemies, until the fall of heavy stones on or near them warned them of their danger.

Immediately Hans saw the Matabili preparing to cast these heavy stones on him, he called to Victor to keep close to the rocks. "They cannot touch us here," said Hans; "but we must use some bullets on them, or they may drop stones on us as we are resisting the men who venture to climb up. Yes," he continued, "that is their plan, and it is clever. These men above hope to keep us back whilst the others obtain a footing on our rock, then it would be all over with us; but we will just teach them a lesson. Now, Victor, we must be quicker than those stones; we must run out and back so rapidly that we shall get the men to hurl their rocks down, but we must avoid them; then instantly, before they have another rock ready, we must shoot them down. They are not sixty yards above us, and we can each drop a running ourebi at that distance. Are you ready now?"

"Yes," replied Victor, and the two men ran out into an exposed position, and, waiting an instant, sprang back under cover of the rock. They were only just in time to avoid two heavy masses of stone that were hurled at them by the Matabili above them; whilst those below shouted defiantly, and instantly commenced again to ascend to their enemies.

"Now for our bullets on those above," said Hans; "we must be quick. I will take the fellow on the sunny side, you the man in the shade."

As the Dutchmen raised their guns, there was a shout of ridicule from those below, as well as those above. "Their powder is done" was the cry, mingled with taunting laughs. This, however, did not affect the aim of the two hunters, who covered each his man, and the two shots fired in rapid succession were echoed from ridge to ridge.

One of the Matabili sank instantly to the ground motionless, and there remained, as still as the rocks around him: the other, who had been busy in hurling stones, rose on his feet, and with a tremendous bound sprang off from the rocks into the air: with upraised arms and struggling body he cleaved through the air, struck against a projecting rock in his descent, and, crashing through the branches of the trees below, fell mangled among his comrades.

The effect of the shot on the other Matabili was instantly visible. Those who were climbing up the rock at once retreated under cover, for they now knew that they were opposed to desperate men, whose ammunition was not gone, and who, it was evident, could use their weapons with skill.

The two remaining men who had ascended the rocks at once endeavoured to escape. One, in his eagerness, missed his footing, and sliding down the incline, bounded off into the air, and was killed by his fall into the depths below. The other, however, managed to effect his escape.

"They will not be anxious to try that again," said Hans. "I wonder what their next plan of attack will be. They can't burn us out, for these solid old rocks are fire-proof; neither are they likely to starve us out. As long as they have no fire-arms we are tolerably certain to be able to defeat them, and to prevent them from ascending this place; so I am curious to know what they will try to do next."

For fully two hours the Matabili were quiet, no sound indicating that they were near.

"Do you think it possible they have decided to leave us?" inquired Victor.

"No, they will not leave us, you may be certain; they will try to starve us out rather, and that reminds me that we may as well eat. We may be busy again before long." Without any loss of appetite from their late excitement, the two men ate heartily, and were soon again ready for a fresh attack.

"Something fresh is going to take place," exclaimed Victor; "they are coming again. What have they there? It is two Bushmen prisoners. Now, Hans, there *is* danger for us. See you what they will do?"

"The rascals—yes, they have made the Bushmen understand that unless they shoot us with their poisoned arrows they will be themselves assagied. Now we must shoot straight for our lives, indeed. Down, Victor, under cover," shouted Hans, and both men dropped behind their barricade just before two poisoned arrows flew over them, and struck the rock behind.

"The Schelms are behind trees, Victor. We shall find it hard to get a shot at them. We must watch and wait for our chance. We must shoot the Bushmen, for no Matabili can handle their weapons. Let us kill them, and we shall have escaped our most threatening danger."

The thorough Bushman of Africa is the most formidably armed man amongst the aborigines. The Amakosa or Kaffir tribes on the eastern frontier of the Cape Colony have for their national weapon the light throwing assagy. This is a spear about six feet in length, an iron head about one-third or one-fourth the length being inserted into a wooden handle. An expert Kaffir will throw one of these assagies with precision about eighty yards, and with sufficient force to penetrate a man's body at that distance.

The Zulu Kaffir and the Matabili use the heavier assagy, which is not so much suited for throwing, but is more fitted for close quarters, and is mainly used as a weapon for stabbing. Both this and the lighter assagy of the Amakosa are far less deadly than is the tiny arrow of the Bushman. The Bushman's arrow is about two feet long, the haft is made of reed, the end of the arrow is made either of hard wood or bone. This end is merely inserted into the hollow reed, and can be taken out and reversed if required, so that a Bushman places the poisoned end of his assagy in a reed-sheath as it were, until it is required for use, when he reverses it, and thus keeps the poison fresh.

The poison itself is said to be a combination of animal, vegetable, and mineral poison. The animal is procured from poisonous snakes, many species of which are common in the country inhabited by Bushmen, among these the cobra, puff-adder, ring-hals, etc., being numerous. The vegetable is obtained from roots known to the Bushmen, and of species of the cactus. The mineral is supposed to be some preparation of copper, which the Bushmen find in the country; but about, this composition there seems considerable uncertainty.

An animal, though little more than scratched with a Bushman's arrow, is almost sure to die, rarely surviving more than one or two hours. The Bushman is a most accurate shot, and can discharge his arrows with such speed, that he will often have three arrows in the air at the same time, the third being discharged before the first has struck the ground.

Knowing the accuracy of the Bushmen's aim, and the deadly nature of the poison they used, Hans and Victor fully comprehended the danger, they now encountered. The Bushman is as active as a baboon; and could these men have been trusted, they would have been ordered to ascend the rocks above the Dutchmen and shoot them from that position; but the Matabili dare not trust them: they had captured these two men, and now showed them that they must shoot the Dutchmen or be assagied themselves; thus the two tiny Bushmen used all their skill and watchfulness in order to save their own lives. The Bushmen finding that the Dutchmen kept under cover and gave no chance for a shot, requested to be allowed to ascend the rock and thus get a shot at their targets. The Matabili, however, would not trust them to do this, as they feared they might go over to their enemies, when once away from the range of their spears; so they directed them to watch their chance of a shot, and if the white men showed even a hand above the rocks, this hand was to be at once struck with an arrow.

Both parties were now watching to obtain a chance of a shot at the other: the white men shifted their position, so as not to give the Bushmen a chance of firing even at the rocks near where they were concealed; and the Bushmen dodged from tree to tree, in order to try to obtain a shot at some part of the Dutchmen.

"I will try what sort of a shot I can make with a Bushman's bow and arrow," said Hans; "I know a fellow is behind that tree stem, so I will try and hit that with one of the arrows of the bow we have."

"Don't expose an arm, though, Hans," said Victor; "for it is death even to be scratched by one of their arrows."

"I will be careful," replied Hans, as he fitted an arrow to the bowstring, and crouching below the rocks they had piled up as a breastwork, drew the bow and discharged the arrow. The little reed flew on, and fell at the side of the tree near which one of the Bushmen was crouching. The little man saw the arrow fall, though he knew not who had discharged it, and, with an eagerness to possess himself of the weapon which quite overcame his caution, he sprang from behind the tree and grasped the arrow which he at once saw amidst the dry leaves and grass. Victor, who was watching the result of this, saw the act of the Bushman, and instantly lowering his gun, he discharged a bullet at him. True to its direction, the bullet struck the Bushman on the shoulder, and passing through his arm, rendered him incapable of again using his bow. The wounded man had not much compassion from his captors; for the Matabili, seeing he could no longer be of service of them, and having a natural hatred of Bushmen, instantly despatched him with their spears, intimating to the remaining Bushman that unless he succeeded in shooting the white men, he would soon meet the same fate as his companion.

Scarcely had the two men taken their eyes off the tree behind which the Bushman had been killed, when Katrine's voice and words caused them to look on the plain to the eastward of their position.

"Hans, Hans!" she called, "look what is coming: there are more Matabili. Are there not two hundred more at least coming to help those who are now here? What can we do?"

Hans and Victor looked towards the east, and there saw a large body of Matabili coming rapidly over the plains, and evidently directed, by some guide, towards their present position.

"They will be too many for us, Victor, I am afraid; what are we to do now, I wonder?"

"Keep down, Hans! keep down!" said Victor; "see what is in your hat!"

Hans instinctively crouched behind the breastwork, and taking off his hat, saw in the crown a Bushman's arrow.

"There's another struck the rock behind us; we must shoot this fellow any how, he is savage now that his brother is killed. There he is, Victor, in that fork of the tree, the rascal, he may hit us from there; but here goes for two ounces of lead in him." The loud report of Hans' gun was followed by the dull sound of the Bushman's body falling to the ground, he being dead before he reached it. From the plain, however, a savage vengeful yell answered the report of the gun, and the additional party of Matabili rushed onwards, their shouts being responded to by their companions around Hans' stronghold.

Chapter Fifteen
Bernhard's Journey—His Success—To the Rescue

Bernhard, upon leaving his companions at the resting-place where the lion had killed the Matabili spy, rode on with speed; he knew that the lives of the females at least depended upon his gaining the Lager of his countrymen, and bringing back aid without delay. He was impelled, by friendship alone for Hans and Victor, to use every endeavour in his power to bring help to them, but even a stronger impulse urged him, viz. that he had fallen in love with Katrine's sister. Bernhard had never devoted much time or thought to the Frauleins, he having always found hunting attractive enough for him; so that there was something quite novel in finding himself incurring so much risk for a couple of girls. When, however, he was thrown into daily communication with one as pleasing as Katrine's sister, and thus could observe her trusting, unselfish nature, he seemed suddenly to awake to quite a new sensation. Thus as he rode on he murmured, "Yes, I'll save her! I'll save her, if it is for man to do it." And onward he rode, with a speed more fitted for a brief ride than for the journey which he was now undertaking.

Onward rode Bernhard. Rivers were forded or swum, plains were passed across, hills ascended, and with but two brief halts, Bernhard continued his journey till the fading light began to warn him it was time to prepare a halting-place for the night. Fatigue to a man of Bernhard's age, frame, and condition was almost unknown, especially when he had been kept up by excitement, as he had been all day; when, however, he determined to halt for the night, he remembered that he had scarcely sufficient food for more than his evening and morning meal, and that before again starting it would be better to provide himself with this necessary.

Allowing his horse to graze as long as there was sufficient light to enable him to see around him, he also cut a large quantity of grass, and placed this near some bushes where he intended to camp for the night. Knowing the caution of most nocturnal wanderers, he cut down some brushwood, and placed this around an open space in which he and his horse would pass the night. Many animals, fearing a trap of some kind, would not venture over these bushes, though most of them could have leaped the obstacle with scarcely any difficulty.

A continued and refreshing sleep, under the conditions in which Bernhard passed the night, were almost impossible. He knew that lions and leopards, hyenas and other carnivora infested the country in which he then was. If his horse should be killed, or even badly mauled by any of these fierce, strong-jawed brutes, his own state would be one of danger; so that to rest was as much as he felt inclined to do, and when sleep made her claims upon him he could scarcely close his eyes before he started up wide awake, as some howling monster scented the horse and its owner, and feared to gratify its appetite lest the dreaded man should have to be encountered.

There are few comparisons more singular than that between the pathless wilds of portions of Africa and the crowded streets of some of our cities. When we walk for hours in London and meet an ever-changing mass of men; when we see streets thronged with thousands, houses over-crowded, and vehicles crammed—we wonder whether our planet must not soon be too densely populated to be a suitable residence for man; but when we travel over immense tracts of land traversed only by the brute creation, and observe these roaming in a state of undisturbed freedom, we almost doubt the fact of men being crowded together in cities, as we believe we have seen them—the two extremes seeming a complete anomaly. We who live in the present century have the advantage of witnessing scenes which our successors will undoubtedly envy us for. At the rate at which civilisation advances, and man and his arts take the place of untrodden nature, it may not be improbable that the wilds of Africa, Australia, and America may cease to be wilds, but will be colonies of various races, whose countries are too small for their requirements. In the year 1967 or 4067 the report that the men of two centuries previous actually hunted such creatures as camelopards, may seem as odd to the then denizens of our planet as it would be to us to think that men ever had the chance of hurling their flint-headed weapons at the mammoth on the banks of the great Estuary of the Thames. The men too of that time may often exclaim, "Ah, those lucky fellows of the nineteenth century who had the chance of hunting elephants in Africa!" Thus the changes that now occur in localities will then have occurred by time, and as it now appears strange to the man who can scarcely find elbow-room for himself, to hear of a country where you may ride for two days and not see a fellow-creature, so will it in a century hence seem strange to reflect on the conditions of the past. Scarcely had daylight began to break than Bernhard gave his horse liberty to feed, he himself being intent on procuring a supply of food for his journey. This he was not long in doing, for the morning was foggy, and he came upon three elands, within a few hundred yards of his night's resting-place. Knowing that he would soon be miles away from his present position, he did not hesitate to fire a shot, and therefore killed one of the elands, selected the choice portions of the animal, and returning to his horse, upsaddled, and at once commenced his journey.

A two hours' ride brought him to a convenient place for a halt, several dead trees yielded firewood, a stream supplied water, and grass was abundant. Making a careful examination of the surrounding country, and seeing no signs of an enemy, Bernhard off-saddled, lighted a fire, and commenced cooking his breakfast. Whilst thus occupied he heard distinctly the sound of a heavy gun; this was to him better than the voice of a friend, and when he heard a second and a third shot, which he found came from some hills about four miles off, he shouted with delight. Seizing his roer, and regardless of the expenditure of his scarce and valued ammunition, he placed the barrels of his gun towards the direction from which he had heard the firing, and in quick succession fired off both barrels. Loading again with a heavy charge of powder only, which he rammed down tightly in both barrels, he waited a few minutes, and again pulled both triggers. Bernhard knew that if the report of fire-arms which he had heard came from any of his own people, the signal which he had given would be soon answered — at least, it would be if it could be heard. In less than five minutes after his signal was given he heard it answered, and he was thus aware that aid was at hand; what that aid was he did not know. Great as was his requirement for food, yet he was more anxious to discover what assistance was likely to be afforded him, so he ran to a rising-ground near and looked in the direction from which the sounds of firing had been heard. He then saw a party of about thirty mounted men riding at a canter towards him, their general appearance seeming to indicate that they were Dutchmen.

His uncertainty was soon set at rest, for as they approached, he recognised familiar forms; and waving his hat as a signal, he was answered by more than one, who, though ignorant as yet as to who he was, were yet aware that a friend was greeting them.

It was not long before Bernhard was the centre of an eager and inquiring circle, amongst whom were uncles, cousins, and other relations of Katrine and Hans. Upon hearing the condition of those whom Bernhard had lately left, there was a general cry of "On, on! let us go help them." Bernhard, however, stopped this eagerness, and made inquiries as to the amount of ammunition amongst the parties, the number of horses, etc.

"We should take extra horses, and as much ammunition as we can carry," he urged; "we shall very likely have to right, and certainly there must be enough horses to carry all the party."

The most experienced at once agreed that this step was necessary, and it was therefore decided that whilst the main body moved forward some five or six should return to the waggons, which were about five miles off, bring extra horses, and all the ammunition, and follow the main body.

Great was the anxiety of all the party to get forward. Hans was a favourite with them all; and the general opinion was, that it would be very odd if Hans had not managed to be a match in some way for any Matabili who might have discovered him. During the whole day the cavalcade advanced with speed, led by Bernhard, and, with but two brief halts, continued their progress, until darkness set in and they were compelled to halt. Bernhard was now in great hopes that he would be enabled to rescue Hans and the girls; for thirty mounted Boers, all well-armed and amply supplied with ammunition, was a formidable force, and one that, against savages armed with spears only, was not easy to withstand. He was therefore much better pleased with the aspect of affairs than he was on the previous night, when he had camped within a few miles of this same locality.

Although a watch was kept and other precautions taken against a surprise, the Dutchmen made no great efforts to conceal themselves: they thus lighted a fire and cooked their provisions, amongst which coffee was one of the items, a steaming tea-cup of which can only be fully appreciated by those who have for days had water as the mere quencher of thirst. Soon after the camp had been formed the party which had been sent back for extra horses regained their brother hunters, and the reinforcement for Hans now amounted to thirty-two hunters, all Dutchmen, and four Hottentots; whilst forty-two horses in all were either ridden or led by the party.

Bernhard estimated that he could reach the ground near which Hans would be concealed by about mid-day on the morrow, and thus, instead of taking a week to obtain aid, he would be able to return in half that time, and with as efficient a force as could be expected. Reflecting upon the probable results of the morrow, he sank to sleep, and enjoyed a night's rest undisturbed by any of the numerous sounds that broke the silence of the wilderness.

Chapter Sixteen
The Fight for Life—Grand Attack of the Matabili—Help arrives—The Meeting of Old Friends—Retreat from the Stronghold

"They may yell, Victor," exclaimed Hans, "but they have not taken us yet: at least fifty of them will not see to-morrow's sun rise, before they capture us. If we had only half a dozen more *Mensch* here, we would give them a lesson; or if we had an unlimited supply of ammunition. Now I dare not fire a shot unless I am certain of my man; so we cannot be as dangerous as we otherwise should be. When these new arrivals come, they will try to scale our stronghold, and we shall then have to use our long spears again."

In half an hour the reinforcement had joined their dark brethren, and there was evidently a consultation going on in the ravine below: there was much talking audible, whilst the men did not show themselves in the neighbourhood. After a time there was a sound as if trees were being felled, and Hans and Victor then knew some plan was going to be put in practice against them. They were not long left in doubt, for, upon a loud yell being uttered, five parties of Matabili, each consisting of above twenty men, rushed towards the rocks, each carrying a slender tree about forty feet in length. These they had cut, and left a few branches on, so that they could be easily climbed. The trees were to be placed against the face of the rock, and in fact were not a bad imitation of a scaling-ladder.

"Our guns for this, Victor," said Hans; "let us thin them as they come; then our spears as they come within reach of them."

To men fighting for their lives as were the two Dutchmen, a shot was a matter of deep importance; and so steady was their aim, that after four discharges the bearers of two of the trees had suffered so severely that they retreated precipitately to the cover of the bush. The others, however, placed theirs upright against the rock, and had they been able to ascend three or four abreast, the fate of Hans and his party would soon have been decided; the Matabili, however, would not quit their shields or spears, and therefore, with only one hand to aid them, and being able to ascend merely one after the other, Hans and Victor had time to reload, and before the most active savage could set his foot on the rock, he was thrust back with the long spears, a second and a third stabbed in the same manner, whilst, dropping the spear and seizing his gun, Hans shot two Matabili who were urging on those before them.

Such rapid slaughter caused a panic among those who were exposed to the deadly aim of the hunters, and they gave up their first attempt of climbing on the rock, and fled amongst the bushes and trees.

"Now, Hans," said Victor, "let us push these trees down: it will take them some time to put them up again."

The two men pushed the tops of the trees which reached to their position on one side, and then by aid of their long bamboos shoved them so much out of the perpendicular that they fell by their own weight to the ground.

Having accomplished this, they were able to turn their attention to their numerous enemies below them, who seemed to be clustering together for a second rush, and another attempt on their stronghold. The whole force had now assembled for a determined assault, and were merely waiting for the signal of the chief who was to direct them. At this instant Hans heard the voice of Katrine, which was audible amidst the din of the yelling savages below. Knowing that she would not take off his attention unless for a special reason, he called out—

"What is it, Katie?"

"Help is near, Hans: I am certain I saw three mounted Mensch ride at a gallop over the far ridge, and enter the bush. I just looked there, and as I looked I saw these three an instant before they disappeared."

"Are you certain, Katie? But three men, unless they could come up here to us, will only be slaughtered if they get into the bush."

"There might have been many more, Hans, and they might have gone out of sight before I looked up; but they must come here in a very few minutes. Oh, the fiends, how they yell!" exclaimed Katrine, as the Matabili, preparing for their rush, shrieked at the top of their voices.

"Don't let us waste a shot, Victor: we must hold on another half-hour, and we may get aid. Rate has seen white men near."

"The Matabili are very numerous, Hans: I hope there will be plenty of aid, if it does come."

"Look, Victor! look! what are they doing?" exclaimed Hans, as the Matabili, suddenly ceasing their yells, turned from the rock, and ran rapidly into the bush.

The two besieged men were not long left in uncertainty as to the change in the Matabili's proceedings, for from the bush below there came the loud report of a gun, followed by a second, and then half a dozen at a time. The threatening yells of the Matabili were changed into shrieks of agony, as they felt the deadly effects of the double-barrelled guns of nearly thirty experienced hunters. For a few minutes the black warriors stood their ground, and even attempted a charge; but their ox-hide shields offering no resistance to the bullets of their opponents, the boldest among them were soon shot, and the remainder fled in disorder, staying not until they had reached the more open plain, or when exhausted and out of breath they could run no more.

The hunters were not yet aware whether their friends and connexions were all safe, but they determined to revenge themselves on their savage foes; so, signalling for their horses, which had been left concealed in the ravines below, and in charge of five of their party, about twenty hunters mounted their steeds, and galloping after their retreating enemies, shot them down without mercy. Out of that yelling and exulting band, which an hour before had been threatening Hans' party with instant death, not half a dozen men remained to sneak by night over the plain, and to report to their chief the disasters that had occurred to them.

Bernhard's anxiety was so great to ascertain the fate of Katrine's sister and the others of the party, that he no sooner found the Matabili in retreat than he came back to the rock from which he had heard the firing, and there recognised Hans and Victor, who with Katrine and her sister were watching their enemies driven rapidly before their friends and brethren.

Upon recognising Bernhard, Hans threw his cap in the air and shouted for joy.

"Come up, Bernhard," he exclaimed. "Come and see our strong kraal; two hundred Matabili could not take it from us. Come up, that we may welcome you."

Guided by the numbers of slain to what he supposed must be the place for the ascent, Bernhard, with considerable difficulty, managed to climb up the rock; but he would not have been able to secure a footing on it had it not been for the aid of his two friends, who pulled him up when no other means of ascent existed. Bernhard's welcome was a hearty one. No formalities or rules laid down by cold-hearted reasoners checked the natural affection of these people: Katrine threw her arms round him, and amidst her tears and kisses thanked him as the preserver of her sister and Hans. The two men, though less demonstrative, were not less sincere in their welcome, and for a few minutes they could think of nothing but gratitude to their preserver, and thankfulness for their escape.

"How did you manage to return so soon, Bernhard?" inquired Hans: "we feared you could not return under a week."

"I luckily came across all our people as they were out on a patrol. They expected some Matabili might be coming near them to spy, and so they came out in a large body, both to hunt and to look out for an enemy. We are not safe any where from Moselekatse, and unless we give him a lesson, we shall be eaten up by him. What weapon is this?" exclaimed Bernhard, as he saw the long lance which Hans had made with the blade of the Matabili's assagy and the bamboo stick.

Hans explained how he had made it, and how effective it had proved against their assailants, whilst he led Bernhard round the small rock, and showed him the method he had adopted to make his retreat secure. All his expedients were fully appreciated by Bernhard, who listened attentively to Hans' description of the Bushmen's death, the attempt of the Matabili to cast rocks upon him, and their last endeavour to climb the rock by aid of trees.

"The rock is not easy to ascend even when friends help you," said Bernhard; "and when you are to be rewarded with a thrust from that lance the instant you reach the summit, it is no wonder the Matabili did not get up. You could not have slept much, Hans, during the last three nights, nor have you had very good dinners. When the men all come back from finishing those rascals, we will have a good feast; and you must tell the Mensch all your adventures. We have been lucky, Hans: few men go through such scenes as we have, and live to tell it. Poor Katie looks worn out, and no wonder; and her sister too is ill. But we have horses for them to ride home, and they shall sleep in peace to-night, for there will be plenty to watch."

The hunters who had followed the Matabili returned slowly from the pursuit, but at length all of them assembled around or on the rock. Much interest and curiosity were manifested by them all to examine the means which had enabled Hans to hold out against such overwhelming odds. Each hunter appreciated the strength of the place after he had climbed up the rock; and so formidable was this ascent, that several declined to attempt it: by raising one of the trees against the rock, and securing this there, they were all enabled to ascend.

The means taken by Hans to cut off his communication with the neighbouring ground, by destroying the narrow causeway that had joined the two, was approved of by the most experienced men, whilst Hans' long spear delighted the hunters.

Firewood having been collected in the ravine below, a fire was soon made, and some dozen or more tin pannikins were brewing coffee, whilst large eland steaks were being broiled, and the victorious hunters and their rescued relatives enjoyed a hearty meal.

Being aware of the strength and cunning of their enemy, the leader of the party decided to lose no time in escaping beyond where it was likely he would be followed; so, as the horses were now refreshed, as well as their riders, the steeds were saddled, and the whole party rode forward, towards the country in which their main body had taken up their residence. Fearing no immediate attack from the Matabili, though aware of the necessity of watchfulness, hunting was carried on only to a sufficient extent to supply the bivouac with food. Eland beef, therefore, was plentiful, and other varieties of game not wanting; so that but little hardship was encountered even by Katrine and her sister during the four days that they took to ride to the lager of their relatives.

Chapter Seventeen
The Boers' Camp—The Plans for the Future—Off to Natal—Treaty with the Zulu Chief—His Treachery—Slaughter of the Boers—The Defence of the Boers

On the return of Hans and the party of hunters to the head-quarters of the Boers on the branches of the Vet river, matters were in a very unsettled state. Amongst the Boers who, dissatisfied with the British laws, had emigrated into the interior, there were dissensions. Some of the men of wealth and influence were for remaining on the ground they then occupied, trusting the lesson they had already given to the Matabili would be a sufficient warning to prevent them from again venturing into the country which the emigrants now laid claim to. A large majority, however, were in favour of another commando against the Matabili, and this party eventually carried the day, and preparations were at once commenced for an expedition against this formidable savage. Others again, and amongst these was Retief, the elected leader of the emigrants, was in favour of treking to the fertile plains south of the Quathlamba Mountains, and near the Bay of Natal. He was induced to take this step in consequence of the reports which he had received from some connexions who had just previously started from Uitenhage and had joined a small party of English at the Bay of Natal.

Finding these dissensions going on, Hans placed Katrine under the charge of an aunt, and placed himself at the disposal of those whom he considered fitted to rule the affairs of the emigrants.

"As soon as things are settled, Katie," he said, "when we have decided where we are to rest, I will build a house, and we will marry; but I doubt if I should be as ready for the trek and for fighting if I left you a young wife behind, as if I left you free; and so we will wait."

The winter passed away, and towards the spring intelligence reached the Boers' encampment that the Matabili, having heard of their enemy's preparation for an attack, had driven all their cattle far into the interior, and had themselves withdrawn so far that to pursue them would neither be a wise nor a profitable proceeding. Thus the proposed expedition against the Matabili was given up, and the whole attention of the emigrants directed to emigrating to Natal A general movement of the camp was immediately commenced, and Hans, attaching himself, with his two companions Victor and Bernhard, to the waggons of Katrine and her relatives, followed the leaders, who started for the long and adventurous journey to the south-east.

During many weeks the emigrants journeyed on, following the track of Retief and his party, who had found a means of passing through the Quathlamba Mountains with their waggons, and in reaching the fertile plains beyond. Here, on the banks of the Bushmen's river, Hans, with a large party of his connexions, decided to halt. The country was well watered and fertile, the climate all that could be wished, and abundance of pasturage for the cattle; thus seeming to possess all those qualifications which the emigrants had sought for when they started on their expedition from the old colony of the Cape.

"We may rest here in peace," said Hans to his two friends. "We shall not have English interference; we have plenty of grazing-ground; there are enough of us to prevent any enemy from attacking us; there are plains under the mountains on which we can hunt elands when we choose, and we can cultivate our land with no fear of having to leave our farms in a hurry. So, as soon as I can build a house, I shall many Katrine, and settle quietly down here. We must take a hunt after the elephant, though, now and then, Victor, just to get some ivory, for the gold is thus easily procured. It was good to trek from the old colony, friends, was it not?"

The party to which Hans had attached himself had been located some months on the banks of the Bushmen's river, and had begun to gather some of the produce of their agricultural labours. About the same period, Retief, the leader of those emigrants who had gone further into the country, paid a visit to the chief of the Zulus, the nation which lived to the east of the Natal district.

It was a lovely, calm evening, early in February, that Hans, having returned from a day's successful shooting, was sitting on the front of his waggon cleaning his gun, and describing his day's sport to Katrine, who was engaged knitting. In all directions round them waggons were grouped, whilst large herds of cattle grazed on the surrounding hills and in the valleys. Every thing looked peaceable, and suitable for freedom and enjoyment, and each emigrant was rejoicing at the fair prospect before him.

"We shall have a large addition to our forces from the colony," said an emigrant named Uys, as he came to Hans' waggon and examined the fine reitbok he had brought back with him; "for the news has gone down that this country is very fine, and is full of game. Retief, too, will make good terms with Dingaan, and that will enable us to live here quietly. We have fought enough with the Amakosa and with Moselekatse; we should now grow corn."

"Yes," replied Hans; "I must grow corn soon and in plenty, for I shall marry in the winter, and therefore shall have two to feed."

"Where is Victor?" inquired Uys.

"He has gone down towards the coast to see his cousin there, and to trade for a horse he wants. I hear the country down there is very fine, and elephants come into the bush every year."

"Yes; that is the truth: there is game in plenty, and the forests contain good timber. Cess, who is this riding over the hill? He will kill his horse if he comes at that rate."

"It is Victor," said Hans. "Something must be wrong, or he would never ride like that, and so near home."

As Victor approached the encampment he raised his hat and shouted, "To arms, men; to arms for your lives!" Such a cry to a people who had long had to deal with dangerous foes was not to be neglected: a rush was made to Hans' waggon, where Victor had reined in his panting steed, and a hundred men were eagerly inquiring what was the danger.

"The whole Zulu army is upon us," shouted Victor. "Retief and all his party are murdered. Between us and the Zulus not a Dutchman is left alive. Men, women, and children are all slain."

Shrieks of horror from the women and cries of vengeance from the men greeted this intelligence, whilst an organised defence was hastily arranged. The waggons were brought together and formed into a square, whilst brushwood was cut to fill up the intervals. A three-pounder gun was mounted on a waggon, and pointed in the direction from which the enemy was expected. Guns and ammunition having been served out to all who could use them,—even the females tended their services as loaders of spare guns,—and the party having sent out mounted spies, they waited in momentary expectation of being attacked.

Victor had now time to give a detailed account of the events which had come to his knowledge, and which subsequent inquiry proved to be in the main correct.

Retief, having entered the Natal district with his party, decided after some time to visit the residence of the Zulu chief, in order to negotiate a treaty of peace, and, if possible, to obtain from him a grant or sale of land.

An English missionary, Mr Owen, was resident at the kraal of Dingaan, and believed he had so influenced the mind of the monarch that a friendly reception would be given to the Dutchmen. The mind of a savage despot is, however, very intricate, and neither Retief nor the missionary had any idea of the plot that was working in the chief's mind. After having welcomed Retief and his party, Dingaan agreed to yield a large portion of land to his friends, the white men, when they had proved themselves friends, and they were to prove their friendship by retaking from Sikonyella a quantity of cattle which this chief, a Mantatee, had captured from the Zulus.

This Retief promised to do, and having first sent messengers to Sikonyella, demanding restitution, they made preparations for attacking him in case of his refusal.

Sikonyella immediately gave up about seven hundred head of cattle, as well as horses and guns, some of which he had taken from parties of farmers, and Retief returned with these, and with a party of about seventy of his best-mounted and best-equipped young men.

Dingaan again welcomed the return of Retief and his party, and actually affixed his signature to a document which ceded to the emigrants the greater part of the Natal district. During all this time, however, a plot had been thickening in the mind of the crafty savage. He had heard how his powerful enemy, Moselekatse, had been defeated by these white men; how he had been compelled to quit his kraal, and retreat into the interior; and he therefore decided that they were dangerous neighbours. With a mistaken, short-sighted policy, he fancied that, could he destroy all those who were now near his country, he would deter others from again venturing near him; but such an act, instead of freeing him from his neighbours, was only likely to bring destruction on his head. His proceedings, however, had been determined on, and his acts may be described as follows.

Having acted in every way so as to gain the confidence of his guests, he invited them to witness a great war-dance, as a fit termination to the visit; and as it was against custom to bring any weapons into the royal presence, the visitors were requested to leave their guns outside the kraal. Dingaan had assembled about three thousand warriors, all armed with the broad-bladed stabbing assagy, and with the heavy knob-kerrie, or clubbed stick. The Boers were invited into the centre of a circle of these warriors, and invited to sit down and drink itchuala, a species of beer; whilst the warriors, striking their shields and beating their feet in time, continued to advance and retire, whilst they shouted one of their popular songs. The very ground seemed to tremble beneath the heavy beat of six thousand feet, and the Boers began to regret that they had left their trusty weapons outside the kraal. The Zulu warriors advanced and retired, shaking their assagies and knob-kerries with threatening gestures, the chief Dingaan watching the effect upon his guests. Suddenly withdrawing from the immediate presence of his men, he from a distance exclaimed, "Bulala," and on the signal the warriors closed in on their victims, whom they outnumbered forty to one, and after a brief struggle,—for the Dutchmen drew their hunting-knives, and fought desperately, slaying several of their enemies,—killed them all, not before they had tortured several who had been the most formidable in the defence.

As soon as this slaughter was complete, Dingaan ordered ten thousand men to dash into the Natal territory, and destroy the white men there located. The Zulus spread like locusts over the land, (A detailed description of the slaughter of Retief and his party was given us by two eye-witnesses, one a Kaffir, who subsequently deserted from Panda, Dingaan's successor, and who was a warrior in Dingaan's service at the time of the slaughter of Retief. This man stated that two Boers had concealed their guns, and had time to use them, but not to reload; thus evincing that some at least of the party suspected treachery. The other account was from a Kaffir named Copen, who spoke English well, and who was a boy at the time in Dingaan's kraal. Both accounts agreed in the main facts.) and, as the emigrants were principally scattered about in small parties, they fell easy victims to their numerous foes.

Some emigrants near the Blue Krantz river were killed to a man, and the place was henceforth termed "Weenen" (Weeping). It was from this neighbourhood that Victor, being fortunately at a short distance from the detachment when the Zulus attacked it, escaped, and was able to ride forward and warn his friends of their danger.

Contrary to expectation, the night arrived and passed with no signs of the enemy; but scarcely had day begun to break than the spies came galloping in, and announced that the Zulus were swarming over the hills, and coming rapidly on to the lager. All was ready for their reception, and before they came within three hundred yards several of their number were laid low by the deadly weapons of the Boers.

Hans, with his two old companions Victor and Bernhard, had selected a position near one of the angles of the square, this being the shape in which the Dutchmen usually drew up their waggons.

As the solid mass of the Zulus charged up to the waggons, an irregular discharge from the emigrants was poured upon them with fearful effect. The three-pounder gun, loaded with bullets, sent its messengers of death among them, and covered the ground with the slain. Even the highly-trained Zulus could not face this deadly rain of lead, and they turned and fled to a secure distance, where they were again drawn up in order by their chiefs, and once more launched against their foes.

Their recent victories over the white men had caused them to underrate their foes; and this, added to the dread of returning to their chief without having carried out his orders of exterminating the white men, gave them great determination in their charges; and though mowed down by scores in their advance, still those in the rear leapt over the bodies of the slain in front, and endeavoured to force an entrance through the rampart made by the Dutchmen.

In their second charge, several Zulus reached the waggon on which Hans was standing; and he, having discharged both barrels of his gun with fatal effect, was for an instant unarmed. The Zulus seemed to be aware of this, and boldly leapt on to the wheel, and with a yell of triumph raised their assagies above their heads, as they prepared for their next spring. Victor and Bernhard, however, saw the danger, and with rapid aim, such as sportsmen alone can take, the savages were dropped from their advanced position; whilst Katrine, pushing a freshly-loaded gun into Hans' hands, grasped his empty weapon, and was soon ready again to supply him with his loaded gun.

Many times did the Zulus renew their charges on their foes, but without avail; and from sunrise to sunset the Dutchmen maintained this unequal contest. As the day advanced the ammunition began to grow scarce, and there was a general demand for powder and bullets, but none were forthcoming; many men having placed their last charge in their guns. Should the Zulus again charge, the fate of the whole party would be slaughter; for if a hand-to-hand fight occurred, the numbers being about forty to one, there could be no doubt as to the result. Fortunately at this crisis a shot was fired from the three-pounder into the midst of the Zulus, and this shot striking some of the Zulu chiefs at a great distance, caused a panic, and a rapid retreat of the whole body, leaving the Boers masters of the field, though their cattle were nearly all carried off.

As soon as the Zulus retired, the Dutchmen assembled, and mounting their horses, sallied out to learn the fate of those emigrants who were scattered about in various parts. Whenever the Boers had been able to collect and form a lager with their waggons, they had beaten off their savage foes; but in other cases the slaughter had been complete.

That night was one of deep sorrow at the lager of Bushmen's river. Fortunately the loss on the part of the Dutch had been very slight, and their victory complete; but the intelligence brought in from all sides was most disastrous. At least 600 men, women, and children had been slaughtered, in addition to the party of Retief. Men with whom most of the survivors had been in the habit of mixing for years, and who were known as the good shot, the brave rider, and the generous-hearted friend, had been slaughtered with wife and children, their mangled corpses being found near those of their family. War in most aspects is bad, but this was a mere wanton massacre; and it was only natural that but one cry should arise from the men, old and young, and also from the women: that cry was vengeance, retribution for all this. "We have the power to teach the barbarian that he cannot slaughter us with impunity, and that mere numbers will not avail. Let us arm and invade his territory," was the exclamation; and this being the general wish, a party of about 400 men was hastily assembled, and placed under the direction of an experienced and gallant leader, Piet Uys, seconded by Potgieter, and was soon ready for the expedition.

Hans and his two friends joined this party, and were anxious to revenge the losses of their friends and relatives.

It was in April, 1838, that this party left the Klip river, and advanced towards Zulu land. Each man was mounted and armed with a double-barrelled gun, and supplied with ample ammunition; and considering the foe against whom they were advancing was armed only with spears, the result of the conflict did not seem for a moment doubtful. The savage, however, as we have found to our cost in Africa and New Zealand, is crafty and practical; he knows both his strength and his weakness, and he appears to know the weak points of our routine system; of these he takes advantage, and not unusually for a long time sets us at defiance.

The party of Boers rode on steadily from their lager at Klip river towards Zulu land. Rivers were crossed, and plains and bush traversed, whilst every caution was taken to guard against surprise. The first night's halting-place was reached, and the party bivouacked, having appointed sentries and reliefs, and detailed the position for each man to occupy in case of attack.

It was a singularly wild scene, this bivouack of some 400 experienced hunters. There were among them lion and elephant hunters, men who had lived for years by the chase; there were others who had fought in several wars against the Amakosa Kaffirs, and had witnessed strange scenes in the land.

"We shall capture all the lost cattle and horses," said the veteran Uys, as he approached Hans, who was cleaning his guns and examining his bullets.

"Yes; and revenge Retief's murder too, I hope. I think it was not wise of Retief to leave his guns behind him, for a savage is ever a treacherous creature."

"Ah! Retief fancied he had won Dingaan over to his side, and he went with so many men because he wanted to show his power to the Zulus: if he had followed the advice given, he would have taken only four or five men, with the cattle that he captured from Sikonyella."

"Do you think we are strong enough, Piet," inquired Hans, "to meet the Zulus in bush country?"

"I think we are; but we will try not to meet them there: we will meet them in the open country. Dingaan has never yet fought against men armed with fire-arms and mounted on horses; if he had he might be more careful than I expect he will be when he hears there are only 400 men come to invade his territory."

"We shall kill many hundred Zulus if they attempt to fight us as do the Matabili. It is only the Amakosa who have been taught lessons, and who keep to the bush, as they know their weakness."

"Zulu spies are out," said Victor, who had returned from some neighbouring hills, near which he had been on watch. "I saw three men running rapidly over the open ground beyond my station; they are going to report to Dingaan our approach."

"We shall be ready for him whenever he shows himself," exclaimed Uys; "and we have our relatives and friends to avenge; so let us remember this as well as that our own safety depends upon the defeat of the Zulus."

"I cannot help thinking," whispered Hans to Victor, "that if we had more men it would be better for us. I understand that some of our people, with some English and deserters from the Zulus, are making an attack on Dingaan from near the coast; if now we all were to join, it would be better. One stick is easy to break after another, but if you tie ten together it is not so easy."

"We must trust to our leaders, Hans," replied Victor, "and fight well for our cause."

Chapter Eighteen
The Boers advance towards Zulu Land—
Their Battle with the Zulus—Hans' Danger—
Lost—The Artifice—The Race for Life

The emigrant fanners advanced through the ceded territory of Natal, crossed the Tugela river, and approached the kraal of Dingaan. Only a few spies were observed in their march, and it was feared that the Zulu monarch had become alarmed, and had retreated into some stronghold in the interior.

Near the kraal of Um kung kunglovo, Dingaan's residence, there was a defile between two hills, and upon the emigrants entering this the Zulu army first showed itself, but, as though fearing the emigrants, the army rapidly retired towards the kraal.

"There stand the murderer's soldiers," exclaimed Uys: "let us follow them." And the emigrants pursued their foes, who shortly showed a front, and, with fearful yells, charged their invaders. Another division of the Zulu army, which had remained concealed until the emigrants had passed it, suddenly emerged and cut off the retreat of the horsemen, who were thus attacked from front and rear. On either side too the Zulus sprang up, and the emigrants were thus prevented from adopting their usual successful mode of warfare; viz. loading whilst retreating or advancing, halting and firing, and again riding away.

It became evident to all the party that their crafty enemy had inveigled them into a trap, and had thus drawn them on, until they had entered this very unfavourable place for fighting on horseback. With a rapidly-arranged system, the Boers directed their fire upon one portion of the mass of their enemies, and thus slaying them by hundreds, cleared a way for themselves out of their difficulty.

Hans, with his two companions, had ridden near their leader from the beginning of the combat. The heavy weapons carried by these three hunters, and their accurate aim, had produced terrific effects on the Zulus, the bullets in many cases having passed through two men and wounded a third. Hans had been one of the first to see the threatened danger of being irrecoverably hemmed in by the enemy, and had shouted the advice, "All fire on the rear Zulus: clear a way out over them."

Had the whole party adopted this plan, there would not have been any great loss on the part of the white men; unfortunately, however, the leader Uys turned from the direction in which the main body were firing, and followed by Hans and about twenty others, dashed through a weak party of Zulus, and thus hoped to escape.

The Zulus, however, were dangerous even to death: several men who had fallen wounded raised themselves as they saw their enemies approaching, and even as the horses trod on their limbs these hard-lived warriors stabbed the steeds which were above them, and, in several cases, wounded the riders. Onward rode the emigrants, however, and their escape seemed certain, although separated from the main body of the party, until they suddenly found themselves on the edge of a ravine, which their horses could not get over. At this time Uys the leader was badly wounded, and his horse sinking under him, he called to his followers to escape, though he could not. At this time Hans' horse received a second wound, and he, finding it could carry him no longer, and that hundreds of the enemy were rushing up to finish the work they had begun on the gallant Uys, he jumped from his horse, and rushed into the ravine, the side of which was densely wooded; and thus, whilst the Zulus were occupied in slaying Uys and his son, who would not leave his father, Hans managed to run or force his way through the underwood, and reached a slope beyond, from which none of his enemies or friends could be seen.

The main body of the Dutch, having cleared a way for themselves by shooting all the Zulus who opposed them, rode on at a gallop till they had cleared the ravine and bushy ground near Dingaan's kraal, and obtained a position in the plains where the Zulus dared not follow them, even had the Dutch waited for them; but finding that the Zulus were a more powerful enemy than they had imagined, and hearing from those of their party who had followed Uys that he, his son, and one or two others had been killed, amongst whom Hans was stated to be, the farmers became disheartened, and returned at once to their head-quarters.

Several of the farmers had seen Hans' horse badly wounded, and when they had escaped from Uys and his son, they saw Hans leave his horse and enter the ravine on foot. They believed he would have no chance of escape, for the enemy were in hundreds, and they therefore reported without hesitation that he was killed, for they believed he must be so. Had either Victor or Bernhard believed that he was still alive, they would have been disposed to venture back in the hope of aiding their friend; but hearing he was dead, they knew they could be of no service, and therefore rode on with their companions.

Upon reaching their head-quarters, and reporting the loss of their gallant leader, his son, and a few others, there was great grief at the lager. All who knew Hans liked him, and expected him some day to be a useful guide to them in all matters of war; so that he was bewailed by all. Katrine bore her grief silently; she would not move from her waggon, and sat rigid and corpse-like for hours, refusing all consolation, and asserting her belief that Hans was not dead.

The emigrants immediately sent messengers to their countrymen, demanding aid; but having heard that the English settlers at Natal Bay, and the other emigrants near there, had been defeated in their attack on Dingaan, they gave up all hope for the present of any favourable results of an expedition against the strong chief of the Amazulu.

When Hans found himself on the slope of a hill, with no signs either of his friends or enemies, he knew his position was one of extreme danger. One of two courses he intuitively knew must be adopted: either to try at once to overtake his friends, or to lie concealed until the night, and then to endeavour to find his way towards the Bay of Natal or the lager of his friends. After a short reflection he decided on the latter plan, and had no sooner done so than he was convinced of its being the safer of the two, for he saw several parties of Zulus on the hill-tops before him on the watch, either to pick off the stragglers, or to observe the proceedings of the retreating enemy.

Having, with the caution and skill which his hunter's experience had enabled him to adopt, forced his way into the densest part of the bush, and left scarcely any trail, Hans remained perfectly quiet, though he was enabled to see the hills on both sides of him, and even to hear the triumphant shouts of the Zulus, as they carried off the spoils of the veteran leader and his son. Hans, however, knew that the slightest movement on his part, even so much as would cause a branch to shake, would most probably attract the attention of his watchful enemies. Thus he dare not move hand or foot, but remained as still as was his brave leader. He had determined to sell his life dearly if he should be discovered, and only to cease using his weapons when he himself was slain. He had some hopes that his countrymen would halt as soon as they had cleared the unfavourable ground from which they had retreated, and either wait there for stragglers to rejoin them, or return and inflict a defeat on the Zulus.

During the whole day Hans remained concealed, and as dusk was setting in he ventured to raise his head among the bushes, in order to examine the surrounding country, so as to decide which would be the safest direction for him to pursue. Whilst thus looking about him he observed a whitish-looking object in the bush about two hundred yards from him, which at first he believed to be a portion of the dress of a white man. After examining this more carefully, Hans concluded that it was the shield of a Zulu, and therefore believed that it belonged to a man who must be on watch there. As long as daylight existed, Hans continued to examine this shield, and finding that no movement whatever occurred, he fancied the owner of the shield was either killed, or it had been dropped by some man in his retreat. When darkness spread on all around, Hans as silently as possible moved through the bush, and being desirous of examining the Zulu's shield, made his way towards it. It was not without difficulty that Hans reached the exact spot on the opposite slope on which was the shield, for it is very difficult to keep to any particular line in a dense forest. He, however, reached the spot, and there found a Zulu dead. The man had been shot through the body, and had evidently sought this retired locality to die quietly.

When Hans saw the thick skin tails that the man wore round his body and neck, and the shield which had proved so useless against the Dutchmen's bullets, he thought that these articles might be of some use to himself. Divesting the body of these scanty articles of attire, he fastened them on himself, and found that they in a great measure covered him from the neck to the knee. Knowing the extreme danger of his position, and the risk he ran of being discovered and at once overwhelmed by numbers, Hans decided on a bold and novel expedient. Divesting himself of his coat, he rolled this up, and fastened it inside the Kaffir's shield. His trousers he cut off at the knee, to which point the tails of the dead Kaffir reached. His felt hat he also fastened up with the coat, and was thus bare-headed and bare-legged, whilst his body was concealed by the Kaffir's strips of skin. In the ravine below him there were some pools of water, in which was dark black mud. To these pools Hans quietly stole, and walking into the water, lifted out handfuls of the mud, with which he covered his face, hair, legs, and hands. Thus besmeared with black, there was no sign of his white complexion, and if viewed from a distance he might easily have been taken for a Zulu even by day. By night, however, it was impossible to distinguish him, and this he concluded would be the case, although he had no looking-glass to guide him. His gun he carried with the shield, so as not to attract attention, and his powder-horn and bullets, being slung over his shoulder, were covered by the long skin strips that fell over his shoulders.

Having performed these various operations, he offered a prayer for his safety, and boldly commenced his journey. He knew that the more he kept to the bush by day the better, but the open plains might be traversed by night. Fortunately for Hans, the night was bright and clear, and plenty of stars shone, so that he could by them find the direction in which he should travel. Hastening onwards, he avoided all the Kaffirs' kraals that stood in his way, and had passed over upwards of three miles without meeting with any obstacles. As, however, he was passing some dense bush, and following a beaten track which he remembered riding along in the morning, he suddenly heard voices at no great distance, and before he could make up his mind whether to walk on or retreat, a voice in Kaffir called out, "Where are you going?"

Fortunately there is a great similarity between the various dialects of South Africa. The language of the Amakosa Kaffirs could be understood by the Zulus, and a Matabili could understand both. Hans had always an aptitude for languages, and had become aware of the principal peculiarities or differences between the Zulu and Amakosa, in consequence of having inquired from those men who had come as cattle-guards to the emigrants, when the latter entered the Natal district. He therefore immediately understood the question put to him, and without stopping replied, "The chief sends me."

The answer satisfied his inquirers, who in the darkness could but discover a figure with a shield, which seemed to them one of their own people, and thus this watchful party allowed Hans to pass without further inquiry, never dreaming that he was an enemy disguised.

During the greater part of the night, Hans continued to walk, and when the first dawn of day enabled him to see objects around him, he entered a dense bush, and there remained concealed. Although his disguise might succeed by night, he was aware that a Kaffir would be curious to see who it was that carried a gun with his shield, and thus he would soon be discovered. Having, therefore, succeeded in escaping one night, he hoped to be able to continue his journey again, and thus he would soon be within so short a distance of his friends that the Zulus would not dare to appear in force near them.

During the day Hans adopted the same caution that he had on the previous evening, and scarcely moved a limb. He saw no Kaffirs until the sun had begun to increase the length of the shadows, when he knew it was past noon. From his retreat he could see far around in all directions, and could thus at once perceive if the enemy approached from any part; but he saw no signs of them during the greater part of the day. As the afternoon passed on, however, he was at once on the alert, when he observed a party of above twenty Zulus following the course he had taken, and evidently tracing him by his spoor. Although he had adopted a Kaffir's attire in most respects, he had not given up his veldt schoens (skin-shoes), for to walk bare-footed would soon have lamed him. The footprint, therefore, which he left, especially when he walked by night and could not see how to avoid mole-hills and soft ground, which took an impression easily, could be easily seen and traced by a Kaffir; and he was therefore tolerably certain that his enemies would trace him to his present retreat. The party of Zulus were still more than a quarter of a mile from him, when he thought of a bold expedient. Partly concealed, as he would be, among the bushes, he trusted that even a Zulu would not be able to see through his disguise; so, standing erect, he shouted "Mena-bo" (the method of hailing a man, like "Hi," "Hullo," in England), and waved his shield to attract attention. The Zulus instantly saw him, and all listened to hear the news, for they immediately concluded that one of their tribe had forestalled them on the spoor, and could give them intelligence of the enemy they were hunting. Hans, pointing with his shield to the hill on his right, and in an opposite direction to that in which he intended to travel, sung out in true Kaffir style, "Um lungo hambili Kona." ("The white man has gone there.")

"Have you seen him?" was the inquiry, called with great distinctness.

"Yes; he went when the sun was up high," was Hans' reply.

Fearing that he might be asked to come to his supposed friends, he shouted, "The chief sends me;" "Hamba guthle;" ("Travel on well;") and, with no apparent effort at concealment, Hans walked rapidly through the bush in the opposite direction to that in which he had said the white man had retreated.

At first Hans believed his plan had proved entirely successful; for the Zulus ceased following the traces of his footmarks, and ran in the nearly opposite direction, looking all the time on the ground for any signs of the white man's footmarks. Hans had made such good use of his time that he had advanced nearly a mile in the direction he knew he ought to travel, whilst the Zulus were endeavouring by a short cut to come on to the spoor of the white man. He could see the Zulus hesitating as they found no signs of footprints, and then he saw them halt and apparently consult. The result of this consultation was soon evident. The party rapidly retraced their steps, and again followed the footprints which Hans had made.

On seeing this, Hans used his utmost speed to reach the banks of the Tugela river, which he knew was not more than two miles from him. On the banks of this river there were wooded krantzs and dark ravines, in which an army almost might lie concealed; and if he were pursued, he believed that in this locality he would have the best chance of escaping the keen eyes of his foes; or if unable to do this, he could fight with the best chance of success.

As he moved quickly on, he lost sight of the Zulus, who had retraced their steps in order to continue their spooring; but he was not left long in doubt as to their proceedings, for upon looking round he saw the whole party on the crest of the hill over which he had passed, running rapidly after him, their shields held aloft, and their assagies waving over their heads. These men had discovered the ruse that had been practised upon them. Even at first one or two suspicious Kaffirs had wished to call the stranger to them, but the fear of stopping the chief's messenger had deterred them. When, however, they found no spoor where the strange Zulu had told them the white man had gone, they became more suspicious, and upon retracing their steps,—and finding that the traces of the covered foot led them to the spot on which the strange Zulu had been seen, and then led on in the direction in which he had retreated, they at once were almost certain they had been cheated by a bold and quick-witted enemy. There was but a moment's doubt in the mind of one or two that the man might have been one of their own people, who had possessed himself of a Dutchman's shoes, and had worn these to protect his feet; but the style of walk was not that of a Kaffir, at least the most experienced men decided that this was not so. Whilst this matter was being discussed, a keen-sighted Kaffir observed on a thorn-bush a small piece of white substance, which on examination proved to be a portion of a white man's garment; and thus it was at once decided that the man they had seen was a white man, who had disguised himself as a Zulu in order to avoid detection.

The rage of the Kaffirs at having been thus deceived was somewhat decreased when, on reaching the crest of the hill over which Hans had retreated, they saw him in the distance moving rapidly towards the Tugela river. Compared to their own speed and power of endurance, they, had but a poor idea of that of any white man. All white men, they believed, travelled on horseback, and were not, therefore, fitted to take long journeys on foot. Thus the mile start which Hans had obtained, they did not consider of so much consequence as that it only wanted about two hands' breath of sundown. The savage usually estimates the time in this way, and when near the tropics, where the angle made by the sun's course with the horizon does not vary much during the year, this method gives very close results. By holding the arm out from the body, and measuring the number of hands'-breadths the sun is above the horizon, the savage knows how far he can journey before it sets. The four fingers only of the hand, when closed and held out at arm's length, subtend an angle of about seven degrees, and as the sun moves obliquely down towards the horizon, the sun being two hands' breadth above the horizon would give it an altitude of about fourteen degrees. Near the tropics this would indicate about two hours, or one hour and three-quarters towards sunset. If, however, a person were at the equator it would indicate about seventy minutes to sunset. It was by the sun's position that the Zulus knew they should have daylight scarcely more than two hours, and they must capture the white man before that time, or they would fail in capturing him at all. They therefore ran with all speed after their enemy, who, finding it was no use attempting any longer to deceive his pursuers, threw off his Zulu attire, dropped his shield, and bringing his gun to the trail, ran forward towards the river.

Hans soon found that he was not in condition for a pedestrian race against such enemies as those who were pursuing him. The Zulu is a born athlete; he is usually a spare man, with not an ounce of superfluous flesh about him; he is kept too in training by constant exercise and no great excess of food, and thus can at a moment's notice run his eight or ten miles, or walk his fifty miles without breaking down. Had the race been one on horseback Hans would have felt more confidence, for to him the saddle was the natural condition, whilst pedestrianism had not so much been practised. Being, however, young and muscular, and prepared by his late hardships for an active life, he was not a very easy prey to his pursuers. He, however, found himself losing ground rapidly, and therefore that it was necessary to put in practice some scheme in order to save himself by his head, if he could not do so by his heels.

The ground over which he had run was grassy, and thus easily took an impression, so that, even had Hans not known that he could be seen by his pursuers, he would have known that any attempt at concealment would have been fruitless, as his traces would show where he had gone. He ran on, therefore, with all the speed he could until he entered the ravine, which led eventually down to the Tugela, and he then tried an expedient which he believed would throw off his pursuers, at least for a time. Having found a hard piece of stony ground, on which a footprint was scarcely visible, and finding that he could not be seen by his pursuers, he left one or two distinct impressions of his foot on the mole-hills, and then retracing his steps for about fifty yards, he trod carefully on large stones or hard ground, so as to leave no traces, and then took a direction at right angles to that he had formerly adopted. The country was here sprinkled with low thorn-bushes, and was rocky and gravelly, so that footprints were not so easily seen and followed as in more open grassy country. Hans having thus endeavoured to throw his pursuers out, stopped for a few minutes in order to regain his breath, and to listen to his enemies' proceedings.

The Zulus came straggling on, eager to overtake their victim, and hoping soon to do so, for they had noticed the want of firmness in Hans' step, and concluded he was like some of their fat men, unable to run far or fast. Noting here and there a footprint which served to show them they were on the right track, the Zulus dashed down the ravine and beyond where Hans had turned and retraced his steps. The whole party had gone nearly two hundred yards onwards before the leaders halted in consequence of finding no spoor; they then spread out in various directions endeavouring to find some sign. Fortunately one of the footprints of Hans had been half concealed by that of a Zulu, who had trodden on the same soft place, and this having been observed, the Kaffirs believed that they might have entirely obliterated other traces in their hasty rush down the ravine. This induced them to seek on further for fresh footprints instead of trying back, and Hans, who could hear their loud voices, knew he should at least obtain a good start even if they did discover his change of direction.

Having regained his breath, Hans decided to move on, not in great haste, but quietly and with care, that he might not be seen by his enemies; for this purpose he moved with the utmost caution over a ridge, and entered a woody valley beyond; he was thus covered from the view of his pursuers, who were still puzzled to find his footprints. He then walked quickly on until he found an open plain about half a mile across, between him and a line of willow-like trees, which he believed grew on the banks of the Tugela. Hans knew that here he must encounter great risk, not so much from the enemy behind, for he believed he should be able to escape them, but from any parties of Zulus who might be out spying, and who would see him and wait in ambuscade for him. He had, however, so firm a conviction that the Zulus behind would only be temporarily puzzled by his artifice that he decided the least risk would be incurred by at once making a rush across this open ground. Waiting a moment to decide for what part of the river he should run, he took one glance around, and then ran off into the plain.

Hans had scarcely gone two hundred yards than he knew he had been discovered by the Zulus in rear, who, immediately they were confused by the spoor, had sent three men to the hill-tops to look out, in order, if possible, to catch sight of him. These spies at once shouted to their companions below, and joining them, the whole body were quickly in pursuit. Hans had, however, more than five hundred yards start, and he knew that he could reach the river long before he could be overtaken. How or where to cross this river he knew not. In some places the Tugela is deep and wide, in other places shallow, the banks marshy, and covered with long reeds. Again the river forces itself between deep precipices, where the baboon alone can ascend or descend. Seeing the willow-like trees, Hans believed that the river might be deep where they grew; and he had therefore selected another part where low bushes prevailed, and where there was an indication of a rapid slope in the ground.

The Zulus were more than a quarter of a mile behind when Hans reached the bank of the river, which he found steep and rocky, the river itself running rapidly over a stony bed. This was just the condition he required; for although he could swim well, yet Hans knew that he could not swim with his heavy gun, nor could he keep his powder dry, and that therefore his last defence would be taken away. On examining the bed of the river he concluded it was not out of his depth, so he instantly decided to cross. Taking his powder-horn in one hand, and his gun in the other, he scrambled down the bank, and selecting those parts where there seemed most ripples on the water, he waded to the opposite bank, the depth in no part being greater than to cover him above his waist, although the rapidity of the stream rendered it difficult for him to retain his footing. He succeeded, however, in reaching the opposite bank without wetting his gun or powder, and he here determined to make a stand: for he thought it possible that some of the farmers might be in the neighbourhood, and that the sound of a gun would call them to his aid. He was also indisposed to give up so good a defence as the river offered. So concealing himself behind some bushes, he waited for his enemies' approach.

Hans had not long to wait. As hounds follow the scent of their game, so came the Zulus to the banks of the river, looked for a moment at the bank, and then leapt into the stream. Four Kaffirs who had outstripped the others in speed, were the first to enter the stream, which was at this point about eighty yards wide; they could only advance at a slow pace in consequence of the slippery nature of the rocks and stones on which they had to tread, and also of the rapidity of the stream. So entirely did they look upon their adventure in the light of chasing a feeble enemy, that they had no idea of any risk as they thus ventured into the stream. They believed the white man's only chance of escape was his speed or cunning in throwing them off his spoor, and they fancied themselves more than a match for these.

Hans watched the men enter the stream, and had noted the leader, a tall, thin, long-legged man, who had invariably taken a decided lead whenever the Zulus had run any distance. He was the first to enter the river, and was midway across before any of the others had advanced twenty yards. Resting his gun on the branch of a small acacia, Hans aimed from his cover at this man, and in another instant the banks of the Tugela re-echoed the novel sound of a heavy gun. The skill of the elephant hunter did not desert him on this occasion; his shot went truly, and the tall Zulu sank beneath the waters of the Tugela, an arm partly raised as the body was whirled down by the rapid current being the only indication of the man's fate, after Hans' bullet had struck him.

The Zulus had fresh in their memory the fatal effects of the white men's guns in the late battle, and those who were already in the stream, and who saw the fate of their fastest runner, instantly turned and scrambled to the opposite bank.

Hans now decided on waiting for a time on this river bank, for he began to feel the effect of a long fast, and of the exertion he had used to escape his pursuers; but a movement of the Zulus on the opposite bank showed him that this step could not be ventured on. No sooner had those who were in the stream when he fired returned to land, than the chief of the party detailed four men to go down the stream, and four up, who were to cross at once, and go round and cut off the retreat of the white man. This plan would at once have prevented Hans' escape, had he not seen the men leave, and had thus become aware of the plot. Taking off his hat, he moved slightly from his cover, so that the Kaffirs might see him, and then crouched down again, as though waiting for another shot. Instead of doing this, however, he placed his hat on a branch where it could be seen by the enemy on the other side of the stream; then lying flat on the ground, he worked his way along, so as not to be seen from the opposite shore. Having thus got out of sight, he rose, and finding he could not be seen, ran rapidly away from the river bank, and finding an old game path, followed this at speed, until he had gone fully a mile from the banks of the Tugela river.

Chapter Nineteen
Unexpected Meeting—Hans tells his Story—The Ambuscade—Greek meets Greek in War—The Country near Natal—The News—The solitary Hunt in the Bush

Believing that as soon as the Zulus found that they had been again cheated they would follow on his trace, Hans ran and walked as fast as he could, avoiding all detached bushes in order to escape any ambuscade which stragglers might have prepared for him. He thus continued his course until it became too dark to find his way, when having chosen a tree, near an open space, where he believed he could have good warning if any enemy approached him, he sat himself down, and began to think how he could procure some food for himself. To light a fire in order to cook was too dangerous a proceeding to adopt, and though almost starving with hunger, yet he could not bring himself to eat raw flesh, and thus he did not see any means of procuring a supper. For two nights he had had no sleep, and though the excitement of his escapes had kept him up, and the water of the river had refreshed him, still nature would not be denied, and he had not long been seated beneath the tree before he felt sleep stealing over him.

"I can sleep safely for an hour or two," thought Hans, "and will then awake, be ready to proceed at daybreak, and shall certainly find some means of procuring food."

Arranging himself so as to be ready to grasp his gun at a moment's notice, he turned on his side, and in a very few minutes was fast asleep, undisturbed by a dream of any kind.

The sun had risen, and was well above the horizon before Hans awoke from his deep sleep, which he did with a sudden start of alarm, as he perceived that it was broad daylight. He instantly stretched out his hand for his gun, but could not find it. Jumping up, he saw that he was surrounded by a large party of Kaffirs, who, armed with assagies and shields, had surrounded him. Without a single weapon to defend himself with, he knew that resistance was useless, and therefore stood calmly awaiting his fate, which he expected was to be assagied immediately. As soon as he stood up, however, several of the Kaffirs called as though to some chief or other person in the distance, and Hans, turning in the direction in which it appeared the person was whom the Kaffirs had called, he first saw the smoke of a fire, and even his strong heart quailed as the thought occurred to him that he was to be roasted alive. His astonishment, however, was extreme, when he saw four white men coming towards him, one of whom was decidedly Dutch in his appearance. "Could these also be prisoners?" was Hans' first thought, "and are we all to be burnt together?" But seeing that the white men carried their guns, he was more puzzled than before. He waited till the men came close to him before he spoke; he then said, "You have caught me asleep; few men have ever done that before." For an instant the men looked at one another, and then the stranger, addressing Hans in Dutch, said, "You must be one of the Mensch, but what, in God's name, are you doing here, and why is your face black?" Hans, forgetting for the moment that he had blackened his face with mud, and that though the water had partly washed off that which had been on his legs, still they had a very Kaffir-like tinge about them, whilst his hair was so matted with mud, that it was unlike a white man's, burst out laughing at the remark of the Dutchman.

"My face may be black," he replied, "but I am Hans Sterk, a true-born Africander."

"You Hans Sterk!" said the other with incredulity. "We heard he was killed with the two Uys." "You Hans Sterk!" the man repeated, as he came nearer, and examined Hans closely, "and how did you escape? You must be a Dutchman by your speech, though in the dim light of the morning I took you for a Kaffir spy, wearing the clothes of some of Retief's murdered men. Come to the fire and let us hear your story."

"Let me eat and drink first," said Hans. "I have been two days without food, and have travelled on foot at a rate that would have puzzled an ostrich. Then, when I'm washed, you shall hear of my escape. But tell me the news. How came you here? and have all my people escaped?"

"We are out on patrol from the Bay, for we, too, were defeated when your people were; and we came up yesterday to pick up any stragglers. Your people have gone back to Bushman's river, but it is bad for them. Their cattle are swept away, and they have little or no food. Their crops are destroyed, and they dare not again attack the Zulus, at least not till they get more help."

Having gained this information, Hans commenced his meal, which consisted of grilled buffaloe. He knew there was a journey before him, so he did not eat to excess; but, having taken sufficient to satisfy his immediate craving for food, he inquired for the nearest stream, and, accompanied by the white men, soon washed off his disguise, and showed himself in his natural colours.

"Then all those Kaffirs are from Natal Bay?" inquired Hans.

"Yes, these are our Kaffirs," replied the Dutchman. "There were many Kaffirs killed in the battle, and these men have come up to look after any of their friends who may be hidden hereabouts. Our people had a greater defeat than yours, and we lost ten or twelve white men, whilst hundreds of our Kaffirs were killed."

"How is it that you don't fear a strong party coming now?" inquired Hans; "for I was followed to within three miles of this place by a party of Zulus."

"We have our spies out, and one is hidden in that tree on the hill there, and if he saw danger he would signal to us at once. A man reported yesterday afternoon that he heard a shot fired from near the Tugela, but as no one else heard it we began to doubt his report. Still we came on this way on the chance of its being true, and we camped last night about a mile from here, and at daybreak crossed your spoor, and followed it for some time, when a spy came in, and said he had seen a man asleep under a tree, and thought he was a Zulu. You were lucky to escape being assagied at once, before we found out our mistake."

"Ah!" said the Dutchman, "there's a signal. Matuan, come here. What does Kangela mean?"

A Kaffir approached at this remark, and looking steadily towards a Kaffir who was signalling from a hill on which the Dutchman had said a spy was concealed, he at once replied —

"Zulus are coming. Not many; we can fight them."

The Kaffir's words were heard with delight by the assembled men, who waited for the Dutchman's directions before acting in any way. "Select three men," said the Dutchman, who answered to the name of Berg, "and let them be good runners. They must draw the Zulus into an ambush. Conceal the remainder, Matuan, hereabouts."

Berg having given these directions, and seen the three Kaffirs despatched in the direction in which the Zulus were advancing, followed the Kaffirs, who had run to some bushes, and were all concealed amongst them.

"Next to cattle, these fellows will like to carry off the spears and shields of their enemies," said Berg, "and we may please them. They are disheartened at the defeat of their people. Our guns will ensure us a victory, so we need not fear the results. We will wait here."

The Kaffirs on the hill had again disappeared, and a traveller who passed this way, and could not read the spoor that was written on the ground, would have fancied that no human being was within miles of him. There were, however, half-a-dozen white men, and nearly a hundred Kaffirs, crouching among the bushes, waiting to slay an enemy.

"I expect the Zulus who have hunted me are those who are now coming this way," said Hans.

"How many are there?" inquired Berg.

"Upwards of twenty."

"Here they come!" exclaimed the Dutchman. "They are in haste to be slain, for not a man will escape."

The three Kaffirs who had been sent on had soon discovered the Zulus, but pretending not to have seen them, they looked about on the ground as though searching for something. The Zulus soon perceived the three men, and taking advantage of the bushes dodged from one to another, till within a hundred yards of the supposed unsuspicious Kaffirs. Suddenly the Natal Kaffirs, giving a shout of alarm, ran back towards where their people were concealed, but not with such speed as to make their pursuers imagine pursuit would be useless. A race then commenced, in which the Natal Kaffirs had more than once to use their utmost speed, on account of the number of their enemy, and to keep beyond the effective range of an assagy. At length the three men ran past the bushes among which their companions were concealed, and one of them uttering a shrill whistle, the pursuing Zulus suddenly found themselves face to face with five times their number of those who, though almost of the same race, were now their deadly enemies. The trained Zulus were not the men, however, to be slaughtered like sheep. They immediately closed together, and feeling after their late run that they stood no chance of escaping by speed from men who had been lying quiet whilst they had been running, determined to fight where they were. Shortening their grasp on their assagies, they moved slowly forwards against the Natal force, a fine example of trained savages. Berg, upon seeing this, called to his people, who were between him and the Zulus, to lie down. The Natalians having learnt to trust their Dutch masters, obeyed instantly, when Berg and his companions fired a volley at the Zulus with the usual effect. Three Zulus fell dead, and one rolled on the ground mortally wounded. The Natal Kaffirs instantly started to their feet, and rushed on to their enemies, and for a minute a scene of skill and agility was exhibited, such as is rarely witnessed by white men. The two opposing parties met, and rapidly exchanged thrusts, which were, however, parried by the ox-hide shield, which, held sideways, turned the stab. Here and there an assagy was hurled at a foe with deadly aim and great velocity, but the Kaffir seeing its approach, either sprang on one side, and thus avoided it, or received it obliquely on his shield, and sent it glancing in another direction. Where there was no great difference in the style of weapons used, or in the skill of the combatants, numbers very soon decided the encounter, and in less than two minutes only two or three Zulus were seen fleeing over the plain with speed, pursued by a host of relentless enemies, who returned before long, shouting triumphantly, and carrying the shields and assagies of their enemies.

Hans and Berg witnessing the Fight between Zulus and Kaffirs.—

Not one out of the party had escaped, and thus Hans, who would be no party to this slaughter, saw the whole of those who had so nearly terminated his existence cut up to a man at the instant that they were under the belief that they were in such force as to be formidable to the small party they were pursuing. Such are the changes which often occur in savage warfare, the strong party becoming the weak, and being again outnumbered unexpectedly.

"It will not be safe for you to join your people by walking from here," said Berg to Hans. "There are many spies out from Dingaan, and you would not be likely to reach Bushman's river. You had better return to the bay with us; then we can talk about our best plan of acting, and you can carry the news up to your people."

Hans agreed to this proposal, and joined his new friends on their return journey to the bay, on reaching which he was delighted at the beauty of the country and the fertility of the soil. Though the settlers had as yet done little towards cultivating the land, yet it was evident that there were immense capabilities for agricultural pursuits, and it was thus considered a place likely eventually to become of great importance. The vicinity of their treacherous neighbour Dingaan alone seemed to be a drawback, but the emigrants had no doubt that with more caution and fresh strength they would be able to overcome this despot, and prevent him from in future molesting the white men.

Hans remained at Natal Bay for a week, and then started on horseback for the head-quarters of his people, which he reached in four days. Hans was received like one risen from among the dead, for his loss had been mourned by his friends, and by Katrine, so that his return was never expected, and was as much a surprise as any thing could be. He found the camp in a sad state, a want of food being actually felt. Having informed the leaders of his party what were the views of the few residents at Natal, and having pointed out the necessity for maintaining a system of espionage on the Zulus, he made preparations for a hunting expedition into the plains under the Draakensberg for the purpose of supplying his people with eland beef. It is a common practice of those farmers who reside in the vicinity of the plains on which large game are found to devote a certain portion of their time to hunting, in order to supply themselves with a stock of meat. This meat is either salted, or made into beltong; that is, it is cut into strips, rubbed with salt and pepper, and hung in a sunny place, where it gets dry, and can be eaten with no further cooking; or it can be placed in water for a short time, and then boiled. Thus provided with a supply of meat, the fanner need not kill his own cattle, but can allow his live stock to increase, and can thus have very shortly a plentiful supply of cows and oxen, so that he has no want of milk or means to draw his waggons.

Running in nearly a northerly direction, and varying in distance from the coast between 100 and 300 miles, are a range of lofty mountains known as the Quathlamba or Draakenberg. From these mountains all the rivers rise which flow through the Natal district, and empty themselves into the Indian Ocean. The principal rivers that there take their rise are the Umzimkulu, the Umkomazi, the Umgani, the Tugela, with its tributaries, the Mooi river, the Bushman's, the Klip river, and the Umzimyati or Buffalo river. The Quathlamba mountains descend into the plains, in many cases, by a series of terraces, which extend several miles, and on which are grassy plains of great extent. These plains being well watered and fertile, were, in the days when the first Dutch emigrants visited this district, inhabited by large herds of game. Troops of magnificent elands, amounting to three and four hundred, would be found herding on these terraces. The hartebeest and wildebeest, the wild boar, the quagga, and numberless other animals, could be seen and hunted. Thus, as the African farmer is by nature a sportsman, this neighbourhood was to him a paradise.

The Englishman in his overtrodden land, but with a love for sport, is compelled to put up with a feeble or artificial imitation of it. The hunting of a half-tame fox, following a stabled deer, or even galloping after the hounds who are hunting the boy who pulls the drag, is considered sport. This substitute, however, cannot fairly be termed sport, though it supplies excitement. It is, in fact, not very different from a steeple-chase, but produces utterly different sensations from those which are engendered when hunting the wildest of wild game in a country where man is so rarely seen that he is gazed at as an intruder, and where hunting is a practical reality and necessity as a means of subsistence, upon which the hunter depends, and not as a mere pastime to kill a few hours, or to endeavour to obtain a little excitement. Very much has been written by those who have never tasted the real sport of the wilderness, in favour of the artificial production in our own land, or those have advanced their opinions who from imperfect knowledge of the art, or from a mere glimpse of some of the minor sports of foreign lands, have found nothing in it to gratify them, whilst from long habit and practice these same men were habituated to English sports. Such persons are not competent judges, and cannot be impartial writers. Let us ask those who, having been accustomed to our English field sports, and having enjoyed all the pleasure of a good day among the turnips, have watched with delight the cautious Rover, or the keen-nosed Fan,—who have lived in the front rank during a twenty minutes' burst over the grass land, enclosed with ox-fences, have at the death been there,—and such will undoubtedly tell us it is good sport, and very exciting. But let these same witnesses tell us what were their feelings as, treading cautiously the rough and tangled buffalo or elephant track, they first comprehended the singular feeling of being utterly alone in the forest, dependent not only for success, but safety, upon their own unaided caution and skill. How fully, too, they appreciated the scene, when a glancing flash of something seemed to dart from out of a tree-fork on to the ground beneath, whilst the light, graceful leopard was recognised as his gorgeous-spotted coat flashed in the sunlight! How thoroughly in harmony seemed the whole scene, as the brilliant trogan or crimson-winged lowry skimmed amidst the festoons of forest vines! The social chattering monkey on the distant branches has long since seen the intruders into his domain, and now performs antics and acts in a manner so like those which illiterate human beings would practise under similar conditions, that we are not surprised at the opinion of those who trace man's origin to his tailed caricature. It is not, however, in the trees, or in the actual living creatures themselves, that all the interest need be concentrated: the very path we tread is a page deeply written. The ploughed field, meadow, or road of England rarely produces much that is noticed as the hunter rides over them. The forest path in the wilderness must, however, be read with care. Here, at our feet, is a record which must be noted. A smooth-looking spot attracts our attention; the leaves are all pressed down, and it is at once seen that some animal has rested there. Down on your knees, and look with microscopic eyes for some sign of the creature. There are one, two, three hairs, all lying together. They are from the coat of a leopard, whose lair we find warm, evincing that he has been lately disturbed. There, beyond, is the mark of a heavy animal; a hoof is impressed on the soil, and we see a buffalo has lately trodden the path before us. So fresh is the footprint that the buffalo probably disturbed the leopard. Now that our large game is near, we scarcely notice the graceful festoons of wild vine, the masses of rich foliage, or the many rare insects that we disturb as we move the bushes. Before us is the spoor, and we follow this, till we hear a slight movement amidst the dense mass of tangled brushwood before us, and for a few seconds we stand with half-raised rifle, watching for some sign to guide us; but all is still, and with cautiously-raised foot we advance one pace, then a second, and are preparing for a third, when, like a thunderbolt, a magnificent buffalo dashes from his dense cover, bounds over a bush as though he were a mere antelope, crashes through the underwood, and scarcely seeming to feel the heavy bullet which has struck him as he fled, is lost to sight in an instant. A few seconds' quiet, and then the crack of a heavy branch being broken is heard; then another and another, and the hunter stands half disappointed as these sounds tell him he has disturbed a herd of elephants who were taking their mid-day siesta in the forest near him, but are now striding through the bush, and carrying all before them. This to some constitutions seems more complete sport than England can afford, though there are men who tell us that nothing can be equal to that which they have seen and daily enjoy in the hunting counties of England. *Nous verrons.* Let the man who angles in his tank, and catches the home-fed gold-fish, tell the Norwegian salmon-fisher that tank fishing is the best sport of the two, and we can but conclude that either his skill or frame is unfitted for the nobler sport, or he has never had the opportunity of seeing more than that of which he is so fond. On the plains there is, perhaps, less excitement than in the bush, when hunting the creatures that are there found; yet to see several herds of wild animals grazing in undisturbed freedom on plains glowing like satin, and through which silver streams wind their way, is to the eye of the man who has been accustomed to crowded cities a gratifying sight. To the hunter who purposes supplying his larder from these herds, it becomes even more interesting; and thus, as Hans and his companions, riding on a commanding ridge, waiting for the morning mist to clear off the valleys beneath them, saw the plains sprinkled with small herds of elands, they rejoiced at their anticipated success, and at once, made their plans for hunting their game.

When disturbed by the sight of man, the antelopes of Africa, to which class the eland belongs, will almost invariably start at a long trot with their heads towards the wind. They pursue this course because they are very keen-scented, and as they meet the wind can tell whether any enemy is concealed before them. Even when they have to run the gauntlet of the hunters, the eland will usually prefer doing so and keeping his head to the wind, rather than run down wind. The only exception to this rule is when the animals know that a very difficult country for hunting is in any one direction. They will then run to this country as to a sanctuary, and can thus escape the hunter; for whilst an eland can descend a steep hill on which are large masses of loose stones at the most rapid trot, a horseman is obliged to dismount and lead his horse until riding becomes possible. Thus it is always one of the objects of a hunter to cut off the retreat of a herd of game from any portion of country in which he knows he could not hunt them with advantage.

A fortnight in the plains enabled Hans to fill his waggons with beltong, and he then returned to the head-quarters of his friends, ready to take any part in the expedition which he knew must be carried out before long.

Chapter Twenty
The Emigrants collect their Forces—Battle with Dingaan, the Zulu Chief—Formation of the Natal Settlement—The Treachery of the Zulu Chief—Brother against Brother

Having partially recovered from the defeat that Dingaan had given them, the emigrants endeavoured to obtain sufficient aid from their countrymen who had hitherto failed to join them, to enable them to attack the Zulus and recover their lost cattle. Not only was this aid promised, but supplies of food and ammunition were sent from the Cape, so that the winter of 1838 was passed over, though not without considerable suffering and privation.

Scarcely had the winter passed, and spring commenced, than Dingaan, who had been carefully preparing his army, and who had been employing his spies so as to learn the state of his neighbours, suddenly gave the word, and in August of the same year the Zulu army suddenly rushed into the Natal district, and attacked the emigrants. The farmers, however, were now on the alert. They had sent out scouts, and these brought them timely notice of the advance of their enemies. The waggons were used as fortifications, and every precaution was taken to make as effective a defence as possible. The result was that the Zulus failed to obtain an entrance into any one of the lagers, and were beaten off with great loss. This victory on the part of the emigrants, although a barren one, had the effect of encouraging those who had before been undecided about joining them, and small parties continued to come in until the beginning of December, when a party of above four hundred and fifty men were assembled, all mounted, and armed with good guns. These were joined by another party from the Bay of Natal, the whole combined being a formidable force.

The leader of this force had formerly been a field-cornet at Graaf Reinet, and was acquainted in a measure with some of the precautions used in military manoeuvres or movements. The advance was cautiously conducted, and each night a camp was formed and defences prepared. The advance had been thus conducted until the Umslatoos river was reached, when Hans, who had joined this party, and had ridden on before in order to guard against surprise, saw the first portion of the Zulu army. Instantly riding back, he gave the alarm, and the camp was at once on the alert, making every effort for defence. Instead of following the plan of Uys, and entering the enemy's country, and thus giving him the advantage of position, enabling him to attack where it best suited him, the new commander had from the first decided on forcing the enemy to attack him, and there now seemed every probability of this desire being accomplished. During the whole night a careful watch was kept, and each map slept with his weapons beside him; but it was not until the first gleams of daylight that the enemy showed themselves.

It was an important day in the history of this now well-known settlement, this 16th of December, 1838, — a Sunday too. On that day a trial of strength took place between the whole of Dingaan's warriors, amounting to from ten to twelve thousand men, and about four hundred and fifty emigrant farmers. Even considering the difference in the weapons, yet twenty to one were great odds; and should the Zulu warriors succeed in forcing the camp, their numbers would enable them to annihilate their enemy, even though they sacrificed thousands in the endeavour.

Forming themselves into a dense mass, the Zulus rushed on to the farmers' defences, and endeavoured to tear a way through them. Met every where with a shower of bullets, the dark-skinned soldiers fell fast, and their first effort was a failure. Nothing daunted, however, they again and again renewed their charge, and for three hours never relaxed their efforts. At length a vast number of the enemy having concentrated on one side of the camp only, a party of two hundred mounted farmers dashed out from the opposite side, and, charging both flanks, poured in volley after volley, which soon discomfited the bravest of Dingaan's chieftains:

"Even as they fell they lay,
Like the mower's grass at the close of day,"

and a panic seizing them, they at length retreated, leaving not less than three thousand men dead upon the field. The emigrants' loss was most disproportionate, three men only being killed, and some half-dozen wounded.

Immediately after this victory the emigrants pushed forward to Dingaan's kraal, which they found burning, he having retreated to the bush with the remnant of his forces. Here, on a hill outside the town, they found the remains of their ill-fated countrymen, Retief and his party, many individuals being recognised by the leather pouches they wore. A fierce retribution had, however, been now taken for the treacherous slaughter of these guests, and the power of the great Zulu chief was broken by a mere handful of well-trained men.

Finding that their ammunition was falling short, and their horses losing condition, the farmers did not consider it advisable to continue their attacks on Dingaan in their present state; they therefore seized about five thousand head of cattle, and gradually returned to their lager.

After this decisive victory the emigrants' position was much improved. They could now venture upon many of those agricultural pursuits which they had before considered it useless to attempt. A town was laid out and named Pietermaritzberg, and at the Bay of Natal another town was formed, now called D'Urban. *Landdrosts* were appointed at both places, and a regular system of government was established, and the Dutch emigrants were under the impression that they would peaceably possess the land for which they and their relatives had suffered so much; but this was not yet to be. The intelligence of the scenes of bloodshed which had been going on between the emigrants, who were still considered British subjects, and the Zulus, had reached the English government at Cape Town, which, justly claiming the district of Natal as a portion of South Africa belonging to England, despatched a party of troops to occupy the district, and to endeavour to put a stop to these scenes of bloodshed. Very serious results might have occurred between the British troops and the Boers, had not the officer in command acted with considerable judgment, he having received orders to seize the arms and gunpowder of the emigrants, in order to stop their slaughter of the Zulus. As it was, however, the English and Dutch maintained friendly intercourse until the winter of 1839, when the British troops were withdrawn, and the emigrants left for a time in undisturbed possession of Natal. The Zulu chief Dingaan gradually recovered his defeat, and recruited his army; but being bent on the destruction of the emigrants, he proceeded cunningly to discover what they were doing. In order to throw them off their guard, he sent to them above three hundred horses which he had captured from them, and promised to return cattle and guns, desiring to make terms with them. The emigrants replied that when he had returned the whole of the cattle he had taken, and had made restitution for the losses he had occasioned them, they would make peace with him, but not before. The crafty Zulu promised to do this, and therefore employed ambassadors to visit the emigrants occasionally, in order to convey messages backwards and forwards, these ambassadors being actually used as spies, in order to discover whether the emigrants continued together in force, or whether they were scattered, and thus offered a chance of success should an attack be made on them. This treacherous proceeding having been discovered by the emigrants, they dared not yet settle down, and they were in uncertainty what to do, when a singular event occurred in connexion with the native politics.

Dingaan had but two brothers remaining alive: one a youth, the other just reaching manhood, and called Umpanda. Umpanda was unlike Dingaan, inasmuch as the latter lived only for war, the former was a lover of peace. Many of the Zulus, having suffered severely in consequence of the many battles in which Dingaan had engaged, were disposed in favour of peace, and of "Panda," as he was sometimes called. This fact coming to the ears of Dingaan, this able savage politician decided upon getting rid of his brother by murdering him. Panda, having friends at court, heard of this decision of his worthy brother, and at once fled, and crossing the Tugela river with a number of followers, stopped there, and sent messengers requesting the aid of the emigrants against his treacherous brother. The result of these negotiations was, that the emigrants, finding that there was no chance of safety as long as Dingaan was chief of the Zulus, decided to aid Panda, which they did, and the result was a great and last battle between the Zulus under Dingaan and the Boers with Panda's forces. During this battle two whole regiments deserted from Dingaan, and joined Panda, whilst the Boers took little or no part in the battle. The result, however, was the total defeat of Dingaan, who was driven from his kingdom far up the country, where he soon after perished; and thus an ally of the farmers occupied the chieftainship of the Zulus, and they could now rest in peace, each seeking the location that suited him best, and requiring his ammunition and gun no longer for the purpose of slaying his enemy, but merely to supply himself with game; and thus the wishes of the emigrants seemed about to be gratified.

Chapter Twenty One
A Hunting Trip—Round the Bivouac Fire—
The Hunter's Tale—Carried off by a Lion—
The Shooting Laws in the Desert—The
Ophir of Scripture—Baboons hunting
a Leopard—The Natal Rock Snake

We have for a time omitted the individual adventures of Hans, and have endeavoured to give a brief account of those events in all of which he was an active participator, and which led to the emigrants possessing for a time the Natal district. So occupied had Hans been with the wars of the time, that Katrine had seen but little of him. Now that affairs were more peaceable, Hans wished to marry at once; but Katrine was mourning for several relatives who had been murdered with Reliefs party, or slaughtered at Weenen; she therefore put it off for six months, a proceeding to which her lover greatly objected. Finding she was determined, however, he had no alternative; and so, to make the time pass as rapidly as possible, he arranged with his old companions, Victor and Bernhard, and three other farmers, to go on an elephant-hunting expedition up the country to the north-east, where it was reported elephants abounded.

The party who started on this expedition each took a waggon, which was drawn by fourteen oxen. Accompanying the waggon was a Hottentot driver and three Kaffirs. From four to five horses were taken by each hunter, so that the party amounted to nearly thirty in all. It was quite an unexplored country where these hunters intended to travel, and so there was an additional interest in this expedition. Guns and ammunition were in plenty, and it was anticipated that considerable profit would be derived from the ivory and skins which would be taken during the journey.

"Well, Victor," said Hans, as the two sat in a tent which had been brought with them, "we have scarcely had a long chat since our battles with the Zulus. Tell me of your escapes."

"I had several," replied Victor; "the nearest, though, was when we went with Uys, and we thought you were killed. There were Bernhard and Cobus and some half-dozen of us who wanted to turn back and look after you, but the others would not. The Zulus were closing on us again, and the hill swarmed with them, but we waited for a minute to try and persuade the others to turn back. During that minute the Zulus closed on us, and a great brawny Kaffir threw his knob-kerrie at me. I tried to dodge it, but it came so quickly I could not, and it struck me fairly on the head. Cess, I fell as if I had been shot. I did not lose my senses, but felt paralysed for a time. The Zulus yelled triumphantly as they saw me fall, and the assagies flew thick about us; but the few men with me were my staunch friends, and a dozen bullets answered the triumphant shouts of the Kaffirs. I think it was old Piet who lifted me on my horse, and holding the reins dragged my horse along, till I got right again, and could hold the reins. I returned the kindness before long; for as we rode through the bush a Zulu started up close to him, and would have had an assagy through him before he could have saved himself, for the Kaffir was quite round on his right side, but I was behind him a little, and just as the assagy was leaving the Kaffir's hands, I sent my bullet through him."

"Those Zulus fought well!" exclaimed Hans. "If they ever get possessed of guns, they may give us trouble."

"Some had guns in the last engagement, but they were not much use to them, and the horses they rode caused the death of one of the party, who being unable to manage his horse, which was running away with him into our camp, the Zulu stabbed himself with his own spear."

"The man was a fool!" exclaimed Hans; "why did he not stab the horse instead?"

"Talking over your battles!" exclaimed Hofman, an old hunter, as he entered the tent. "Ah! we have had plenty of fighting for some time to come, and we may talk about it now, for there will be peace in the land for some time. We have been fortunate in our last battles, though we ought not to have been beaten before. It all arose from underrating the enemy. Though we had guns, and they had none, yet when you fight in bushy country, and there are twenty to one against you, even a savage armed with an assagy is not to be despised. I fought against the Amakosa tribes when they attacked Graham's Town, and I know how these Africans can fight. You will see more fighting before you die, Hans, depend upon it."

"I am ready to defend my own and my home," replied Hans, "though I have no wish to shed any more human blood; though I can say I never shot a Kaffir, unless it was to save my own life."

"Now we shall have to try our strength against dangerous game, instead of against savages," said Hofman, "and that will try your nerves at times. I know that I never found in any battle I have been in such nervous work as the first time I shot a lion, and that I did in self-defence, and when little more than a boy."

"Tell us the tale, Hofman," said one or two of the party, who had all assembled in the tent, and were busily occupied in smoking.

"It is not much of a tale," replied the hunter, "and Hans there, I know, has had many more narrow escapes; but it was when I lived under the Winterberg. I had been over to our neighbours, who lived twenty-five miles from us, and I rode an old horse that was almost past work. I was to ride there and back in the day, and bring some seeds with me for the farm. Well, I had ridden there and got the seeds, and should have soon returned, only there was somebody there I liked to stop and talk to, and so I waited rather late. It was near sundown when I started, and I had a good three hours' ride before me. This I did not think much of, though I had to pass a place called Lions' Fountain, where lions were usually seen, and if they were not seen, their footprints always were, showing that they lived in the neighbourhood. I rode on, however, and as it got darker I rode quicker; but before long I found the old horse was knocked up, and could not go beyond a walk. I knew my father was fond of the old horse, so I determined to dismount and lead him. I did so, and walked slowly enough, for the horse would not hurry himself. Presently I found him snorting as from fear, and getting quite lively, for which I could not account at first; but noting that the old horse kept turning his head as though looking at something, I strained my eyes to see what it was. I was, as I said, young at the time, and so you may not be surprised when I tell you my heart beat quickly when I saw, not a single lion, for that, I think, I might have felt a match for, but no less than four lions trotting along about sixty yards from the side of the waggon-track I was following. I could scarcely believe my eyes at first, but the night was clear and starlight, and there was light enough for me to see that. What was most strange, too, was that one lion seemed to be afraid that the others should take his prey away from him, for every now and then he would turn on them, and with a smothered growl rush at them, sending them scampering away like cur dogs; then he would trot up again within forty yards, and go along in the same direction. This he did once or twice, till I began to think he was taking care of me, and didn't mean to eat me or the horse. I was armed with only a single-barrelled gun, and that not a very large bore; so I did not feel at all a match for four lions, and began to try and remember some prayers I had heard might help one at a pinch like this; but I couldn't well call to mind any thing suitable, and was beginning to think I had better leave the old horse and run for it, when the big lion, having driven off the others to some distance, came up within thirty yards of me, and right in my path. If I led the horse on, I should be nearest the lion, and I believed he would kill me first, and the horse afterwards. I hesitated what to do, and had I been more experienced, I believe I should not have done what I did; for a wounded lion is a terrible creature, even worse than a hungry one. However, I determined to fire at him. Aiming at his forehead, I pulled the trigger, and instantly bolted behind the old horse. Before I could see what happened, I waited a moment, expecting to hear the monster roar; but there was no sound, except of creatures scampering away in the distance; and when I looked to see where the lion was, there he lay dead. My little bullet had struck him between the eyes, and killed him on the spot I remember it all now as if it had just happened, and I think I never was more alarmed than on that night."

"You were once carried off by a lion, were you not, Hans?" inquired the last speaker.

"Yes, I was carried a hundred yards or more, and scarcely had my skin broken. A lion is like a cat in that; he can hold a live creature in his mouth, and not damage it, just as I have seen a cat carry a mouse, and when it put the mouse down the little creature would run away just as though it hadn't been touched."

"I heard you had been carried, Hans, but never heard all the story. How was it?"

"I was out after porcupines, and was lying down one night near a porcupine's hole, waiting for him to come out. I had no gun, but only my hunting-knife and a large knob-kerrie, with which to knock the porcupine on the nose; for that, as you know, kills him at once. I did not hear a sound until I found the grass near me move, and a lion put his paw on me, and holding me down by it, gripped my back and lifted me up. The brute pressed his claws into me, but luckily my leather belt prevented his teeth from damaging me, and he carried me by holding on to my belt and coat. If either of these had given way, I should have soon been laid hold of in a far more rough manner. I knew the nature of a lion well enough to know that if I struggled I should have my neck broken or my head smashed in an instant, so I did not struggle, but quietly drew my knife, and thought what was best to do. I thought at first of trying to stab him in the heart, but I could not reach that part of him, and his skin looked so loose that I feared I could not strike deep enough, carried as I was. I knew it would be life or death with me in an instant, so turning myself a bit, I gashed the lion's nose, and cut it through. The lion dropped me as I would drop a poisonous snake, and jumped away roaring with pain. He stood for an instant looking at me, but I did not move, and he did not seem to like to carry me again. More than once he came up to within a few yards, licking the blood as it poured from his nose; but there I remained like a stone, and he was fairly afraid to tackle me again. I know a buffalo and an ox are very sensitive about the nose, and a cat, if just tapped on the nose, can't stand it; so I thought a lion might be the same, and so it proved, or I should not be here to tell you the story. I think we may have good sport up the country," continued Hans, "and lions may be plentiful."

"I don't go out of my way to shoot lions," replied Hofman. "There is more danger with a lion than even with an elephant, and when you have shot a lion, what is he worth? His skin will not fetch thirty rix-dollars, and his teeth are only used for ornaments. Now if you kill an elephant, he is worth twenty or thirty pounds at least. So I will leave the lions to you, Hans, and I will go after the elephants; but shall we arrange our shooting laws?"

"Yes, we had better do so now," replied Hans, "before we come to any large game."

"Well, my plan always has been, let us shoot for food in turns; or if we all shoot together, divide the meat amongst us. When we come to elephants, let it be that the first bullet entitles the shooter to half the ivory; and whoever puts in another bullet, to a share. What say you to this, men?"

"It is not good," said Hans; "for men will shoot wild in order just to get a bullet into an elephant, and may thus spoil sport. I propose that whenever we are together, and kill our game together, we mark the tusks, and all share alike. If we are alone, and kill alone, the tusks belong to whoever kills. We are honest men and tried; none of us will shirk his fair risk, and no man will shoot the worse because he knows his friend may get a share of the ivory."

"Hans' plan is the best," exclaimed several.

"I have seen friendships lessened by the disputes over dead elephants," exclaimed Victor, "and Hans' plan will prevent disputes. If you and I fire together, we may both think our bullet struck the elephant first. It is better to share, or to shoot alone."

"My Kaffir tells me we shall find elephants in plenty up the country. Now if we could but capture a young elephant, and bring him safely back to Natal, we should make much money, for I hear in England they will pay large sums for a live animal from Africa."

"The English must know very little of Africa, and of the game here," said Hans. "They are, I have heard, all crowded together in that country, and have no elephants or large game wild, so they must wish for our land, and some of them come out here to see what sport is."

"There is more in the land we shall hunt in than game," said Hofman; "and if we are lucky, we shall find it. For, though ivory is valuable, gold is more so."

"Gold!" exclaimed the hunters in one voice; "what makes you think there is gold there?"

"About two years ago I met a man at Algoa Bay, who came from the Faderland. He had come in a ship from Delagoa Bay, and he said that from Delagoa Bay inland, and to the west, gold was found in the rivers. He showed me that he had some gold dust, and that this he had bought from natives. The country about there is very unhealthy, and oxen or horses don't live well; therefore white men can't go in from there to find it. He said, too, that the country called Sofala was really Ophir, and that the Patriarchs got their gold from about there."

"I think, Hofman," said Hans, "if you search for the gold, I will be content to hunt for elephants. One is certain, the other is risky."

"We are out to hunt elephants, Hans," replied Hofman, "and that is what we will do; but if we at any time find ourselves near rivers where there are no elephants, we might look for gold."

"Yes, that might be done," replied Hans, "but my gold shall be skins and ivory. Hark to the hyenas! how they yell to-night! There is a lion about, I should fancy."

"A lion or a leopard," replied Victor. "It is very strange how the weaker animals often club together to defend themselves against a stronger one. Before I left the borders of the old country, I more than once saw my cattle beat off a hyena. They would form a circle, and show a bold front of horns, and run at the hyena if he came near them."

"For that there is nothing equal to a troop of baboons," said Hofman; "they are as cunning and as wise as men. I have watched them often, and they set one of their number to watch for enemies; and if he does not do his duty, the others will beat him. I often amused myself by trying to stalk near the baboons that lived near me when I was near the Winterberg, and they never but once were caught asleep. I managed once to get quite close to them without the sentry seeing me, and then stood up and ran at them. I was soon sorry I had ventured amongst them, for they were savage, and so powerful they could have torn me to pieces had they attacked me; but they at once bit and tore the sentry, who scarcely attempted to defend himself, just as though he knew he deserved to be punished. I can tell you a strange story about these baboons.

"There came into our neighbourhood a leopard, and he lived well for some time, till we hunted him, and he had to keep to the bush. Now it turned out that the leopard killed a baboon, and ate him. The baboons feared to attack the leopard, as he would be too much for them, but they had decided on revenging themselves on him. They therefore followed him about, but at a cautious distance. After a time the leopard wanted to drink, but no sooner did he go to the water than the baboons came around threatening him, and they were so active that the leopard could not attack them successfully. The leopard started off to leave the country, but the baboons followed, barking and screaming after him. For three days the baboons followed him, and would neither let him eat nor drink, when the leopard became quite weak from thirst and want of food. There were so many baboons, too, that they never let the leopard rest, and thus he was worn out As soon as the baboons found he was weak, they assembled around him, and attacked him in earnest, and killed him in a few minutes. I had missed the baboons from my krantzes (steep ravines), and I heard from the neighbours that they had seen baboons following and worrying a leopard, and at last the baboons were heard worrying something, and this turned out to be the leopard, which was found dead and fearfully mangled."

"I have heard that same thing before," said Bernhard, "and I know the baboons are capable of it; they are very wise."

"Yes," said Hans, "they are useful too; for whatever a baboon eats, a man may venture to eat also. This is the case with monkeys, too. A man ought never to starve, if he lives near where monkeys are; for you can watch what fruit or sorts a monkey eats, and that will show you what you may venture upon. You have been down at the bay for some time, Hofman," continued Hans; "can you tell us any thing about the large snakes that are there?"

"Yes, I can. There are very large snakes there, but these large snakes are not poisonous. They live in the long grass near rocks or old trees, and feed on birds, small buck, and such things. They will not attack you, I believe; but they could kill a man, as one I shot there had killed and eaten a calf. It was about twenty-five feet long, and two men could not lift it. There are snakes said to be much larger than this one, and I have heard from the Kaffirs of a snake near the coast as long as a span of oxen; but this I cannot speak to, for I never even saw the spoor; yet they may grow to a great size. But there are puff-adders, cobras, ring-hals, and many snakes there, and it is not good to walk much in very long grass. There are elephants, too, near the bay, but the bush is very dense, and the elephants are fierce; it does not do to attempt shooting them there."

"We have a fine country about us," exclaimed Hans, "and now that Panda is chief of the Zulus we may rejoice at leaving the old colony to come here. The game was nearly all gone from about there, and the place was worn out. My father shot elephants near Algoa Bay, and all the game was to be seen in the colony; but now there is nothing there, though it is not so far from us. It will be a long time before the elands are driven away from the plains here, and there are buck in plenty. We can go after elephants when we choose, and now that we have won our land we may enjoy it. Good luck to us on our trek, Karls! and I think now we will sleep, and by and by we may sit up at night to becroup large game; so we had better sleep now, when it is not so plentiful."

The advice of Hans was relished by all the party, who having directed two Hottentots to watch, and to call others in succession, the hunters sought their waggons, and wrapping themselves in their blankets, lay down to rest in these vehicles, which to the hunter are like a ship to a sailor.

The camp was soon quiet, the only sounds being the low guttural voices of the Hottentots, or the low tones of the more harmonious Zulu, as the Kaffirs talked over the scenes of the past few months, and wondered at the power of the white man, which had enabled him to break the strength of the mighty Zulu chieftain who had so long been the terror of those tribes, which, having either fled from him or from other nations near, had settled at Natal, had welcomed the arrival of the white man, and had at once accepted him as an ally: the distant moaning of a wolf, and the shrill barking cry of the jackal, being the other sounds that plainly told that the wilderness was around.

Chapter Twenty Two
Elephants found—The Hunt—The Evening at the Camp—An Elephant Adventure—Encounter with a Kaffir Spy—More Elephants—Strange Men—Hans made Prisoner

During the first few days of their journey the only game that the hunters encountered were elands, buffaloes, and antelopes of various kinds. Of these numbers were killed, so as to supply the camp with food, and also to lay in a stock of beltong for the future; for in some parts of Africa the game suddenly disappears, apparently without cause, and the hunter finds it extremely difficult to obtain even the necessaries for his daily meals. More than once there had been expectations raised in consequence of elephants' footmarks having been discovered, but on examination these proved to be old, and the elephants were evidently journeying northwards when they left their traces on the ground. The party had now reached the sources of the Pongola river, and the traces of elephants were most numerous.

"We must have passed many herds of elephants in the forests," said Victor, as he rode beside Hans, and followed the spoor of some bull elephants which was very fresh, and which had been traced since daybreak. "We should have stopped and hunted them."

"We can do that on our return, if we do not obtain enough ivory hereabouts to fill our waggons; but I think this country much better suited for hunting than the thicker bush further down. We can always ride our horses here, which we could not in the bush we have passed; and so our success here will be probably greater. We ought soon to sight these elephants, for the spoor is quite fresh. Hark! did you not hear a trumpet? There are elephants near, and we shall get them to-day. Where are the rest of our party?"

"They have all gone after the spoor that led along the river's bank, and I don't think that was as fresh as this; but need we wait for them? They may have found their game, and will not wish to join us."

"We will ride on," said Hans. "It was among those trees in that slope I heard the trumpet, and see! there is a bull elephant. Pull up; let us watch him awhile; he is a magnificent tusker, and there are at least half-a-dozen others. Victor, we must get nearly all these. We shall have a good day's work to do that, though, for they will carry away many bullets. Ah! there was a shot from down to leeward: so the others have found elephants. See! the bull has heard the shot, and is alarmed."

It was true that the sound of a gun, though probably not an unusual sound, was yet one that alarmed the elephants, for they collected hurriedly together, and strode away at a rapid pace.

"I wish we could have lodged our bullets in them before they became alarmed," said Hans; "but we may do that now, if we ride on before them, and keep a little wide. The elephant has very bad sight, and he may not see us."

Hans and Victor galloped forward in the direction in which they had seen the elephants, taking care not to follow exactly in their footmarks, and in a very short time they saw the huge animals had collected under some spreading acacias, and were elevating their ears to endeavour to hear if any danger threatened them, whilst their trunks were raised to catch the scent of any foe.

"Now," said Hans, "we may drop an elephant before we give them the alarm. They don't know what to fear; they only know not what to make of the sound of a gun. They have not been much hunted, it is evident, or they would not stop so soon after being alarmed. We will now fasten our horses to these trees, and stalk the elephants; then we can retreat to our horses, and follow them on horseback."

"We ought to put four bullets into that large bull first," said Victor; "then the others, not having a leader, will not know what to do."

"We will stop his getting away, Victor. I can hit him in the leg, and can then take him between the eye and the ear. Unless your bullet is very large, it is between the eye and the ear that you had better shoot, on the chance of a death-shot. I have killed many of my elephants by hitting them there."

The two hunters fastened their horses to a tree at about 300 yards from the elephants, and then commenced stalking their noble game. The elephants, although but lately disturbed by the discharge of a gun, had recovered from their alarm, and stood beneath the trees, occasionally raising their ears to listen; but the cautious advance of Hans and his companion was conducted so quietly that even the acute hearing of the elephant could not discover that an enemy was near him, and the two hunters succeeded in reaching a tree that was within eighty yards of the largest bull without being seen or heard by their formidable game. The stake for which these men were playing was too important a one to allow of a single chance being thrown away. Thus no word was uttered by either, and merely a signal was given by one or the other to draw attention to some fact which it was necessary to notice. The breaking of a dead stick by treading on it would have been fatal to their success, and thus it was necessary to watch where each foot was placed, in order to avoid such a contingency.

Upon reaching the corner of the tree Hans signalled to Victor that they would fire at the same time, and without delay; for the elephants were getting uneasy, and were uttering short sharp cries, which seemed signals of danger. The great bull of the herd, whose polished white teeth protruded far out of his mouth, stood broadside to the hunters; but his watchful manner and uneasy movements indicated that he might at any moment turn and retreat, or at least alter his position; so Hans, taking aim between the eye and the ear, fired, whilst Victor, aiming at his fore-leg just above the knee, fired at the same instant. The aim of Hans was true, and his bullet found its way through a mass of bone to the elephant's brain, for it fell dead to the shot, and there was, therefore, no need for the second bullet. The instant the sound of the guns was heard, the remaining elephants retreated over the bushy ground with a headlong, reckless speed. Trees that stood in the way were knocked down, the noise of their being broken sounding like the crack of a rifle. There are few things which give one a greater idea of animal power than the headlong rush of a troop of elephants through a forest. The elephant is usually a quiet animal, and when it moves through the bush it proceeds with scarcely any noise, its feet being well suited for walking quietly. When alarmed, however, it rushes forward almost blindly, for its great weight causes it to move onwards in nearly a straight line, rapid turns being almost impossible. Thus if a tree stand in its way, and is of moderate size only, the elephant runs against it, and breaks it off. On several occasions we have had opportunities of measuring the diameter of the stems of trees thus broken off, and we have found many which were eight inches in diameter. The noise caused by a number of such trees being snapped in two, one after the other may be readily imagined.

As soon as Hans saw the elephant fall, he said, "Bring up the horses, Victor; I'll cut off the tail, in case any one comes this way."

Hans had completed his work before Victor had reached him with the horses; so, having reloaded his gun, he ran back to meet Victor. The two then mounted their horses, and rode after the remaining elephants, which by this time had gained a long start; but elephants which have led a quiet, unhunted life for a considerable time soon get too fat to keep up a rapid pace for any length of time, and stand no chance with a horse, except for a few hundred yards. If, however, the huge animals are not hurried, they will continue striding on at a speed of eight or ten miles an hour for some time. After about a mile's gallop, the hunters were once more near their game, and now quite a different kind of sport commenced to the stalking which had been previously practised. Riding forward, so as to be slightly in advance of the elephants, the hunters pulled up their horses, jumped off, and as the animals shuffled past, sent their four bullets into the largest elephant that remained. Feeling itself hit, the creature turned on its assailants, and with upraised trunk and shrill piercing shrieks rushed on. To mount their horses and gallop off was a momentary proceeding with both Hans and Victor; but so furious was the savage animal's charge, that it was nearly catching Victor's horse, and did not cease to pursue until it had followed its enemies for several hundred yards, when, finding further pursuit useless, it followed the other elephants. It was not allowed to go so quietly, however; for the hunters, having reloaded, followed it, and with a second volley brought it to the ground.

"We must let none of those elephants escape," said Hans, when a second tail was added to that previously taken. "Bernhard is with the other party, and depend upon it they will kill more than an elephant each. There are fine tusks in those elephants' heads on before us, and the creatures are so blown they cannot run fast now. Two more each will make it a good day's sport."

Setting spurs to their horses, the pursuit was once more carried on, and with a discharge of several bullets four more elephants were laid low.

"Now," said Hans, "I will say the sport is good. We can return to our outspan to-night, and can tell what we have done, not boastfully, but as men who have done well. I hope the others have been as successful."

On returning to camp, Hofman said—

"Come into my tent to-night, Karls, and eat there; we will then talk over our day's sport. What have *you* done, Hans?"

Hans briefly related the results of his day's work, and described the size of the tusks which his elephants carried.

"You have done better than we have," said Hofman, "for we have only shot seven amongst us, and two are not full-grown bulls."

As might be expected, the conversation during the evening was mostly about elephants and elephant hunting; and as we may learn much about the habits of this singular animal, and the method of hunting it adopted by the Africans, we will relate some of the anecdotes connected therewith.

"You ask me where I shot my first elephant," said Hofman. "It was where few men now hunt elephants, because there are not many there now, and because it is a dangerous place to hunt them in. It was in the Fish-river bush in the old colony. That bush, as you know, is very thick and thorny, and if they would only lie close, and didn't leave a footmark, a hundred elephants might live there peaceably for years even now; but when I was quite a boy there were not many men could say they had walked ten miles in the Fish-river bush. My father used to go down to Graham's Town about twice a year to get various things he wanted, and when he went he generally took me. I was little more than fifteen when he went down on the occasion I will tell you of.

"We had to pass the Fish-river bush on the way from our place down to Graham's Town, and as we were going along I saw near the road,—or rather waggon-track, for it was nothing more,—a broken tree. I turned into the bush to look, and then saw what I knew was the spoor of an elephant. I didn't say what I had seen, for all of a sudden I got very ambitious, and I thought I would make myself a name, and not be thought a boy any longer. I knew that we outspanned about half a mile further on, and as the day was very hot, I asked my father if he would go on after a short outspan, or wait a bit.

"'I'll wait till near sundown,' he replied, 'for it is full moon to-night, and we can trek better in the night than in this heat, and we can sleep a little now.'

"'I'd rather go and shoot,' said I, 'if you'd lend me your big gun.'

"'What do you want the big gun for?' inquired my father. 'That is for elephants or rhinoster, and you will find nothing bigger than a buck.'

"'I can always shoot better with that big gun,' I replied.

"'Very well,' said my father. 'Don't lose yourself in the bush; but you can't do that with the sun shining as it is.'

"'I'd like Blueboy to come with me, father; he'd carry my buck.'

"Now Blueboy was a bush-boy who was *fore-looper* (Fore-looper is the leader of the team of oxen; he holds a string fastened to the horns of the first two.) to the oxen sometimes, and who had taught me more spooring than any one else, and I wanted to consult him about this elephant.

"'Oh yes! take him,' said my father. So, beckoning Blueboy, I told him I wanted him to come with me, and the little fellow was glad enough to come, as we always had some sport together.

"'There's the gun,' said my father; 'it's loaded with two bullets. I'll just give you two more bullets, and two charges of powder, for you must not waste the ammunition. Mind you're back an hour before sundown.'

"This parting advice I hoped to comply with, and Blueboy and I walked off.

"I kept quite silent till we were away from the waggons, when I instantly said, 'Blueboy, we are after an elephant.'

"'Yes,' said the sharp little fellow in his broken Dutch, 'I thought so. I saw you go into the bush where the tree was broken. When did elephant break tree?'

"'The marks were quite fresh, Blueboy; I think not long before we got there.'

"'We shall see when we look,' was his reply.

"We hurried on, and entered the bush, Blueboy going first. He carefully examined the ground, picked up the grass, and at length rushed at a small broken branch as though he had seen a treasure. After turning this over once or twice, he pointed to the eastern part of the sky, and said, 'When sun there, elephant here. He may now be far off, may be close here; we see soon. Follow me now.'

"I followed him, but with difficulty. He moved like a snake among the bushes, as noiseless as a bird, and as quick as one. We went nearly a mile, when we came to a steep bank, at which Blueboy stopped, and whispered to me, 'We find him here; water near, and he very hot. Elephant love water. Now come slowly.'

"We moved down the bank, and came to a large pool of water, which was muddy and bubbling. I knew from this the elephant had only just drunk there. Presently I heard a sound as of water being poured out of a narrow-necked bottle, when Blueboy, turning quickly, pointed to some bushes below us, and there was the elephant half buried in bushes, but his back visible above them. I now felt very excited. I knew it was very dangerous work, but I fancied I might be successful. All depended on a surprise. I had heard so much about elephants, and had in imagination so often shot them, that I knew every vital part, and where it was best to fire; so, though I had never seen an elephant before, I knew lots about them. I noticed that the bank was above the elephant, and about twenty yards from it; so if I could get to the nearest place, I should get a good shot in safety. To get to that place I had to retrace my steps, and make a guess at the whereabouts; so pointing this out to Blueboy, he at once led the way, and soon pointed out where I must go. 'Fire both at once,' he said, pointing to my barrels. 'You aim well first time, badly second.' I crept to the edge of the bank, and was almost afraid as I saw the elephant so close to me. I aimed on the shoulder, just outside his ear, and pulled both triggers. I was knocked right down by the recoil, and fell among the bushes, and the elephant went off very fast for nearly a hundred yards. We could see him plainly, and I began to fear I must have missed him. I didn't know then how tough elephants were, and how much shooting they required.

"Well, the elephant then stopped, and pulled up some grass, and seemed to be stuffing it into his wounds, for he was losing strength very fast; and then he turned and climbed up the bank, and went away through the bush towards the road we had come with our waggon.

"'He'll take to the old track,' whispered Blueboy; 'we shall get him again at the tree he broke to-day. Come along quick now, and get there before him. You'll never do any good following, for you will have to fire at him from behind.'

"I didn't think we should see much of him by going on before, but I trusted the quick-witted bush-boy, and tried to follow him, but he went away again so quick I called him to stop.

"'No, no,' he replied; 'you must come on, the elephant will get there first else.'

"I ran on as well as I could, and in time we got to the tree.

"'Is bullet there?' said Blueboy, pointing to the gun.

"I had not had time to load yet, so I set to work, and put in my remaining bullets. I had scarcely done this before I saw Blueboy point to the bush before us. He pointed eagerly, and said, 'Oliphant kom, oliphant kom,' and I heard a very slight noise, as of an animal moving in the bush. I collected my thoughts, and determined to try again what I could do; and having cocked my gun, stood ready.

"I first saw the elephant's head, but had been taught not to fire at this, if the elephant was facing me; so I waited, and soon saw the chest of the great creature. I aimed steadily, and fired at the chest both barrels, as before. As I fired, Blueboy pulled me on one side. I saw a mass of bush pressed down, and was knocked down by a branch of a tree; but though not much hurt, I couldn't get up easily, as the tree held me down, but I forced myself out after a bit with Blueboy's help. I didn't know at first what it was had knocked me down, but Blueboy said, 'He dodt, he dodt,' and on looking round I saw a great black mass among the bushes, and there was the elephant lying dead.

"I went up to the creature, and was astonished with its size; it was, as it lay, far higher than I was. I noticed that there were big tusks, and this delighted me too. I didn't know that to cut off the tail proved ownership, so I left the animal, and with no little excitement went off to my father at the waggons. He was just getting up from a sleep, and upon seeing me said,—

"'Well, where's the buck? I heard a shot: did you miss him?'

"'I fired all four bullets, father,' I said.

"'And missed with all four. That won't do; you must shoot with a smaller gun, boy, or you'll waste powder and lead.'

"'I didn't miss with one bullet, father; I hit with all.'

"'Then you've killed your buck; and where is it?'

"'It wasn't a buck, father,' I said.

"'Not a buck! What was it then? Not a buffalo; you don't mean to say that you've fired at a buffalo?'

"'It was bigger than a buffalo,' I answered.

"My father looked at me incredulously for some time, but I couldn't wait any longer, so I said, 'I've shot an elephant with large tusks.'

"My father jumped off the waggon-box as if he'd been shot, as he exclaimed, 'Shot an elephant! You—you shot an elephant! Where is he?'

"'Ja, bas, (Yes, Master), he's shot an elephant!' exclaimed Blueboy. 'I showed him where the elephant was.'

"'Get a hatchet—get your knives!' shouted my father to the Hottentots; 'the boy has shot an elephant!' and off we ran, I leading, till we came to the place where the elephant lay. There he was, sure enough, and my father was delighted. We didn't get the tusks out in a hurry, and then we cut up lots of meat, and took the trunk, and a foot, and carried these with us to Graham's Town. Just for curiosity lots of people bought the elephant's flesh to taste, and the teeth being fresh weighed very heavy, and fetched a good price.

"'Keep the money,' said my father; 'that shall be your first prize; and I now give you my gun that you shot the elephant with;' and here, Hans, you see that mark in the stock. That stands for the first elephant I ever shot."

"There are plenty since then," replied Hans. "See, your stock is covered with cuts."

"Yes, I've made the old gun do her duty. She has tried her hand at several kinds of things, and has settled Amakosa, Zulus, and all; and what do you think besides, Hans?"

"Lions in numbers, I suppose."

"Yes, that is true; but this one mark is for a white man. Not for a true Africander, but an English-Dutch fellow. This gun shot him, and well he deserved it."

"How was that?" inquired all the party, to whom the information was news.

"I'll tell you here, for we are friends; but don't mention it again, for few people know it, and I might not be liked by some people for having done what I did, though in my heart I feel I was right, and according to the laws of war I was right; still I don't want it talked about. Have I all your promises?"

"Yes," was the universal reply.

"Well, then, it was when the Amakosa had been beaten back from Graham's Town, that I, who was in the town at the time, saw a fellow half clothed among the Kaffirs. I watched this fellow for some time, and when the Kaffirs rushed on and fought bravely, this fellow stayed behind, and only urged them on. The more I looked, the more certain I was that the fellow was a white man, rubbed over with something to disguise his skin; but I knew the walk and look of the fellow, and fancied if I should see him again, I should know him. We beat the Kaffirs off, as you know, and they lost hundreds in the battle. I stayed in Graham's Town for some days, but was going down to Algoa Bay in a short time, when, as I was going to a store, who should I see before me but a fellow whose walk I could swear to. It was the fellow I'd seen with the Kaffirs.

"He walked on and turned into the store, so I followed him, and found him buying powder and lead. I waited till he had gone, when I inquired of the owner of the store who he was.

"'He's an officer's servant,' said the owner.

"'Have you ever seen him before?' I asked.

"'Never,' he replied; 'but he told me he was an officer's servant.'

"I bought what I wanted, and then went out, and seeing the man walking on before me, I quickened my pace, went to my house, got my gun, and traced him to a low Hottentot house. Having seen him housed, I suspected at once he would wait there till dark, and then go off somewhere; so I set watch, and sure enough it was no sooner dark than out he came, and walked right away out of the town, and away over the hills.

"I followed him cautiously, but more than once he stopped to listen; but I was as cute as he was, and dropped on the ground immediately he stopped, so that he could not see me, and then on we went again. As it got darker, I followed by the sound, and kept rather closer; but this wasn't very safe work, for if he had liked he might just have waited behind a bush till I came up, and then shot me or stabbed me; but I was very careful, and as long as he kept to the open country I felt I was a match for him. After a while, though, he struck into the bush, and took a narrow path, and then I thought it wouldn't do to follow him, for he would be sure to hear me if I kept close enough to hear him; so I reluctantly gave up, but I had seen enough to make me suspicious.

"I now thought of returning, and should have done so at once, but determined now I was so far off to wait a bit, and see what might happen; so taking shelter under a bush, I sat down on watch. I hadn't sat long before I saw a gleam of fire away in the bush towards where the man had gone, and this shone out pretty clearly. 'That's your camping-ground, my man,' I said, 'and I'll have a trial to find out what your company is.' I determined to creep up near enough to this fire to see what was going on, and started at once. I had to walk a good mile before I came near the fire, and then I crawled along on all fours till I got a view of the fire. I was sorry for myself when I found where I was, for I saw nearly fifty Kaffirs, some of them wounded, and all of them armed with assagies or muskets, and with them was the man I'd seen in the town. He was giving the chief Kaffir some powder, and seemed well-known among them. I think I could have shot the fellow from where I was, but I knew I should be assagied to a certainty if I did; so marking all I saw, I crawled back again, and off I went to Graham's Town.

"The next day I went to the store-man, and told him what I had seen.

"'If that blackguard comes here again, then,' said the man, 'I'll have him taken, and it's death to sell ammunition to the Kaffirs.'

"'He fought against us, too,' said I; 'that I can swear to.'

"'He must be a deserter from some regiment,' said the store-man, 'for he is just like a soldier in all his ways.'

"Two or three weeks after this I was out looking about Graham's Town for some pouw (a bustard), for they came there sometimes, when, in a bush path, who should I see just coming close to me but the deserter and spy! He'd got a gun, a single-barrelled one, and seemed looking out for game. Forgetting the risk I ran in my eagerness, and never thinking whether he might not have a lot of Kaffirs with him, I said, 'You're a Kaffir spy and deserter; you come into Graham's Town with me.'

"'I'm a spy, am I?' said the fellow; 'and who the d—l are you?'

"As he said this, I saw him cock his gun, which he still held at his side, and bring the muzzle round towards me.

"'Turn your gun the other way,' I said, 'or I'll fire!'

"'Fire, then!' said the Schelm (rascal), as he raised his gun and aimed at me.

"The gun hung fire a little, I think, or quick as I was he'd have hit me; but I jumped on one side behind a bush, and then back again, so as not to give him a steady shot. Bang went the gun, and whiz went the bullet I think it struck a branch, and thus turned; any way it missed me. The fellow was off like a duiker (the duiker is a small, quick antelope), but he'd an old hunter to deal with. I caught sight of him as he jumped, and he never got up again when he came to the ground. I didn't care to meddle with him, for I didn't know who might be near him. I knew I'd saved a court-martial some trouble, and a file of soldiers some ammunition, so I reported at Graham's Town what I had done. A party went out at once, but they found the body stripped, and the man's musket gone, and no one could identify him except the owner of the store, and a Hottentot woman, who said he had been a soldier, but had been supposed to have left the colony long ago. The Hottentots in the house where I had seen him said he had come there to get a light to light his pipe, and sat talking with them till it was dark. This might or might not have been true, but he never fought against his white countrymen again, nor did he sell any more ammunition. This long notch is for him, and I think I did my duty to my fellow-men when I shot that fellow, who would have murdered me if he could have shot quick enough, as well as aid those rascally Kaffirs against us."

"I have always heard there were deserters from the English soldiers who aided the Kaffirs in this outbreak," said Hans, "and it seems your man was one of them."

"Yes, there were several deserters among the Kaffirs, but, as is usually the case, they received very rough treatment at the hands of their new friends, who, knowing that they dared not leave them or rejoin the English, made them work like slaves."

"Do you think," inquired Hans, "that the Amakosa Kaffirs fought as bravely when they attacked Graham's Town as the Zulus have done lately against us?"

"Yes, I think they did. All savages fight well; there is no want of courage amongst them; and when they are assured by their prophets that bullets won't touch them, and assagies will be blunted against them, they will fight like demons, and will rush up to the very muzzles of the guns without fear or hesitation. The Amakosa, however, fear the Zulus, and have an idea that the Zulu is brave and very strong. This is because the Zulu drove the Fetcani down the country from the East, and the Fetcani, taking a lesson from the Zulus, drove the Amakosa Kaffirs before them, so that the latter sought the aid of the English against these invaders, whom they then defeated."

"Most of those who now claim portions of the country seem to have won it from some one weaker than themselves," said Hans. "We lost the country we had won, and the Kaffirs seem to have lost their country, or a great part of it. I hope we shall never lose Natal."

"Natal is too far away to make people anxious for it," replied Hofman; "though if people knew how fine a place it was, they would come to it from many parts of the world. I wonder the Portuguese never took possession of it, as they have Delagoa Bay close to it."

"They have enough land there, and don't want more, so I have heard," replied Hofman. "They send parties to hunt elephants near this. Did you see any spoor to-day, or do you think your elephants had been hunted lately?"

"No, my elephants knew what a gun was, but they did not seem disposed to trouble themselves much about it; for though they ran at first, they soon stopped again, and I thus shot my first elephant on foot."

"To-morrow we will collect our ivory, and we must search for fresh game, for the elephants will trek from here. We shall have much work, so we will do well to sleep now."

With this parting advice Hofman made his brief arrangements for sleeping, a proceeding that was followed by all the other hunters, and the camp was soon in a state of repose. The horses were fastened to the waggon wheels, the oxen tied to stakes driven into the ground, and thus prevented from straying or wandering where they might tempt a hungry lion or hyena, and with but few exceptions every human being slept, for hunters sleep lightly even when tired, and the oxen or horses soon give an alarm, should any danger threaten.

By the aid of their Hottentots and Kaffirs, the hunters had cut out all the tusks from their elephants by mid-day, and these being carried to the waggons, were placed therein, each owner's mark being cut on the tusk. After a hasty meal, it was decided to hunt during the afternoon, and return before sundown to a new outspanning-place which had been agreed upon. Some very likely-looking ground was seen from a hill, and which lay in the north-easterly direction. This country was not at all known by the hunters, and, in fact, to this day it is not well explored. Two parties were formed, one of which was to take the more easterly direction, and then to return by a southerly course; the other to take the more northerly, and return by a westerly and southerly course. Thus the whole country would be hunted thoroughly. Hans and his two companions took the more easterly course, the companions on this occasion being Bernhard and Victor.

"I know we shall get ivory down by that dark-looking forest," said Victor, as he pointed to a distant slope on which were masses of trees. "Elephants will be found there, if there are any about."

"It looks good elephant ground," said Hans; "and it will be well to try it. There is none better looking round about."

"It was unlucky you lost your far-seer, Hans; that would have told us what game there was about us."

"Yes, it was unlucky; but let us dismount, and let our horses feed awhile, whilst we look closely over the country. I can recognise an elephant a long way off, if I take my time in looking."

The hunters dismounted, and knee-haltering their horses, sat quietly examining the distant country for several minutes.

"I can see an elephant," at length said Hans. "Come, Victor, your eyes are good; look in a line with that distant pointed tree; look at that third cluster of forest trees, and on the right side there is an elephant. Watch, and you will see him move."

"I see him now you have pointed him out, but I could not say it was an elephant; it might be a buffalo or rhinoster."

"No, an elephant is more square than either, and does not look so pointed; it is an elephant, too, by the way it turns. We shall have more sport to-day, but it will be a long ride to get to those elephants. We ought to drive them this way, and therefore ought to go round from the other side, and that will make our ride six miles at least; so we had better let them feed well now. They will be quite fit for a gallop after a six-miles' canter, though they are full of grass."

"The country would be fine for elephant shooting about here. The loose sharp stones damage their feet, and they would rush from clump to clump of wood, so that between them we should get shots from the saddle; don't you think so, Hans?" asked Bernhard.

"Yes, we should be very successful here, and I think our trip altogether will be a lucky one. When we return, we shall have plenty of dollars' worth of ivory, and I shall then be quiet for a while."

Having upsaddled their horses, the hunters rode towards the forest, near which Hans had seen the elephants. The country was one magnificent field of flowers and game. Bucks bounded in all directions, whilst the most stately antelopes continually crossed their path. The stately koodoo, the noble water-buck, the striped eland, and many other creatures rarely, if ever, seen in England, except in our museums, were seen in numbers. But the game upon which the hunters were bent was elephants. No temptation could induce these men to fire a shot at less noble game, for the sound of a gun would alarm the country, and disturb the elephants; so that there would be but slight chance of finding these acute-scented, sharp-eared animals after they had been alarmed by a shot. Riding steadily on, therefore, with an indifference to the animals that they disturbed, the hunters reached the position they desired, and there saw the game they expected. There were but four elephants, but they were all bulls, and with fine tusks, and were browsing without any signs of alarm.

"That elephant alone to the right I will take, if you like," said Hans; "you ride for the other two."

"Yes, they seem all alike in tusks, so you take him. We will ride down on them, and shoot from the saddle," said Victor.

The three hunters separated slightly, each riding down towards the elephant he had selected, and each regulating his pace in such a manner that he should reach his elephant at the same time that the others did. Hans was the last to reach his elephant, as he had the farthest to go, but was nearly ready to fire, when the double shots of Victor and Bernhard alarmed his elephant. Firing rather hurriedly, he aimed high, and his bullet striking the animal in the head, enraged it, so that it charged him instantly with a fierce trumpet Hans, being well mounted, easily avoided the charge, and the elephant continued on its course, thus travelling in the opposite direction to that in which the elephants ran which Victor and Bernhard had wounded. Hans quickly pursued his elephant, and firing at it behind the shoulder, lodged his two bullets there. This the huge animal seemed to be indifferent to, and still charged on with great speed. Loading as he rode at full gallop, Hans continued bombarding the elephant, but apparently with no great effect, and he found himself far away from his companions, and riding in the opposite direction to that in which they had gone.

Powerful as was the elephant, still it was mortal; and as the heavy gun of Hans was discharged time after time close to the animal's side, the bullets passed nearly through it, and at length compelled it to cease struggling for life, and resign the combat. Standing near a large tree, against which it leaned for support, the animal received its death wound, and fell to the ground, breaking off both its tusks as it came to the earth.

Hans immediately took the saddle off his tired steed, and allowed it to graze, whilst he sat down beside his prize. He estimated that he had ridden about eight miles away from the spot on which he had first started the elephants, and in a nearly easterly direction. The country was entirely unknown to him, and there was no sun to guide him as to the points of the compass, but the instinct of a hunter would tell him which way he should go in order to retrace his steps, or he might follow his spoor back. He determined to rest about an hour, and then to ride back; so, lighting his pipe, he enjoyed a quiet smoke. Whilst thus occupied, he was surprised to hear human voices near him, and still more so when he saw a party of about a dozen men, some of them partially clothed, and all armed with guns, who were coming rapidly towards him. Hans' first idea was to mount his horse and ride away; but he saw that before he could reach his horse the men would be close to him, and if they intended to injure him, they could easily shoot him at the short distance which they would then be from him. The fact of their having guns rather disposed Hans to think that they must be partially civilised, and that therefore he need not fear them as enemies.

It was evident that these men, having heard the report of his gun, had come to search out the cause of so unusual a noise in this neighbourhood, and the elephant soon attracted their attention, and with a shout as they saw it they ran rapidly down towards it. Hans stood up as they approached, and showed no signs of fear; and when they came close, he noticed that three of the men were evidently half-castes, and one seemed the leader of the party. The men saw Hans, and immediately transferred their attention from the dead elephant to him. He spoke to them in Dutch, then in English, but they seemed to understand neither language; so he said a few words in Zulu, which were equally unintelligible. The men spoke rapidly amongst themselves, and Hans could not understand what they said, and was at a loss to comprehend from whence these hunters—for such they seemed to be—had come. After several attempts at communication, the chief shook his head, and pointing to the west, then at Hans, seemed thus to signal that it was from the west that Hans had come. Hans, who was accustomed to aid his imperfect knowledge of language by signs, immediately nodded his assent to this pantomime, and pointing to the men around, then to the east, thus inquired whether these hunters came from the east. The chief nodded to this, and thus explained to Hans that he must have come from the neighbourhood of Delagoa Bay, and was probably a cross between some natives there and the Portuguese.

Whilst this communication was going on between Hans and the chief, some of the men had pulled the teeth from under the elephant, and had cut off the flesh that hung to them. They then lifted up the teeth, and seemed preparing to carry them away. To this appropriation of his property Hans objected, and made signs to the chief that the men should place the tusks on the ground. The chief uttered a few words to the men, who immediately dropped the tusks, and stood waiting for further directions. The chief now came close to Hans, and commenced making signs, which, however seemed to Hans unintelligible. He was, however, endeavouring to discover what these signals meant, when his arms were grasped from behind, his gun taken from him, and in the struggle which ensued he was thrown violently to the ground, and there held by three of the men of the party. Though strong enough to have mastered any one of the strange men singly, still Hans was no match for three of them; and thus he ceased to struggle on finding himself disarmed, and surrounded by such a force. Immediately he was thus quiet, some leather straps were produced, and his hands were firmly tied behind him. His legs were then tied by a powerful strap, so that he could walk by taking an average length-pace; but if he attempted to go beyond this, he could not do so: thus running was out of the question.

Whilst this sudden attack, and being thus bound as a prisoner, made Hans very angry, yet he knew that it was no use showing this anger; he therefore submitted quietly, and began to hope that as there seemed no intention of murdering him, he might be merely kept a prisoner for some time, and then released.

"Perhaps they will steal my horse, gun, and ivory, and leave me here unable to follow them," thought Hans. "If so, I shall have a long journey on foot to reach my people." This idea, however, was soon relinquished, when Hans saw the chief mount his horse, take his gun, and whilst others of the party carried the tusks, three men, who seemed detailed especially to him, signalled to him to walk on before them, and after their chief. Pulling long knives from out of their belts, they signed to him that these would be used if he did not willingly comply, and thus threatened he followed, as best he could with bound hands and encumbered legs, the leaders of the party.

Hans could tell that the direction in which he walked was nearly east, and therefore away from where his people would be expecting him. None of the Dutchmen would be likely, therefore, to come across him or to find him, so that a rescue was out of the question. The only chance seemed to be that Victor and Bernhard might come in search of him, and might trace him up; but then two men against twelve men armed with muskets might result only in the death of his two friends.

Chapter Twenty Three
Hans carried away—His Fellow-prisoners—Slavery—Thoughts of Escape—Carried off to Sea—The Voyage—Pursued—The Chase—The Night Battle—The Repulse—The Capture

With no hesitation as to the direction in which they were to travel, the party who had so unceremoniously captured Hans marched on till near sunset. It was evident they knew the country well, and had decided in which direction they were to proceed. They talked freely amongst each other, and Hans was often apparently the subject of their conversation, but he could not comprehend a word of their language. It was no compound of either Dutch, English, or Kaffir, and he therefore concluded it must be Portuguese.

Hans could not understand why he should be taken prisoner. He had not, he believed, committed any crime, and was merely hunting in a free country; but having failed to think of any likely reason, he did not further trouble himself about the matter. When the sun was so near the horizon that the shadow of the trees made the forest through which they walked nearly dark, the party halted. Some wood was quickly gathered, a fire was lighted, and some elephant's flesh was broiled; Hans was given his share of the food, and also supplied with water. He was carefully tied to one of the men of the party, whose duty it was to watch him, and thus all chance of escape was prevented. The party then set one man to act as sentry, and, forming a ring round Hans, laid themselves down to sleep. Bound as he was, Hans could not for a long time sleep; but at length, long exposure to danger having rendered him very much of a philosopher, he slept as soundly as the remainder of the party.

The sun had scarcely risen on the following morning before Hans and his capturers, having breakfasted, again travelled on to the eastward. The march was continued till mid-day, when a halt was made, and one or two shots were fired, apparently as signals. After a short interval these shots were replied to by other shots, and soon after a second party of very similar-looking men appeared from the south, and brought with them three Zulus, bound in the same manner as Hans. An immense number of questions and answers passed between the two parties of men, those who last arrived evidently describing to their friends some adventure which had happened to them, and which from the action Hans supposed to be a fight of some kind, probably with a hunting-party of Zulus, some of the members of which were taken prisoners.

Hans was quite sufficiently acquainted with the Zulu dialect to have made inquiries from his fellow-prisoners as to the manner in which they had been captured, but as this would have been merely through curiosity, he thought it more prudent to keep silence, and not to let his captors know that he could speak the language of his dark-coloured fellow-prisoners; besides, he believed that he would soon be able to overhear enough of their conversation to find out in what manner they had been captured; and in this supposition he was correct, for he soon gathered enough information to know that the Zulus had been out hunting, and were surprised by their capturers, who shot several men who offered resistance, but seemed more inclined to take prisoners than to kill. The chief whom Hans had seen at first, came up to the Zulus, and commenced feeling their arms and bodies, as a purchaser pinches cattle. At first a feeling of alarm came across Hans, as he fancied he had fallen among a party of cannibals, who captured men to eat at their great feasts; but this he could not reconcile with the half-civilised look of the men, and their having guns. Only one other explanation seemed probable, however, and when this occurred to him, Hans was surprised he had not thought of it before. Rumours had often been heard amongst the old colonists that up the East Coast the white men used to persuade the natives sometimes to go on board ship, and then to make them prisoners, and sell them in distant lands for slaves. Hans now thought that he and the Zulus could be captured for no other reason, and this idea was little less satisfactory than was that of being eaten by cannibals. That a Kaffir could be thus captured and sold, Hans did not doubt; but it seemed to him impossible that a white man could be thus treated, and he therefore hoped that, as soon as he reached the head-quarters of wherever he might be going, he would be liberated.

For four days the party marched on through a country in which there seemed no inhabitants. Game was shot occasionally, and the Zulus, as well as Hans, were well fed, this convincing Hans that he and they were destined to be sold for slaves, as a fat, plump, healthy-looking slave would always fetch more than one who was thinner or weakly-looking. At the end of the fourth day Hans saw the sea, distant only a few miles, and near the sea he saw, as he advanced, several huts built two stories high, and indicating much more architectural skill than the kraals of the Zulus.

Several men, women, and children came out from these huts to welcome the return of the expedition, which had evidently been out slave-hunting. They all looked at Hans with great interest, but took not the slightest notice of his remonstrances or earnest appeals for liberty. He was taken with the Zulus to a large hut, in which there were benches and large wooden rails. To these were attached chains and fastenings for the hands and legs. The men were evidently accustomed to the work of securing prisoners, and fastened Hans and the Zulus in a very few minutes, shortly afterwards bringing them some boiled rice and milk; then locking them in, left them to their own resources; a man, however, being placed on guard just outside of the hut to watch them, and to report if any attempt was made to escape from their fetters.

On the morning after his arrival at the coast, Hans was surprised to find that he was taken away from the other prisoners, and was conducted to a distant hut, where some coloured men were assembled, whom he had not previously seen. As soon as Hans arrived, one of these men commenced clipping his hair and beard, until as little was left as is found on the woolly pate of a Zulu. It was in vain Hans remonstrated against this outrage; the men paid not the slightest attention to his words, and seemed not to understand them; and as his hands were fastened by irons he was completely in their power. Having clipped his hair to their satisfaction, the men produced a vessel in which was a thick black composition. Removing Hans' clothing from his neck and arms, they deliberately painted his face, neck, hands, and arms with this composition, which shortly dried; and Hans, judging what his lace must be from what he could see his hands were, knew he must look very like a negro or Zulu. The Ethiopian singers whom we are accustomed to see in our streets are not nearly such good imitations of black men as Hans was after his wash.

Hans concluded that this disguise was effected in order that it should not be known that he was a white man; but he remembered that though his hands and face were blackened, yet his tongue remained white, and he could speak Dutch, and his knowledge of English was sufficient to enable him to converse with tolerable freedom; so that if it was intended to conceal his nationality, that was hopeless.

On his being taken back to the hut where the Zulus were confined, he discovered how complete had been his disguise, for his late companions did not recognise him, and believed that a stranger had been brought to them.

During ten days Hans was kept a prisoner in the hut, along with the Zulus, but on the morning of the eleventh day some change was evidently anticipated by his jailors. The men who had been on guard came in early to the room, and by signs intimated that the prisoners were to follow them. The irons and shackles were taken off, and with a hint that a spear would be used should any attempt be made to escape, the Zulus and Hans were conducted towards the beach. Hans soon saw what he supposed was the cause of this change. Near the shore, and partly sheltered by a woody promontory, was a long, low, small vessel. Her look was what sailors would decidedly term suspicious, and such she really was. The prisoners were taken to a shed near the coast, and were immediately visited by half a dozen sailor-looking men, all of whom were dark, ruffianly-looking fellows. Hans spoke in Dutch and in English to them, but obtained no attention, the sailors either not understanding him, or else purposely declining to listen to his complaint. After what appeared to be a bargain between the sailors and Hans' capturers, the former brought some rope from their boat, and tying Hans and the Zulus together, led them down to the boat, their capturers following them with cudgels and spears to employ force should any resistance be offered.

Upon reaching the boat, the prisoners were dragged in, and ordered into the stem, where they were compelled to lie down. The boat was pushed off and rowed to the vessel.

No sooner did Hans get on board the vessel than the horrible smell which he encountered, and the first peep down below, convinced him that all the tales he had heard connected with slavery were true. Upwards of two hundred dark-skinned men were crowded together and chained like wild beasts to the deck, and to benches. Hans, who had all his life been accustomed to the pure air of the open country, who had left the least sign of a town to obtain the freedom of the wilderness, found himself thus brought into that condition of all others which was to him the most repulsive. That he should be chained like a wild beast, and brought into contact with some hundreds of foul natives, whom he and all his class looked upon as little better than animals, was more than he could endure. "Even death is better than this," he thought; and with a sudden wrench he drew his hands from the fastenings with which he was held, seized a handspike that was near him, and in an instant had felled two of the sailors that had brought him on board. Several of the ship's crew who were standing near, on seeing this sudden attack, recoiled from Hans; but being armed with pistols and cutlasses, Hans' career would soon, have been terminated, had not the captain, who witnessed the proceeding, called to his men, and given them some directions which Hans could not understand. The captain, seizing another handspike, approached Hans, as though to decide by single combat the question whether or not he was to obtain freedom; at least such was for a moment Hans' idea. Concentrating all his attention and energy towards defeating the captain, he approached him cautiously, his handspike in readiness for a blow, when having reached nearly the required distance, something flashed before Hans' eyes, a noose settled over his shoulders, and before he could understand what had occurred he was jerked to the deck, and there pinioned by half a dozen sailors.

Protesting in alternate Dutch and English, Hans was dragged down below, and placed in irons alongside of some Africans, whose nationality or language he was unacquainted with. At first Hans supposed that his words had been unintelligible to those to whom he spoke, but after some hours a sailor came down, and seeing him said—

"You speak Ingleese."

"Yes," said Hans; "I am a Dutch farmer: why am I made a prisoner like this?"

"Captain pay silber for you; that why," said the sailor. "If he get more silber from you, he let you go, not without."

"I have no silver to give him here," said Hans; "but if he could send any one with me to Natal, I could procure plenty of silver, enough to pay him back more than he gave for me."

"Ah! captain no like go to Natal; English gun-ships sometimes there; he no go there; no, he sell you in America."

With this remark the man left, and Hans was now alone amidst a crowd; for the black men around him had no sympathy with him, and did not understand a word of the language he spoke.

Hans had now time to look around at the scene in which he was a partaker. At least two hundred negroes were crowded together between decks. There was no attempt at cleanliness, and the foul state of all around convinced Hans that a fearful mortality would shortly overtake the negroes. The heat was suffocating, and the ventilation scarcely perceptible. A hot steamy atmosphere pervaded the hold of the vessel, and rose from it as from a furnace. In such a situation Hans looked back longingly to his free life in the forest and on the plains of Africa, and he reflected, like many people, on the immense value of that which he had lost, and which he had not half appreciated when he possessed it. "What would I not give," said Hans, "even to be the fore-looper of a waggon, so that I might see the light of day, and breathe the fresh air of heaven! Oh, Bernhard, and you, Victor, how happy are you, and how little you know of the sad fate of Hans! Poor Katrine too, you will wait expecting me for many a long day, and you will wonder why I have not come back; but I may never be able to tell you how hard a fate is mine."

The day after Hans came on board he began to experience the style of treatment he would receive from the hands of the sailors. The fact of his having knocked down two of them seemed to have drawn special attention to himself, for whenever food was brought down for the slaves, the very worst was given to Hans, whilst kicks and cuffs were freely bestowed upon him whenever an opportunity offered.

At daybreak on the third day the vessel's anchor was weighed, and with a fair wind from the north-east she ran offshore and steered down the coast. As long as the ship was protected by the headland, she did not feel any influence from the waves; but no sooner was she out at sea than, being a very small vessel and drawing but little water, she was very lively, and danced merrily on the waves. Hans had never been to sea before, nor been on board ship; and cooped up as he was in the close, foul atmosphere between decks, he was very soon, in addition to his other miseries, suffering from sea-sickness, and was thus utterly prostrated, and unable to do more than rest his head and wearied limbs as best he could, and wish for some release from his sufferings.

As the day wore on, and night once more came, Hans believed that no human being could be in a more miserable plight than he was. He reflected upon his sensations when he discovered that Katrine had been carried off by the Matabili; he thought over his feelings when he fought on the solitary rock with Victor, and when a rescue seemed very improbable; but there was excitement and uncertainty in those conditions, whereas now there seemed not even the remotest chance of any help coming to him. He was on board a vessel, a chained prisoner, and determined men his jailors; and thus his fate was sealed.

For three days and nights the little vessel rolled steadily on her course, at the end of which time Hans had in a great measure recovered from his sea-sickness, and had begun to plan some means of escape. He had made up his mind that death was preferable to a life of slavery, and it is surprising what a desperate man will plan and very often accomplish. Hans decided that the only possible means of escape was to induce the slaves to mutiny. If the slaves could be freed from their irons, and could be organised in any way, they would number more than ten to one of the crew, and thus the vessel could be captured. What to do, then, Hans did not know; but he thought that if all the sails were taken off the vessel, and she was allowed to remain still on the ocean, some ship would be sure to see them, and give the aid he required. The great difficulty was to get up any organised attack, for, except the Zulus who had been brought down the country with him, there was no one with whom he could communicate. The Zulus did not seem to understand the language of the other slaves, and thus it was impossible to obtain any uniformity of action. Still Hans thought over every possible chance, and decided that if no other means presented themselves, he would, by the aid of the Zulus alone, endeavour to do something.

On the fourth day Hans found by the motion of the vessel, that some change had occurred in the weather, or in the sea. Instead of rolling steadily onwards with an easy movement, the ship jerked and plunged very uneasily, seeming sometimes as though rushing furiously onwards, and then suddenly being checked in her course. There was, too, a great commotion among the sailors, and the noise made by the wind in the rigging of the vessel prevented even the groans and yells of the slaves from being heard. During the whole of the fourth day and night these conditions prevailed, heavy seas striking the small vessel, and spray in abundance finding its way down amongst the crowded human beings below. The night was a long and dreary one. The hatchway which led down to the slaves' den was narrow, and scarcely allowed enough ventilation to prevent suffocation. The darkness was such that not even a hand could be seen when held close to the face, and as Hans could not sleep, his torture in being thus confined was almost unbearable.

The first signs of daylight had just begun to appear, when Hans heard a shout on deck, followed by the sound of rushing feet; then a series of shouts, and what appeared to him execrations, uttered in a language which he could not comprehend. He endeavoured to discover what was the cause of this sudden commotion, and after a time he believed that either the ship had met with some accident, and was likely to go down, or her direction had been changed for some reason with which he was not acquainted. As the daylight increased, he could obtain glimpses through the hatchway of the masts, and he then found that the vessel was crowded with sails, and from the bounding sort of feeling, and the rushing sound of the water, he knew the vessel must be forcing her way with great speed. For what reason this sudden change had been made Hans had no idea, but that there was some cause for anxiety there seemed to be no doubt, for the crew were so fully occupied that none of the slaves had received any food up to mid-day, and consequently their groans and yells were incessant. Without apparently being influenced by these sounds, shortly after mid-day some of the sailors rushed down among the slaves, and after inflicting several lashes on the more noisy, they unlocked the irons of about half a dozen slaves, among whom was Hans, and signed to them to go on deck.

Hans willingly complied with this request or order, for even had it been to meet his death he would willingly have purchased a few breaths of fresh air at this price. Upon ascending to the deck of the vessel, the sight to Hans was one of wonder and astonishment. He had seen the vast plains of Africa extending far as the eye could reach in all directions, and had admired the extent of these, but never before had he at all realised the vastness of the ocean. As he held for an instant to the shrouds on the ship's side, he saw around him a wide expanse of water, tossing and dancing as though possessed with life. He saw vast masses of water come rushing after the vessel, foaming as though eager to swallow her up; then the little vessel, rising as though by instinct, seemed to allow these to pass beneath her, whilst she rested for a few seconds, before again springing forward in her mad career. Hans had scarcely time to observe even this, before he was dragged to the after-part of the ship, and was given a pail with which he was directed to bale out the water that had descended into the hold of the vessel. At first Hans was inclined to refuse this, but a moment's reflection told him that it might be wiser to obey, and wait for some chance of a mutiny at another time. He therefore lowered his bucket by the rope which was attached, and empted its contents over the side as directed.

Whilst employed in this manner, Hans observed that the sailors were continually looking astern, even ascending the rigging in order to obtain a better view of something. His trained eyes soon observed an object on the horizon, but at a considerable distance, and this object he knew must be a ship. Nothing of her was visible but a mass of white sails, which were seen when the little vessel in which he was rose on the summit of a wave, and were lost sight of as she again descended. The short glance that he had given at the distant ship caused a heavy log of wood to be hurled at him by the captain, who, pointing to his bucket, indicated that he was to go on baling. Hans, believing that the distant ship might be one which was in pursuit of the slaver, was so anxious to watch her that he at once set to work baling vigorously, fearing that if he did not do so, he might be sent down below, and another slave liberated to take his place.

During an hour or more Hans remained near the stern of the vessel, and continued his labours as well as the motion of the vessel would allow him to do. In this interval the strange vessel astern had evidently gained on the slaver, there being a taller mass of canvas visible than when first Hans had noticed her. The captain of the slaver seemed to be aware of this fact, and though the masts seemed to bend under the heavy press of canvas on them, he yet sent some men aloft in order to get another stern-sail on his vessel. This extra sail, small as it seemed to be, yet added to the speed of the slaver, which now bounded over the water like a fresh horse on the springy turf. During another hour Hans could see no difference in the apparent distance of the chasing ship, and he began to fear that this chance would fail him. Could he venture to cut any of the many mysterious ropes that held the sails, he would, he knew, temporarily stop or retard the vessel; but he knew not what to cut, and he did not possess a knife, even had he known. Thus he was helpless in this particular, and had to continue working, only resting occasionally when an opportunity occurred of doing so.

Nearer and nearer the sun travelled towards the horizon, and yet the pursuing vessel seemed scarcely to decrease her distance from the slaver; and if night should come before the distance was decreased, it would be very probable that the slaver might escape. Hans, although totally unacquainted with nautical affairs, could yet see that such a result was very possible, and therefore, as the afternoon passed on, his hopes fell, and he became at length disheartened, especially when he noticed that the distant ship had suddenly begun to increase instead of decreasing her distance. It was some time before the cause of this increase in the slaver's rate of sailing became apparent, and even then Hans could not quite comprehend it; but the fact was, that the slaver was very light, and was built mainly for running before the wind. Her sails were large, and she thus sailed in a light wind better than could a larger, heavier ship, to which a strong breeze was better adapted. Thus as the wind was falling lighter, she gradually increased her distance from her pursuer, and bid fair to escape out of sight. The wind, which had decreased from a fresh breeze to merely a light air, ceased altogether about sundown, and before dark the slaver was becalmed, not having even enough way on her to enable her head to be kept in one direction. The last rays of the setting sun just illumined the royals and topgallant sails of the distant vessel, and at this Hans cast a lingering look as he left the deck and was sent below, and again chained to the benches. Some of the negroes, who had been taken on deck for various labours, had seen the pursuing ship, and were evidently under the belief that she was an enemy of the captain's, and therefore was a friend of theirs. A great deal of talking was going on amongst these men, evidently with reference to what they had seen on deck, though their words were unintelligible to Hans.

Night closed in, and all was silent on deck. The groaning of the bulkheads could alone be heard as the vessel rolled lazily on the now tolerably quiet sea. The effect of the fresh sea breeze, and the labour he had undergone, rendered Hans sleepy, and though his position was a most uncomfortable one, he yet managed to sleep for short intervals. From one of these brief minutes of repose he awoke, and heard the sailors on deck talking in subdued tones. The rattle of swords or some such weapons on the deck was audible, whilst the ring of a ramrod, as bullets were rammed down, was a sound which to Hans' ears was very intelligible. What all these preparations were for he could not imagine unless it was that the captain and crew expected the slaves to mutiny, and were thus making preparations to meet them.

When the sailors appeared to have loaded several muskets, all was again quiet on deck, and no sound seemed to indicate that there was a living soul there—the groans of some of the slaves, and the snores of others, being audible to those only who were with them.

For some time this quietness continued, when Hans heard a slight movement on deck, and some loud whispering. His being near the hatchway enabled him thus to distinguish sounds in the open air. Several sailors hurriedly ran to and fro on the deck, and Hans could hear that nearly if not quite all the crew were on deck.

Suddenly the captain of the slaver called out in a loud voice, as though he were hailing some one at a distance, and Hans distinctly heard from the sea a voice in English call out, "What ship is that?"

There was some hesitation on the part of the captain of the slaver, for no answer was at first returned; but when a second demand, "What ship is that?" was uttered, one of the crew, who had before spoken to Hans in English, answered, "Portugee ship, Pedro: what you want?"

"I must come on board," was the reply from the sea; for Hans could not tell in what sort of vessel the inquirer was, though he hoped a rescue was at hand. He strained every muscle to try and free his arms from the irons that held him, but without effect; for he feared that perhaps the inquirer, whoever it might be, might not venture beyond inquiries, and thus would avoid seeing all that he must see should he come on board. The inquirer, however, was not satisfied, as his remark indicated, and the sound of oars was audible amidst the stillness which followed. Presently the grating of a boat on the vessel's side was heard; then the fall of a heavy substance, the crashing of planks, and a heavy splash in the water, followed by the shouts of men, who, some crushed, others struggling in the sea, were able to call for aid, and thus announced their distress. A loud cheer given by English lungs responded to their calls, and three other boats, which had before kept back in the darkness, now dashed at the slaver.

The captain of the slaver was a desperate man, and his all was risked in the vessel he now commanded. Having either suspected that the ship which had chased him would send her boats to capture him, or having heard an incautious speaker or the imperfectly muffled oars, he had made his arrangements for defence. Supported from the mainyard arm, he had suspended three or four solid iron bars, each of which exceeded a hundred pounds in weight. A man with a sharp knife was placed close to this, with orders to cut the rope by which the iron was held immediately a boat came beneath him. The man obeyed his orders well, and the mass of iron, having gained great velocity by the distance it had fallen, stove in the boat, killing two men in its descent. Four boats had been sent from the ship in order to capture the slaver, and the three that remained pulled eagerly forward to avenge their first check. The crew of the disabled boat were struggling in the water as their comrades came near, and, as is too often the case, the sailors could not swim, and were therefore in great risk of being drowned. The boats, therefore, were checked in their advance, in consequence of stopping to take up their comrades.

Whilst thus delayed, their position could be distinctly seen from the slaver, because of the phosphorescence of the water, which gave a line of brilliant light following the boat like a comet's tail in the skies. The captain of the slaver saw his opportunity, and directing his men to fire at the boats, he set the example by discharging both barrels of his fowling-piece at the leading boat; and then waiting a short time, followed this by a shot from each of the double barrels of his pistol. His men, being all well-armed and desperadoes, knowing that their lives would be sacrificed if they were captured, and believing in their present superiority of numbers, fired with a deadly aim at the boats, and immediately afterwards dropped behind the bulwarks, where they were comparatively secure from the irregular discharge delivered from the boats.

The English sailors did not, however, retreat, though fully half their number were already either killed or wounded. Having aided their companions to get into the boats, they pulled on to the slaver, and were preparing to board her, when the slaver crew, having reloaded, poured another shower of bullets on to their assailants with almost as fatal an effect as before. To attempt a further assault would have been merely a reckless throwing away of life, and this the commander seeing, he ordered an immediate retreat, which seemed the signal for a general discharge of fire-arms from the crew of the slaver.

Hans' heart beat rapidly as this tumult went on, whilst all the slaves had uttered groans and savage yells. The hold of the vessel seemed more like a den of infuriated beasts than a prison filled with human beings. The slaves all seemed to comprehend that those who were attacking their vessel were their friends, and that they had been defeated; and their groans and yells were therefore redoubled when the boats pulled away from them. The noise they made caused the infuriated crew to come amongst them with whips and canes, which they used freely in all directions, thus quelling in a measure the disturbance.

After the din and tumult of the combat the silence on the deck of the slaver was a most painful contrast to Hans, who believed it improbable that another attempt could be made to take the slaver before the following day, because the distance of the ship to which the boats belonged was so great that they could not reach her and bring a stronger force before daybreak, at which time there was usually a fresh breeze on the coast; so that Hans feared his fate as a slave was decided.

Before daybreak Hans could feel by the movement of the vessel that a light breeze had sprung up, and this he now knew was just the style of wind that would best enable the slaver to creep away from the heavy ship in pursuit of her. He therefore obeyed unwillingly the order of one of the crew, who came down below to drive him and half a dozen other slaves on the deck to aid the sailors in pulling on the braces, etc. The night was rather foggy, and but few stars were visible; but Hans noticed that the clouds seemed to pass rapidly before the stars, as though the wind up high blew stronger than down below. From this fact he hoped that an increase would take place in the wind soon after sunrise, when there might be a chance of the large vessel again overhauling the slaver.

Hans remained on deck till the first streak of light appeared, but as the sea-line was not visible on account of the fog, he could not obtain a view of the vessel that was pursuing the slaver. As the light very rapidly increased, Hans looked eagerly astern in hopes of seeing the ship there. He was not aware that the vessel's course had been altered, and that it was no longer astern that he must look for the ship. He noticed that the sailors were all anxiously looking out in a different direction, over the slaver's quarter in fact, and there all was foggy. Soon, however, the fog rose, and there, to the surprise of the slaver's crew, was the strange ship, distant scarcely more than two miles. To Hans it seemed little short of a miracle how she had reached such a position; but the fact was that the breeze which had enabled the slaver to move on had been first felt by the ship, which had brought it up with her, and she had thus seen the manoeuvre of the slaver in changing her course before the fog had hidden her from view.

All sail was already spread on the slaver, and nothing more could therefore be done. Light as she was, and built entirely for running before the wind, she was able to maintain her distance from the ship, and for several hours the two did not alter their position. To the captain of the ship this must have been a sad trial of patience. He knew that if he could once come within gun-shot of the slaver, he could capture or sink her in a few minutes; but there she was tantalisingly just out of gun-shot, and maintaining this position, if not increasing her distance. Steam-vessels in those days were not common off the coast of Africa, and slavers or pirates had to be captured by sailing vessels alone.

Hans feared that the second chance of release would be lost, and he began to speculate upon what could be done to enable the vessel following them to come alongside. He believed that it might be possible to cut some of the many ropes which held the sails, and thus cause them to fall, and by this means to bring the slaver under the guns of the English ship; but the knife was wanting to accomplish this. Thus, though Hans thought over every plan, he could see nothing quite practical, or that could be effected without enormous risk.

As the day advanced it was evident that the slaver had the best of the race, the light breeze favouring her, and by sunset the English man-of-war brig—for such she was—had dropped back to nearly five miles' distance.

When darkness had completely set in the captain of the slaver altered his course, and ran in towards the shore. He had for two days sailed in the opposite direction to that in which he wished to go, the English brig having stood in his way. He now wished to let her pass, and thus renew his original intention of running over to the coast of South America, where his slaves would soon be disposed of. Having steered for about an hour in the direction of the coast, the captain ordered the vessel's head to be kept south-west; and thus he expected to run past the English brig, and avoid her in the darkness. It seemed impossible that any eyes could distinguish the vessel even at the distance of half a mile, and the crew of the slaver were unable to see the brig shortly after sunset. Whether it was, however, that they possessed admirable glasses on board the brig, or some light was visible on board the slaver, the change of course of the latter had been seen; and scarcely had she altered her course, and had begun to beat up wind in a south-westerly direction, than the crew of the slaver found themselves within half a mile of the brig, which was steering towards them. All was immediately hurry and confusion on board the slaver. Her course was altered, and additional sails were ordered to be placed on her, which, now that she was again put before the wind, she could carry. The English brig, however, was determined to put a stop to this, if possible: altering her course to suit that of the slaver, she also prepared to carry additional sails, but at the same time showed her intention of endeavouring to stop her quick-sailing enemy. The flash of a cannon, followed by the whistle of a shot over the ship, which was accompanied by the report, showed that she was in earnest. In rapid succession shot after shot flew over the brig and between her masts, yet none struck a mast, yard or spar. Already had the slaver begun to draw ahead, when a shot from the brig struck the main-mast of the slaver, and so nearly cut it in two that it could not bear the pressure of the sails upon it, and the next instant it snapped like a reed, and a mass of canvas and rope fell partly on the deck, and was partly supported by the mainyard, and immediately checked the speed of the vessel.

The captain shouted his directions to the men to clear the deck, whilst he swore at his luck; for he now saw that capture was almost certain. He dared fight the boats of the brig, but he had no means of successfully combating a vessel armed as she was. Finding that capture was almost a certainty, he called to the mate next in command, rushed to the side of the vessel, and lowered a boat which hung there; then rushing to the cabin, he brought up a heavy bag, apparently containing gold, and before any of his crew were aware of his intention he had left the vessel with the mate alone, and thus hoped to escape to the coast, which was not more than fifty miles distant.

The lucky shot which had struck the slaver's mast enabled the brig to come alongside, and several shots having been fired into the rigging, the slaver became unmanageable, and entirely lost her way, lying a wreck on the water. The brig, having come close to her, hailed to know if she had surrendered; but as no one except Hans seemed to understand what was said, no answer was at first returned; so Hans shouted in reply, "The captain has left the ship in a boat. Come on board, and free us."

Still fearing treachery, the commander of the brig would not despatch a small force to take the slaver, but sent two boats of armed men, who at once polled alongside, and springing on deck ordered the slaver's crew to throw down their arms. This order, given as much by signs as by words, was at once obeyed, and the crew were rapidly sent into the two boats, and transferred to the brig. Hans was at first taken for one of the crew, but the irons on his legs indicated that he was a slave, and his explanation of himself was considered so satisfactory by the officer sent to take charge of the slaver, that Hans was sent on board the brig to the captain to give all the information he could relative to the slaver.

Hans' account of the manner in which he had been captured, and also the manner in which he had been treated on board the slaver, enraged the captain of the brig, who was already irritated at the loss of some of the best men of his crew. He therefore determined to run up the coast, and, if possible, discover the head-quarters of these slave-catchers, and destroy it. Hans was quite delighted at this proposition, for all that he had suffered was still fresh in his memory, and he considered that if this slave establishment remained, some of his companions might be captured when on their next hunting expedition; so that he was most anxious that it should be destroyed.

The captain of the brig at once made his plans, which were that the slaver only should run up the coast after she had got rid of her slaves and the crew. Thus the slave-catchers would imagine she had put back for some reason, and might not be alarmed as they otherwise would be if the brig showed herself. The only objection to this plan seemed to be the delay which must occur before the slaver could return, for it would be necessary for her to go at least to Simon's Bay in order to get rid of her slaves. This plan, however, the captain of the brig decided on, and therefore, placing a portion of his crew with an officer in charge of the slaver, he sent the prisoners on board her, and secured them so that they could not interfere with the regular sailors, and gave directions to the officer in charge to make sail for Simon's Bay, and return as soon as possible.

In the mean time a boat which had been sent in pursuit of the captain and mate of the slaver returned, having found the boat they had escaped in bottom upwards, and no signs of its late occupants, who with their treasure had gone to the bottom, or been eaten by sharks.

Chapter Twenty Four
Off to Simon's Bay—Mutiny of the Slaves—
Their Repulse—Ship on Fire—The black
Demons—The Zulus' Escape—The Vessel sinks

Although the slaver had been the scene of so much misery to Hans, yet when he knew that she was going to the Cape he begged the captain's permission to go in her. He was anxious to get back to Natal, or at least to let his friends know that he was alive and well. The captain of the brig did not like to let Hans go, because from him he hoped to discover the head-quarters of the slavers; but Hans informed him of all he knew, and urged that he could tell no more even if with him, for he did not know what part of the coast the slavers lived on, except that it was not far from Delagoa Bay. After vainly endeavouring to persuade Hans to stay with him, the captain consented to his going in the slaver, and so Hans once more set foot on this ship, though under very different conditions from those with which he had previously boarded her. He was now given a hammock in the captain's cabin, and was able to roam about the ship without hindrance. By dint of soap and much scrubbing he had succeeded in rubbing off the composition that the slavers had painted him with, and he therefore now looked a thorough white man.

It was not considered safe to free the slaves and allow them all to come on deck, but a portion of them were liberated at a time, and brought up to the fresh air; and when these had been again secured, others were allowed to come up, so that during the twenty-four hours every slave passed a certain portion of his time in the fresh air.

The wind being fair for the slaver, she ran rapidly with the current that runs down the coast to the south-west, and was supposed to be about forty miles south of Cape L'Agulhas on the day after she had parted company with the brig. Towards the evening of this day it fell calm, and at sunset there was not a breeze stirring. Hans was leaning over the side of the vessel, talking to the lieutenant who commanded her, when the sun-setting attracted their attention.

"We shall have enough wind before the morning," said the lieutenant, "for the sun looks windy."

"Yes, that is the truth," replied Hans. "How long will it be before we get to the Cape?"

"We could drift down there in little more than two days even if there was no wind, for there is a current of three miles an hour running down this coast; but with a fair wind we shall get there in less time. Where shall you go to when you get to the Cape?"

"I must get up to Natal as soon as I can," replied Hans; "but I know not how to do that I have no money, and know no one there. Hark to the slaves! they are more noisy than ever."

"Yes," replied the officer, "they are just letting out some, and chaining up others. It is disagreeable work having slaves on board, but there ought not to be all this noise; something must be wrong."

This last remark had scarcely been made than from the hatchway leading to where the slaves were confined four of the sailors rushed up on deck, two of them bleeding from wounds in the face, whilst the other two were helping them along. They shouted, "The slaves have mutinied, sir," "Look out, sir," "They have freed themselves," and ran towards the officer and Hans. Closely following these sailors nearly a score of the negroes rushed on deck, yelling like maniacs, and flourishing portions of planking and benches, with which they had armed themselves. From the shouts which arose from below, it was evident that the negroes had possessed themselves of the means of unfastening their chains and handcuffs; and thus the situation of the prize crew was rather critical. The trained sailor, however, saw that instant action was the only chance. Calling to the two sailors to follow him, he drew his sword, and rushed at the nearest negro, whom he cut down at one blow. Drawing a pistol from his belt, he shot another, and was looking round for another victim, when the negroes, panic-stricken by the sudden exhibition of power, rushed to the hatchway, and tumbled one after the other down amongst their companions, leaving only their two slain comrades on deck. "On with the hatch," shouted the lieutenant; and the two sailors, who were now joined by the man who had stood by the wheel, and by the two wounded sailors and Hans, placed the hatch over the hatchway, and immediately secured it so that no man could come up.

"Who's below?" inquired the lieutenant of one of his men.

"Steel and Roberts, yer honour. They're torn to bits by this time."

"How did this occur, men?"

"Just the devil in these fellows, sir. We was taking them quietly down, after giving 'em a look at the sea, when one of 'em whistles, and at once the whole lot turns upon us, snatches my cutlass afore I could get hold of it, knocks down Steel and Roberts, slices those two across the face, and so begins it. I knocked two of 'em over with my fist, but them niggers' heads is tarnal hard, and fists is no account against a hundred of them fellows, when they have your cutlass, too; so I comes up to you to tell you, sir."

"Are all the men on deck?" asked the lieutenant. "Yes, sir, all."

"Get the arms out of the chest, Jones. Let each man have fifty rounds of ammunition. Four men keep watch over this hatch, and shoot any slave who attempts to force it up. Blake, you take two men, and see that the slaver's crew are quiet. Give them a hint that we are not to be trifled with, and then wait for orders."

These directions having been given by the lieutenant, he reloaded his pistol, and turning to Hans, said, "The two hundred slaves, if on this deck, would murder us, and throw us into the sea, in spite of our weapons; but if we can keep them under hatches, they can do nothing, though they all get free of their chains. If a breeze does spring up, we shall be in Simon's Bay in twenty-four hours, and we can then obtain force enough to defy all these savages. Two of my men are murdered, I fear, and I can give them no aid even if they are not. These savages are like infuriated wild beasts when they have once tasted blood, and to open that hatch now would risk all our lives. You have no weapons," he remarked, seeing that Hans had neither sword nor pistol. "Go into my cabin; you will find a double-barrelled pistol above the cot in which I sleep. We may all want to use our weapons."

Hans entered the cabin, and found the pistol, with which he returned on deck, when he immediately joined the lieutenant, who was directing his men how to oppose the efforts of the slaves to force the hatchway; one or two thrusts with a cutlass, and the exhibition of a pistol, being found effective to check these attempts on the part of the slaves.

Yells and groans were uttered for some time by the slaves, when a loud voice, as of one directing them, resounded above the tumult, and all was for a time hushed. The lieutenant, with Hans and the crew, fancied that a combined effort would be made to force the hatches up, and they therefore prepared to resist this; but as time went on, and no resistance seemed to be offered, they began to think this attempt would not be made.

Darkness came on with great rapidity, as it always does in the tropics; and before any attempt was made by the slaves to force their way on deck, the sun had gone down, and darkness had set in. Finding that there seemed no immediate cause for action, the lieutenant asked Hans to come with him into the cabin, and eat something, an invitation which Hans willingly accepted.

"Whenever we English have any fighting," said the lieutenant, "we always like to eat I don't know if it is so with you Dutch."

"I am English on my mother's side," said Hans, "so I suppose that is why I am hungry; but man must eat if he uses great exertion, and fighting requires exertion."

"Have you ever seen a man killed before to-day?" inquired the lieutenant. "I will not say it boastingly," replied Hans, "for no man should boast; but I tell you as the truth that in fair fight—fighting for my life, or for my goods, of which I had been robbed—I have shot perhaps as many black men as you have now on board this ship."

"Have you, indeed?" said the lieutenant, his opinion of Hans being thereby much enhanced; "then you have had to fight in Africa?"

"To fight!" said Hans. "Have you not heard of our battles with Moselekatse and Dingaan, and how we defeated them? Have you never heard of Eus, Pretorius, Retief, or Landman?"

"Never heard of one of them," was the calm reply of the lieutenant. "Are they niggers?"

What would have been Hans' indignant reply to this remark there is no saying, but a shout from the sailors caused the lieutenant and Hans to rush to the hatchway, before approaching which they saw some suspicious-looking smoke rising from the side of the ship.

"What is it?" shouted the lieutenant, as he approached his men.

"The slaves have set the ship on fire, yer honour," replied an old sailor.

"Curse them!" said the lieutenant; "they will destroy themselves and us too."

"The boats will swim, I think, sir," said the sailor, "and we can reach Simon's Bay very soon. We needn't be burnt, unless yer honour thought it a point of duty to be so. Them slaves and slave crew might make the best of a burning ship, and perhaps the sooner we get out of the ship the better for them, as they could then put the fire out."

"And let them re-take the slaver; eh, Roberts? What would the Admiral say to us then, if it were found that the slavers had driven us out by a little smoke?"

"It wouldn't do, yer honour; but the slavers, nor the slaves either, won't stop the flames on this ship, for she's built of pine-wood, and she'll be ablaze from stem to stern in half an hour."

The sailor's remark seemed very likely to be verified, for the ship being, as he said, built of pine-wood, and having been long exposed to the heat of an almost tropical sun, was so dry and inflammable that the fire caught the timbers, and burnt as though it were fed with shavings. In order to get at the situation of the fire, it would be necessary to go into the hold where the slaves were, and thus it would be necessary to raise the hatch. With above two hundred furious savages, who had just murdered two white men, in the hold, the lieutenant knew no chance existed of putting out a fire, which, whenever it occurs in a ship, requires a thoroughly well-disciplined body of men to be called together in order to put it out. "Take three hands with you, and lower the quarter boats," said the lieutenant to one of the men. "Sterk, will you stay here, and help to guard the hatch? I will put a few things into the boat. We must lose no time, I see; the ship is like tinder."

During the few minutes that the officer was absent, the fire had made great progress, and the yells and shouts from the slaves were almost deafening.

"We must free the slavers from their irons," said the lieutenant. "We must give them a chance. Come along and help me, you two." And with the aid of Hans and a sailor the lieutenant freed the crew of the slaver, and signed to them to follow on deck.

"Now into the two boats, men!" said the officer. "If we have any room, we'll save whoever we can. Stand by to let me in, for I'm going to free the hatch, and let the slaves up. They must have a chance for life, and God help them! for I see no possibility of human aid being of benefit." The sailors having hurried into the boats, the lieutenant seized a handspike, and knocking off the fastening of the hatchway, left it so that a very moderate amount of strength would force it up. He then lowered himself into the boat, and ordered the men to pull away a short distance from the slaver, where he purposed watching the struggle that he hoped might take place between the crew and the fire.

"I could do nothing else, I think," said the officer to Hans. "I have the lives of my men under my charge, and if I had waited on board, these slaves would have tried to murder us. Now they have a chance for their lives, but I run a risk now. If the slaver is burnt, and her crew and slaves go down with her, I may be called cruel for having left them to themselves, whilst I saved my own and my men's lives. If the fire is put out, I must again go on board, though we lose half our number in the attempt, or I should never dare show myself to the Admiral. Ah! there's a specimen of the negro's habits."

The slaves, upon being able to raise the hatches, rushed on deck, shouting and yelling like demons. Seeing some of the slaver's crew, who had also come on deck, they rushed at them, and with such weapons as each possessed a fight took place on the deck of the doomed vessel. Utterly reckless as regards the fire, which was now raging, and illuminating the deck, the two parties fought for revenge and life. The numbers of the negroes soon enabled them to overcome the slaver's crew, who were stiff from their late confinement, and the negroes were consequently masters of the ship. The use they made of this temporary possession was not to endeavour to quell the flames, or in any way to make preparations for their own safety; but, rushing into the cabins, they searched for plunder, and more particularly for drink, which, however, did not consist of any thing more than a few bottles of inferior brandy. For the possession of this brandy terrific struggles took place, handspikes and planking being used for weapons. To view this scene from the boats was like obtaining a temporary view of the imaginary infernal regions on which so many civilised beings delight to enlarge and dwell. The raging fire, which now was catching the rigging, was below the mass of yelling, dancing, fighting blacks, who seemed only intent on a few minutes' maniac-like orgies.

Standing calm spectators of the scene, Hans observed the Zulus who had been his fellow-prisoners. Though nearly black in colour, these men were unlike the negro in features, and seemed altogether a superior race. Though he had so lately been engaged in combats against the Zulus, yet when Hans saw these men thus calmly awaiting their death, he was desirous of saving them.

"See those men standing near the mast," said Hans: "they are Zulus. I should like, to save their lives."

"How can you do that?" inquired the lieutenant. "Will you let them come in the boat?" inquired Hans.

"Yes, if they can get in; but I cannot allow the boat to go near the slaver: she would be swamped in a minute, and all our lives would be sacrificed."

"I will try to make them understand," said Hans, "if you will help them into the boat if they swim to us." Saying this, Hans called in a shrill voice, "Mena-bo," at which the Zulus started up, and looked eagerly in the direction of the boats, which they could just perceive by aid of the light given by the burning ship. Having thus called their attention to him, Hans called in the Zulu language, "Jump into the water, and swim to me, or the fire will soon kill you."

The Zulus for a few seconds seemed to hesitate, but looking round at the fire, which was rapidly closing round them, the three men stepped on the side of the vessel, and jumped feet first into the sea. In an instant afterwards their heads appeared above water, as they swam rapidly towards the boats, into which they were dragged by the sailors.

"The men are all mad," said one of the Zulus to Hans. "They put fire to the ship to free themselves, and now they will not put water to the fire."

"Are the white men dead?" inquired Hans, referring to the sailors who had been attacked in the hold.

"Yes, and they would be cold by now were they not kept warm by the fire... It is all fire where we were."

The escape of the Zulus had either not been noticed by the negroes, or they supposed it was an act of desperation on the part of these men; for no notice was taken of it, the negroes still continuing their frantic proceedings. The slaver was evidently burning inside more than out. The flames every now and then shot up, whilst at two places in her hull they had forced a way out. Every now and then there was a hissing sound, as though water had fallen on a red-hot surface, and steam in abundance came up from below; the flames again arose, and after a time the same hissing occurred.

"I believe," said the lieutenant, "the flames have eaten a way through her somewhere, and the water is entering her; that is what causes the steam. It is so; look! she is settling down."

As he thus called attention to the slaver, all eyes were turned to her. The flames, which had previously risen half-way up her masts, suddenly ceased, whilst a sheet of white steam arose in their stead. The vessel's hull gradually descended; and the boat's crew had but just time to obey the command to "pull and together," and to move the two boats a safer distance from the ship, when the beautifully-modelled slaver, her yelling cargo of demons, and her mutilated bodies, sank together beneath the smooth surface of the ocean. Though she went down gradually till within a few inches of the water's edge, she yet raised a large wave by her submergence, which lifted the boats, and caused them to dance for some minutes. The darkness was fearful after the late glare of the burning ship; and so awful was the sight of this crowd of human beings, hurried into a next existence whilst their spirits were stirred with feelings of murder and rapine, that a dead silence of near a minute prevailed in the two boats, the sailors even being awe-struck at the catastrophe.

Adventures of Hans Sterk | 187

The voice of the lieutenant first broke the silence, and it seemed to all a relief to hear a human being speak.

"I will light a lantern, that we may keep together," said the lieutenant, "and to show any poor struggling wretch, who may not have gone to the bottom, that there is help at hand. Keep near us with your boat, Jones, and we'll pull off in ten minutes."

"Ay, ay, sir," was the reply. "There won't be any come up again alive. A sinking ship takes down her crew with her."

Allowing about fifteen minutes for a chance of saving a life, during which time the lieutenant pulled over the spot beneath which the slaver had sunk, he consulted a compass which he had placed in the boat, and taking the rudder, directed the men to arrange themselves at the oars, and to commence their long pull towards Simon's Bay.

"If no wind comes against us," said the officer, "and the sea remains smooth, we shall reach Simon's Bay by steady pulling before to-morrow night: so give way, men, and let's make the most of smooth water."

Chapter Twenty Five
Off in the Boats—The Storm—A fair Wind—A Council—They Steer for Islands—Land

It was soon found that a lantern was not necessary to enable the second boat to follow that in which were the lieutenant and Hans. The singular and beautiful phosphorescent light caused by the dipping of the oars and the passage of the boat through the water was so brilliant, that even the faces of the crew were visible every now and then to each other, whilst a long star-spangled wake trailed behind the boats, and showed long after, where they had passed. To the sailors accustomed to traverse these regions there was nothing new in this sight, though they fully appreciated the advantages of it as a means of keeping a straight course, and of being able to follow the leading boat. To Hans and the Zulus it was a subject of wonder and admiration. The latter in some manner connected it with the burning ship, and seemed to consider that the latter had been the cause of the apparent fire in the water. The attention of the crews of both boats was, however, soon drawn to the brilliancy of the ocean by a shoal of porpoises, which, rushing along near the surface of the water, occasionally rolled half over as they took breath, and again pursued their pathless course.

"We shall have a wind against us before long, I fear," said the lieutenant, "for those porpoises usually go up towards where the wind will blow from."

"Can they feel the wind when in the water, and before it blows?" said Hans.

"I don't know what they feel," replied the lieutenant; "I only know that when they swim in calm weather in any direction, the wind usually comes from that direction in a few hours. Give way, men; we'll near the coast as much as possible before a wind comes, and the current is strongest about ten miles off land."

"What makes this current run down the coast?" inquired Hans. "Water won't run up hill, at least on shore. Is it lower at the Cape than up by Natal?"

"Well I don't know why it is exactly," said the lieutenant; "but it has something to do with the trade winds. As long as I know where the current runs, I am satisfied; I don't trouble myself about why it runs. Here comes a breeze, and right in our teeth. It must not blow too hard, or we shall have some difficulty in keeping our course."

The sea, which had previously been as calm as a pond, soon became broken even with the slight breeze that was blowing. The wind and current being opposed to each other caused the waves to break more than they otherwise would have done, and seen from the small boat, these waves soon began to appear dangerously large. As the breeze gradually increased, it was found too dangerous to force the boat against the seas, and thus she was obliged to change her direction and go with them. Orders were given for the men to nail up some tarpaulin round the stem, and to sit close together, so as to keep out as much as possible any water that might otherwise come in as the seas broke over or near the boats. Men were also told off for baling, and thus every precaution was taken to prevent the boats from being swamped.

If the breeze did not freshen, there seemed every probability of the boats keeping afloat; but as a constant wind would for a time cause the seas to increase, the sailors became very anxious, and began to strain their eyes in all directions for the chance of catching sight of a ship or land. The course in which they were was not far out of that of homeward-bound vessels, or those which might be bound from India to the Cape, and thus there was a fair prospect of being picked up. Still the night was so dark that no vessel without lights could be seen, unless within a stone's throw. Thus daylight was anxiously looked for.

The day at length dawned, and a beautiful fresh morning it was. A breeze which in a ship would have been only sufficient to fill all her sails, was to the small boats too much to be pleasant or safe. Still by the aid of repeated baling, they were kept comparatively free of water. No sign of a vessel, however, appeared, and it approached noon, when the lieutenant, arranging his sextant, prepared to find out where he was. After waiting several minutes, he was at length satisfied that he had obtained the sun's meridian altitude, and having from this deduced the latitude, he announced that the boat was not more than thirty miles from land, though what part of the land she was opposite he could not exactly tell. "My chronometer is not a very trustworthy one, and this knocking about in the boat may have unsettled it; but if it is near right, I fancy we are actually west of the Cape; and this is possible, if the current has been very strong."

During the day the breeze somewhat abated, and by sunset it was again nearly calm. The direction in which he was to steer was now a matter of considerable uncertainty to the lieutenant: whether he should place any trust in his chronometer, or steer according to what he believed his true course. Considering the rough use to which his chronometer had been subjected, he decided that he would steer a westerly course, keeping a little north, so as to make the Cape, and thus reach Simon's Bay.

Soon after the sun had set, a breeze sprung up from the north-east, and this being nearly favourable, a small sail was set on each boat, and they by this aid dashed merrily onwards. For the first few hours of the night the wind was not too strong for the boats to carry a sail, but it afterwards came on to blow so hard that it was no longer possible to do so. The sea, however, was not, even with this breeze, nearly so dangerous as it had been when the wind and current had been opposed to each other; and though it was necessary to keep the boats before the wind, yet both were comparatively dry.

"If this wind lasts," said the lieutenant to Hans, "we shall be carried far past the Cape, and how to regain it I don't know, for we shall have the current dead against us, and we have neither water nor provisions for a long voyage. There is only one cask of water, and the biscuit is, I fear, wet with salt water, so that our provisions are short; but there is no help for us; we must go on as long as this wind and this sea last, and trust to being picked up, though I believe we may be three hundred miles from the Cape."

During the whole of the night the boats kept a westerly course, and before the wind. As morning dawned, the horizon was anxiously scanned in order to find a ship, but the ocean seemed deserted, and mid-day came without any signs of a vessel. The officer again tried to find his latitude, and decided that he was still upwards of twenty miles south of the Cape. From an observation he had made in the morning, he also concluded that, allowing every likely error for the chronometer, he must yet be many degrees west of the Cape, and was drifting rapidly westward. Having come to this conclusion, he signalled for the second boat to come close alongside, when he said—

"Now, my lads, we have drifted so far from the Cape that I fear with these small boats, and such a sea as we may have to meet, we can't reach the Cape before our provisions and water are all done. We have, then, two chances: we may hang about here, and take our chance of being picked up by a vessel, or we can run on with all speed, and try to make some islands which lie out westward. I'm not sure we can get water on those islands, but we may do so, and I believe they have no inhabitants. As this is a question you are all concerned in, I'll hear what you have to say."

The sailors talked among themselves for some minutes, and then Jones, who was in charge of the second boat, said—

"We think, sir, that we should make sail for the islands. We don't lose our chance of sighting a ship by doing so, though it be a bit away from the outward-bound course; but if a gale comes up, we just go down in these cockle-shells, and that's all about it. I have heerd from whalers that there is water in some of them islands, and any way we get a bit of a rest, and with our boats we can go out and look for ships when the weather suits. We think, sir, that's our best chance."

"I am of the same opinion," said the lieutenant. "Has any one else any thing to say?"

"We all think that's our best chance, sir," said several of the men.

"Give way then, my lads," said their officer. "We ought not to be more than two days reaching the islands. We have guns, and so ought to be able to get birds or seals; and if we can only find water, we may get on well."

The north-east wind, which assumes almost the character of a trade wind off the Cape, and which blows sometimes for weeks together, continued steadily for the next two days; and the boats during part of the time being able to carry sail, made rapid progress through the water, so that on the morning of the third day all hands were eagerly on the look out for land.

It was about ten o'clock in the morning that Jones, in the second boat, called the lieutenant's attention to what he thought was land about south-west of them. The telescope being used to discover what this was, revealed the fact of land, which was rather low, and was estimated at not more than ten miles' distance. The boat's course having been altered to enable them to make direct for this land or island, as it was known it must be, the lieutenant called to Jones to bring his boat close, in order to tell him what should be now done.

"I'll take the lead, Jones, and we must have a man standing up in each boat to look out for broken water. I think it will be better to go to the leeward of the island, and land there, unless we can see some kind of a bay. Don't you follow too close, for in case we strike a rock, or are swamped, you must be far enough off not to fall in the same way."

"I've heerd, sir," replied Jones, "that these islands are surrounded by long sea-weeds that make boat navigation rather difficult; but if you know where the channel is, then you are all right, as weeds and rocks don't come near the surface there."

As the boats neared the island, the lieutenant used his telescope in the endeavour to discover if any ships were there, for he believed it possible that whalers might have made use of this island, as afterwards he found had been the case. The wind seemed to have blown itself out towards mid-day, and shortly after it fell quite calm, and as the boats neared the island, the sea had considerably diminished.

Upon reaching within about a mile of the shore, the surface of the sea began to be sprinkled with sea-weed in abundance, which was some of it floating, and other portions evidently growing from the rocks beneath. Advancing slowly and cautiously, the lieutenant directed the man who was steering, and thus threading his way through thick masses of weed, approached sufficiently close to the shore to see where the surf was breaking. Having noted a headland jutting out into the sea, the sailor, from his knowledge of the general form of coasts, concluded that behind this he would very probably find a bay, and such proved to be the case. This bay was covered at the water-line with a white sand, up which the waves washed; but there seemed no sign of rocks near this, and thus it appeared in every way suitable for a landing. Steering the boat carefully round the promontory, the lieutenant made for this beach, and watching his opportunity ran the boat up, so that as the sailors jumped out, and seized her to haul her up, they were high and dry as the waves receded. The second boat, being thus guided, followed the example of the leader, and was also securely beached, the men jumping out, and being rejoiced to stretch their legs once more, after being cramped on board their small boats for so many days.

Chapter Twenty Six
Game found on the Islands—Want of Water—Water at Last—Sea-lions—Fish and Eggs—A Ship—Rescued and Carried to Simon's Bay—The Traveller among the Cockneys

"Carry the boats up high and dry," said the lieutenant; "out with the sails and oars; cover them with the tarpaulin; then get out the water casks and biscuit bag. Let's see what provisions we have."

These orders were rapidly obeyed by the sailors, who never for a moment forgot their discipline, and acted just as though they were on board ship. The water was found to be very low, there being scarcely more than two pints for each man. At this all looked blank, for so essential is water that it is a matter of certain death, at least to a great many, to be without water for many days. Having divided the biscuit into as many portions as there were men, the lieutenant gave each his share, saying, "We shall be able to keep this biscuit for any voyage we may make; for on this island we shall get birds. We can shoot as many birds as we require for food, so be careful of the biscuit." Whilst these arrangements were being made, the Zulus had been wandering along the shore, looking at the ground in various directions, and pointing out to each other something which had attracted their attention. Returning to Hans, who alone understood their language, they said, "*Amasondo m'culu kona*" ("There are large footprints there.")

"Of what?" inquired Hans.

"We don't know," replied the Zulus. "The game lives in the water that makes these footmarks."

Hans, guided by the Zulus, went to the shore where the footprints were visible, and there saw a spoor which to him was quite new. Several footprints of a large animal were to be seen, and near these some circular cuts in the sand, as though an arc of a circle had been traced with an instrument. Though well acquainted with the spoor of all South African animals, yet Hans could not remember any similar to this. The Zulus, however, with a quickness of perception often possessed by semi-wild men, pointed out to Hans that there were only marks of two feet, then that the circular scrapes were marked over these footmarks. One of the Zulus then lay down on the sand, and dragged himself along by his hands only, thus indicating that the creature must progress much in that manner. Still, neither Hans nor the Zulus had ever seen any creature at all like this in South Africa.

Returning to the sailors, Hans asked the lieutenant if he knew of any creature that had only two legs, that was large and heavy, and lived in the sea, but could come on shore.

"Yes, seals, and sea-lions," replied the lieutenant.

"Then they come here," said Hans; "there is spoor of the creatures on the beach."

"Then we are safe for food, and that is something: for we shall not starve as long as seals or sea-lions can be captured or shot. As soon as all is made snug here, we'll examine the island."

In half an hour every item of the stores being safely secured, the lieutenant left three men in charge of the boats and stores, and two others with directions to collect all the dry sea-weed and pieces of wood or reed that they could find. These were to be heaped together to make a fire, for great numbers of birds were seen flying about, this island seeming to be a favourite resort or breeding-place for many sea-birds.

The lieutenant, with Hans and the Zulus, and the remaining men, went in shore to examine all that was to be seen. The island was rocky and barren, and destitute of vegetation. There seemed no stream or rivulet, or fresh water of any description, and no living creatures except birds. The centre of the island was elevated about three hundred feet, and from the top of this a good view, it was expected, might be obtained all around. Ascending to this plateau, the lieutenant and Hans were both occupied in looking round the horizon for some signs of a vessel, and the latter was therefore startled by hearing one of the Zulus in a loud voice exclaim "*Amanzi!*"

"Water!" shouted Hans; "where?"

"There it is," said the Zulu, pointing to a hollow piece of ground which they had passed, and in which there was a large rocky basin about thirty feet across, and in which there was water. A rush was at once made to the place by the whole party. Officer and sailors, Zulus and Hans, were each equally interested. Upon reaching the side of this pool, or reservoir, a clear mass of water some six feet deep was visible; it was evidently the deposit of rain water which had drained from the neighbouring slopes. Stooping over this, Hans reached his hat into the pool, and bringing it up full of water, drank a few mouthfuls, and announced it to be fresh. A loud hurrah from all the sailors answered this statement, and several of the men immediately employed several ingenious methods to obtain a good drink of the fresh water. A temperance advocate would have been delighted, could he have seen these stalwart, hardy men so anxious to obtain merely cold water, yet not one man present would have been willing to exchange this well of fresh water for its quantity in wine or spirits; for every experienced man knows that there is nothing which quells the thirst so effectually as water or tea, the latter being essentially water, merely flavoured by a herb.

"There are very heavy rains here," said Hans, "and this pool is the result of them. We shall not want for water."

"No; we are favoured," said the lieutenant; "for there must be times in the dry season when no water is here. We have sea-weed for fuel, we can get birds and sea-lions for food, and thus we can live for some time. We must then try to get to the Cape."

"Ah! I am afraid that much evil may happen before I can get away from here and regain my people," said Hans. "They must all think me dead, and so I am anxious to return among them as soon as possible."

"Yes, I can fancy that you are," said the officer; "and so am I anxious to get to my ship. We shall have some more work up the coast, I expect, with these slavers, though it does not pay when their ships are burnt. However, we must be satisfied at having reached some land, and found food and water. If we had not obtained water here, we might have dug each other's graves. We will go to that peak and look round, and judge of the size of our island. I should like to go all round it before I return to the boats—so come along."

The whole party ascended the highest peak on the island, from which a view was obtained all round. The island was very small, and appeared alone. It was evidently a volcanic production, and might possibly be of no great age. In many places the birds had congregated in such numbers that they had covered the ground with manure, the thin soil thus produced was merely waiting for some seeds to be brought there by strong-winged birds which had swallowed them in distant regions, and would then drop them in his locality, where, taking root, they would produce the first vegetation.

After scanning the horizon with his telescope, the naval officer examined the shore, which was visible from this peak nearly all round the island. Scarcely had he directed it to one part of the shore nearly on the opposite side of the island to that on which he had landed, than giving the telescope to Hans, he told him to look at the shore and say what he saw. Hans, taking the telescope, directed it at the spot indicated, and immediately exclaimed, "There is *wilde* (game) there. What are they?"

"They are sea-lions," said the lieutenant, "and we can eat them, and can make tents out of their skins. There are scores of them, and we must manage to shoot them."

"Are they very shy?" inquired Hans.

"I think not. They don't know much about men on these islands, I expect, but still we had better stalk them."

"Yes, that must be done, and let no one shoot who is not certain where his bullet will go to at a hundred yards."

"Now shooting these creatures is more in your line than mine, as you are an elephant hunter," said the lieutenant; "so you just arrange the matter, and tell me what to do, and I'll direct the men."

"I don't know any thing of the animal," said Hans, "and each animal ought to be hunted differently, so I cannot give safe advice; but I think we must approach them along shore, for if we go down this way they will smell us."

"That's a thing I should not have thought of, unless you had told me," replied the lieutenant. "Of course if we go to them from windward they will smell us. Very well; we'll go along shore, and what then?"

"We can stalk them then, and I think at eighty yards we ought to be able to kill them at a single shot. Perhaps, too, these creatures don't know what the report of a gun is, and we may reload and refire before they think of escaping."

"We'll try that plan, and so perhaps only two or three of us had better go after them, or the others may be seen. Let us take two men, and leave the others to gather eggs."

Hans and the officer, with two seamen, at once started after the sea-lions, and taking the coast-line found that on the rocks there were plenty of oysters, which were fixed to the solid rock, but could be opened on the spot. Hans was quite at home in this stalking expedition, but found much fault both with the lieutenant and the sailors. The latter, especially, would speak every now and then, and seemed not to understand in the least the signals which Hans made to them. In spite, however, of the clumsy manner in which the sailors and their officer practised stalking, yet the sea-lions were approached to within eighty yards without being alarmed. At this distance the hunters were concealed by some rocks, and Hans now signalled that the four should fire. One of the sailors, however, stopped Hans as he was raising his musket, and whispered—

"Them brutes, sir, can only hop, and not very fast either. Won't it be better to board them, and shoot them at close quarters? I and my mate can't make certain of hitting at this distance?"

Hans, who did not understand every word of this, but comprehended the drift of the speech, replied—

"You and your companion run forward, as soon as I have fired; then you can try your plan, I mine."

This plan being agreed upon, Hans took steady aim at a monster that was lying apparently asleep on the beach, and fired, whilst the lieutenant selected another victim. Upon the report of the gun being heard all the animals raised their heads, and began with a most awkward motion struggling to reach the water. The sailor had been quite correct as regards the speed at which the lions could move, for without difficulty the sailors overtook them long before they reached the water, and each putting the muzzle of his gun close to the head of one of the lions, killed it at a single shot. The monster that Hans had wounded had almost reached the sea, when noting the success of the sailors' method of attack, he ran up to this creature, and discharged his rapidly-loaded gun into its head. Thus three lions were killed, the lieutenant having either missed his aim, or wounded his lion so slightly that the creature easily escaped to the water before he could again discharge his gun.

All the lions that had been shot were very large, and measured nearly fourteen feet in length. Hans, being aware of the skill of the Zulus as skinners of creatures, shouted to these men to come and aid him, and shortly after they, followed by the remainder of the sailors, came down to examine the sea-lions, and aid in carrying back the flesh to the boats. At this work the Kaffirs were quite at home, and bore on their shoulders huge pieces of sea-lion, enough to last any man but a Zulu at least a week. This was borne to the shore, where the boats had been left, and a fire having been lighted by the aid of a flint and steel, the flesh was cooked, and though not probably affording a dish that an epicure would select, yet by hungry men who for several days had eaten nothing but biscuit, the solid food was relished. Having partaken of dinner, as the lieutenant called this meal, he assembled the men round him and said, "We can live here for a long time, as you can see, for we have food and water, and can get tolerable shelter; but none of you would be satisfied to live here long, so we must try all we can to escape. To do this, we must keep a watch from daybreak till dusk upon the top of the hill, and try to catch sight of a vessel coming from the west, because that is the direction from which we may expect them. Then, if we have due notice, we may pull out in the boats, and attract her attention by firing a gun, and so get on board: so that two men must take duty on the hill. This will come round in turn for each of you, as I'll keep the roster. Two men must always remain with the boats, but the others who are not on duty may go about the island; only take care to be all ready in case a ship is signalled. You'd better take the boat-hook and tie a handkerchief to it; the waving of that will be the signal that a ship is in sight."

"There are fish about here, sir. If you'd like, I'll try and catch some," said one of the sailors.

"There are turtle too, sir. I saw one when you were away: he swam past that point."

"Catch as many fish and turtle as you can. We will share every thing whilst we are on shore here, and each man must do his best to procure food for the whole of us," said the lieutenant. "We can get egg; and birds, fish and turtle, and sea-lions, and so shall have a variety of rations."

During the remainder of the day Hans, with the lieutenant, and attended by the two Zulus, roamed about the island. The Zulus had found some pieces of wood on the beach, evidently the spars of some vessel, and having borrowed a knife from one of the sailors, they had cut these into knobbed sticks similar to their knob-kerries. With these they soon exhibited their skill against the birds which swarmed over many parts of the island, and which were so tame that they would allow a man to approach within a few yards of them. The knob stick was thrown at these birds, and in an hour the Zulus had knocked down a dozen or more birds.

As the sun drew near the horizon, the various parties of two or three returned to the meeting-place near the boats, and exhibited their trophies. Two moderate-sized turtle, four rock cod of goodly size, a large sack nearly full of turtles' eggs, about two dozen sea-birds, some of them as large as wild geese, were brought together. There was plenty of dry sea-weed, and this served for fuel, so that the men were busily occupied in cooking their respective prizes, and reckless as sailors generally are, they were now as cheerful and happy as though surrounded by plenty, and able to obtain a supply for all their wants. Immediately after their evening meal, the men selected the most comfortable situations, and were soon fast asleep.

Hans and the lieutenant, however, sat talking for a long time, until they also felt disposed to rest, when they followed the example of the sailors.

The first streaks of dawn awoke the party, and after a meal the lieutenant and Hans walked round the island, and ascended the central peak. Scarcely had they been there many minutes, before the naval officer, who was using his telescope to scan the horizon, exclaimed, "A sail in the west, and a large ship, or I am mistaken. Look, Jones! What do you make her out to be?"

"A full-rigged ship, I think, sir. Shall I hoist the signal?"

"Yes, up with the oar. We must get the boats out at once, and pull hard, or she will pass too far off."

The oar waved on high, with a crimson handkerchief fastened to it, was seen by all the wanderers, who very soon assembled near the boats, and were joined by the lieutenant and Hans. The boats were run down to the water, launched, and manned, and in a few minutes were pulled away from the island, impelled by the fresh and vigorous arms of the sailors, who were now aware that there was some object in pulling. The ship, which had been easily distinguished from the peak on shore, could not be seen from the boat, and this fact was somewhat puzzling to Hans.

"Why is it," he asked, "that the ship cannot be seen from out boat, though it could from the peak of the island? There is no hill to see over."

"It is because the world is round, and we can only look straight forward. I expect that when we are able to see that vessel's sails, she will be nearly twelve miles off from us; so that now she is more than that, but that will enable us to cut her off in her course."

"I never noticed this on shore," said Hans, "though we have large flats there."

"None so level as the ocean," replied the officer: "that alone shows every thing in its beauty. You will not, I expect, ever like your inland life again, after having seen the real sea."

Hans looked astonished at this remark, and hesitated a minute before he replied. He then said, "Do you mean to compare this salt, dull-looking water, over which you creep in a boat, and fear getting drowned every minute, to our beautiful flowery plains or forests amongst which we can ride? Why, you cannot get on a horse here ever."

"And never want to," replied the lieutenant. "I always tumble off when I do; but that's not often. When a man can ride over the waves. I don't see what he wants with a horse on dry land."

"Ah! you don't know what the plains are, that is evident," replied Hans, "or you'd be discontented with the sea."

"There's the ship," said the lieutenant; "she's coming along fast. We must hoist a flag now. A red handkerchief must be our flag. Easy with the oars, men; we've way enough."

The ship came steadily on, and when within about two miles of the boats she lowered her studding sails and made indications of lying to, so that the lieutenant at once knew his boats had been seen. The captain of the ship was standing in the rigging, watching the boats, and on coming within hailing distance inquired where the boats were from. The lieutenant answered him, and pulling alongside was soon with his boat's crew on the deck of the ship, his boats being hauled on board also.

The vessel proved to be an Indiaman bound for Madras, and was a well-appointed vessel in every way. The lieutenant and Hans were immediately given accommodation in the after-part of the vessel, whilst the sailors and Zulus were quartered amongst the crew. The captain of the Indiaman, having heard the account of the lieutenant, was surprised to find the island was so well supplied in various ways, as was the small rock which he had passed so often on his outward-bound voyage, and which he had always looked upon as a mere barren rock. Having no intention of putting into Table Bay, he asked the lieutenant whether, if he altered his course and kept closer in to the land, he would be able to get into False Bay, and hence to Simon's Bay by the aid of his boats.

Knowing how much value these Indian traders set upon their time, the lieutenant at once accepted this proposition; so the captain, steering slightly more northerly, kept a course which would bring him within a few miles of the Cape of Good Hope, at which point, if the weather were favourable, he proposed lowering the lieutenant's boats, and starting him on his short voyage into the bay.

The distance which had taken the boats several days to pass over, was run by the Indiaman in about fifty hours, and when the entrance to False Bay was directly north of them, the boats were lowered, and the lieutenant, with Hans and the crew, were wished a hearty farewell; and being supplied with some provisions in case of need, commenced their few hours' rowing expedition, and shortly pulled round into Simon's Bay, approached a man-of-war there lying at anchor, and having gone alongside, the lieutenant, with the systematic method induced by discipline, went on board and reported his arrival.

No intimation having been received either of the capture of the slaver or of her destruction by fire, the arrival of the lieutenant was a great surprise to the admiral at the station, and Hans, from having been captured by the slavers, soon found himself an object of curiosity and interest. The account which the lieutenant gave of him to the naval officers was so flattering, and the account given of his proceedings on the island and in the boats so much to his credit, that he stood in no need of friends. From the Indiaman he had received presents of various articles of clothes, of which he stood much in need, and having received invitations to dine on shore with various official people who were interested in his adventures, he was additionally supplied with all necessaries by the officers of the ship.

The residents of Cape Town and the vicinity are proverbially hospitable, and many of them being of Dutch extraction, Hans' adventures, and his experience of the Matabili and Zulu warfare, were the very subjects on which they were deeply interested. It is sometimes surprising how little the inhabitants of one part of the world know about the lives and occupations of those in another part, but at the Cape, in former times, it was more singular still to find the residents there knowing little or nothing of the principal events occurring up the country, or if they knew of the general facts, these were in transmission so perverted or distorted as to be very far from the truth when they reached Cape Town; so that Hans, both from his nationality and experiences, was sought as a guest by many of the leading merchants at the Cape.

Having despatched to some friends in the eastern frontier letters which he requested might be sent by the first opportunity to Bernhard and Katrine, Hans had no objection to partake for a time of the hospitality offered to him at the Cape. To him it was an entire novelty to sit down to formal dinners, and to live in the ceremonial manner which it struck him was adopted by the people with whom he now mixed; yet he was not long before he fully appreciated the good things which were set before him. Though Hans was deficient in many of those necessary items of education and refinement which belong to civilised and polite society, yet from his known wild life these were overlooked, and as he warmed with his subject, and described in brief graphic language, either in English or Dutch, the scenes through which he had passed, and gave in detail his adventures in elephant and lion hunting, his hearers forgot that he had used his knife to carry his peas to his mouth, and had seemed unconscious he had so long delayed eating his fish that the table had been kept waiting for him.

Very many of the residents of Cape Town and the neighbourhood were men who had either come to settle there from Holland or England, or had been born at Cape Town, and had never travelled far from it. Thus to these men the wilderness of Africa was as much an unknown land as are the Highlands of Scotland, with their sports, to the London cockney, whose travels have been confined to Richmond, Kew, or Greenwich. As a natural consequence, Hans was often supposed to be inventing tales when he was stating the most sober matters of fact; and not imagining for a moment that his hearers were doubting his veracity, he rarely gave any of those additional details which might have smoothed the difficulties to belief; consequently, amongst many of the fast young gentlemen of the Cape, who had never themselves travelled a hundred miles from the Table Mountain, Hans was termed "the lying Dutchman."

Two months were passed by Hans at Cape Town and its vicinity, when an opportunity occurred for his reaching Algoa Bay by sea, a merchant having a vessel which was about to sail for Port Elizabeth from Table Bay. Some Dutch merchants, having subscribed amongst themselves, offered Hans above one hundred pounds to enable him to purchase horses for his journey from the colony to Natal. This sum Hans accepted as a loan, being unwilling to be a debtor whilst he had the means when he reached Natal of repayment; and bidding good-bye to many kind friends, he set sail from Table Bay on the brief voyage to Algoa Bay, the port of the eastern frontier.

After a fair-weather voyage of eight days, Hans once more set foot on the eastern frontier, and losing no time in this part of the colony, he at once purchased a horse which would do to carry him until he went farther inland, where horse-flesh was cheaper and better; and having at Cape Town purchased a good double-barrelled gun, Hans joined the waggon of a Dutch trader who was bound on an expedition across the Orange river, and was once more leading the life of a South African Boer.

It must often have been a subject of thought and comparison in the mind of a man who has seen both the life of the natural and civilised man, to compare the relative advantages and disadvantages of each. By the natural man, we refer to one who leads a life of nature, who gains his bread by the sweat of his brow in agricultural labours or in hunting, who considers the necessities of life to consist in food and raiment, and in a dwelling which is wind and water tight, and who, possessing these, thirsts for nothing more. The majority of South African Boers lead this life. They by inheritance are possessors of a certain quantity of cattle and horses. These increase in the natural course of events, and if taken care of, the horses especially soon multiply, for a couple of horses may be counted on to produce about two foals in two years: thus in six years the two have increased to eight. About the sixth year the first foals may begin to produce stock, and the increase then becomes doubled. About the eighth year it becomes trebled, and so on. Thus, in a suitable district for horses (and many parts of the Cape colony are admirably suited for them), a boy presented with a mare may ten years afterwards be the owner of upwards of a dozen horses, the produce of this one present, and his cattle having increased in like manner, he may begin to live upon his stock. The time of the youth may then be occupied in cultivating a certain portion of ground, in hunting as a means of supplying food, and in watching his stock; and thus he has but few cares or anxieties, and lives what may fairly be termed a natural life. He is at least twelve hours a day in the open air, and enjoys consequently most robust health.

Let us compare the daily occupations of this man with those of hundreds of thousands of men of similar position as regards a first start in life among civilised nations. A youth is educated, but he must gain his own living, because his predecessors have not been able to do much more than secure the means of living and of educating their children. The youth is found a situation in an office in one of the cities of Europe. In this office it is competition, a race for wealth, and none but the hard worker can hope even to avoid ruin. A youth thus started leads a life probably as follows. He rises early in the morning, hurriedly eats a breakfast, walks down to the train, is carried rapidly to a smoky city, enters an office in which the light of the sun is a rarity, labours in this office amidst a crowd until near the hour of sunset, again enters his train, and amidst the darkness is deposited near his dwelling, where the remaining hours are occupied. Day after day, and year after year, this life is passed, until the man becomes fitted for nothing else, and cares for nothing else, even his recreations often being partaken of as a matter of business. It seems strange to reflect that perhaps on the very spot that is now the scene of such artificial life, our ancestors, before Caesar had 'taught them to clothe their pinked and painted hides,' may have enjoyed the greatest freedom, may have hurled their darts at the bounding stag, or transfixed the passing salmon, and each day may have enjoyed sport and feasted upon their game in a manner which few of these day-labourers are able to do.

Here, however, is the singular comparison of lives of the two divisions of mankind, and Hans having for a time seen the civilised man's life, and having partaken in a measure of this, could not, now that he was once more free, imagine how any man could endure the life which he had seen many pursue in their offices or on board their ships. The life of the sailor he considered strange and unnatural, but that of the clerk he could not comprehend. Long and patiently he thought over what he had seen during his visit to Cape Town, for that locality was to him the most advanced civilisation he had seen; but he could come to no other conclusion than that a mistake had been made by those who selected this life. A conversation which took place on this subject between Victor and Hans some time after his return to his own people may well explain his view of the subject, and though anticipating the future slightly, we will venture to insert it here.

"What is Cape Town like?" inquired Victor. "Is it much bigger than Graham's Town?"

"Yes, much bigger. There are many houses, and these are large, whilst the shops are supplied with every thing."

"Do the people there want much more, then, than we do in the country, that the shops are so well supplied?"

"Yes, Victor, that is so. We here are accounted rich if we have plenty of horses and cattle, a waggon, or perhaps two, two good guns, a house that keeps out the rain, and just clothes enough to change about. It is not so in the great towns. Your house must be very large. A man is poor who is not able to eat his breakfast in one room, his dinner in a second, and to drink his tea in a third. You may not sit in a room whilst your servant places the dinner plates on a table: that would show you were poor. You must not eat your dinner either in the same clothes that you would wear at breakfast: that would show you were a poor fellow. There are regular clothes for eating dinner in; and, Victor, the young frauleins come to their dinner with scarcely any clothes on."

"Is this true, Hans?"

"It is, Victor. We turn up our sleeves when we skin an eland, and we take off our coats and turn down our collars when we are too hot. The frauleins in the towns turn down their dresses far lower than we do, and their sleeves are turned up higher than we turn ours."

"Cess, this is strange. And you saw all this, Hans?"

"I did, Victor, and much more."

"What more did you see, Hans?"

"I will tell you. I saw a Roebargie officer come into a room where there were many of these frauleins. He had never seen one of them before, but looking at one, he asked a man near to take him to her. He went up, Victor, bent his head very slowly, then—I tell you truth—he seized the fraulein round the waist, and as some music played he ran round the room with her, twisting round and round like a wounded pouw."

"That, I have heard, the folks do in the towns. The Hottentots, too, are fond of it, though they don't run about in the same manner. But what do the men during the day? Is there much game about there?"

"This, Victor, is the strangest thing of all. The men pass all their lives in the stores or in the shops, or they just walk about the town, or go in parties to ride out and ride home again. There is no game at all there, or so little that no one goes after it.

"Then, Hans, I will tell you what it is. The Mensch have no means of proving themselves men by riding and shooting, or training their oxen and horses, or even spooring, as we have here. We can make a mark on a man, and we know him by his deeds. We know you, Hans; you are a safe man to stand near one when a wounded lion is preparing to make his spring. You can be trusted to stop an elephant in his charge, and you can tell at a glance a buffalo's spoor from an ox's. In the towns they can't do this, and so they amuse themselves with these trifles. And do they not try to exceed each other in their clothes, Hans?"

"Yes, they do; and by this means they show how much money they have."

"You are not sorry to come back to the country again, Hans?"

"No, Victor, I am not. The town men, I knew, laughed at me because my clothes were not like theirs. I should like to see some of these spoc-karls (The Boers are fond of terming a man whom they consider a dandy a spoc-karl.) on wilde paard, hunting an angry bull elephant. I think we should laugh then."

"Yes, Hans; and they laughed at you because you were not clever at what is not a manly business, and we should laugh at them because they could not do what it requires a man with a head, heart, and hand to succeed in. I don't think we shall ever want to live in a town."

Chapter Twenty Seven
Hans tires of the Towns—Reaches the Wilderness—Adventures with Wild Beasts—Meets his old Companions, and starts for his old Haunts

To a man with the habits and training of Hans Sterk, the journey from the eastern frontier to the locality north-west of Natal Bay, in which his friends were residing, was merely a pleasant trip. He had to pass over many hundred miles of wild country, in which were savage men and beasts, the former of which would not hesitate, should the opportunity occur, to slay a solitary traveller for the sake of his gun or clothes, whilst the latter would consider a white man a very good meal for dinner or supper.

As Hans intended to pursue his journey alone, should no other means present themselves, he trusted that his knowledge of the habits of wild beasts, and his weapon, which he well knew how to use, would enable him to defend himself against any number of these enemies. He also hoped that he should be able to gain from his countrymen such information as would enable him to judge where and when he must travel in order to avoid any enemies who might endanger his safe transit across the country.

Thus Hans without hesitation left the last lager of the farmers near the Orange river, and with no other guide than an old waggon-track, and the knowledge that he must ride in a north-easterly direction, he started for the pass in the Draakensberg mountains by which he should be able to reach his friends near the Bushman's river. Having exchanged the horse which had carried him from Port Elizabeth for another well suited to carry pack-saddles, and having bought a hardy, well-trained, shooting horse, Hans was amply provided for a week's ride. The country through which he intended riding was well supplied with game; there was water in abundance; and thus to the hunter supplied with ammunition there was all that might be needed to be obtained on the journey.

During two days Hans rode steadily onwards, passing principally over plains where ostriches scoured away on seeing him. Herds of gnus and bontebok bounded over the plains, and many solitary antelopes started from their lairs as he approached them. As these old familiar sights once more greeted him, Hans felt a sensation of freedom which he had in vain sought for since his capture by the slavers. As he looked around at the free, open, untrodden country, and saw the creatures on it, he went back in memory to Cape Town and the life led there, and he could not help being thankful that he had been to that town, in order that now he might more fully appreciate his free life. Having brought with him some cooked meat and biscuit, he had no need of shooting in order to supply himself with food; and thus on the third evening of his ride he stopped near a narrow ravine where a clear stream ran over the rocks, and where there were several fine trees, underneath which broken branches were scattered in abundance, and where there was consequently plenty of fuel for fire. Having knee-haltered his horses, so that they could not stray far, Hans started with his gun to examine the edge of a vlei or marsh into which the little stream flowed, and where Hans believed he might find some game.

Having reached the edge of this vlei, Hans commenced examining the ground to look for spoor, as by that means he could tell what creatures he might probably find there. The first footprint that attracted his attention was that of a buffalo, which from the size of the hoof and the wide-spread toes he concluded was a very old bull. This buffalo, from the freshness of the spoor, was evidently in the reeds not far from him. Being a thorough sportsman, Hans was not one who shot for the mere object of killing. He, on the present occasion, wished to obtain fresh meat, and a small buck was what he wanted, an old bull buffalo being rather too tough. As Hans decided to seek for some other game, he noticed a movement in the reeds about fifty yards from him, and there saw the bull buffalo stalk slowly out, raise its head as it scented danger, and then trot slowly away in the opposite direction. From curiosity Hans stood watching this noble-looking brute as it moved apparently unwillingly away from a danger which it would have readily encountered. Having reached a covert about two hundred yards from where Hans stood watching it, the creature entered this, crushing the long canes as though they were nothing stronger than grass, and expecting there to obtain a sanctuary. As far as Hans was concerned the buffalo was safe; but his attention was soon drawn to an object which, scarcely visible above the long grass, seemed rapidly advancing to the reeds in which the buffalo had retreated. At first Hans supposed this to be a buck, but a glance which he obtained as the animal bounded over a tangled mass of reeds showed him it was a full-sized lion. The defenceless state of his horses at once occurred to Hans, whose first thought was to return to them; but being convinced that the lion was in pursuit of the buffalo, he determined to wait in order to see the result of the combat. The buffalo was evidently aware of some danger, for it did not rest amongst the thick canes, but slowly stalked out on the opposite side, thus giving to Hans a good view of itself. The lion soon followed, and as the buffalo turned about and sniffed the air, the lion with a rapid bound sprang on the buffalo's shoulder, and endeavoured to drag it to the ground. The great height and giant strength of the buffalo prevented the lion from at once succeeding, and with a bound and a shake it shook off its foe. In an instant, however, the lion with a savage roar was again on its prey, which with its claws and teeth it tore fearfully.

Hans, who had been an idle spectator of this combat, almost regretted he had not done something to prevent the lion from killing the buffalo, but it was too late now to save the animal. The sight, too, was one which Hans had never before witnessed. He had often found the remains of creatures that lions had killed and partly eaten; he had also seen a lion kill a zebra, but that was an almost instantaneous event. To see somewhat of a combat between a lion and a buffalo in their native desert, the one the most powerful among the carnivora, the other the most formidable among the bovine species, was a scene to be remembered.

"What would they say to this in Cape Town?" thought Hans, as he saw the buffalo, after dragging the lion some distance, and vainly striving to cast him off, sink to the ground, and shortly after lie quietly down, as though merely fatigued by a day's journey.

Since his arrival in the eastern frontier, Hans had enjoyed no real sport. To a man who has tasted the excitement of large game shooting, the sport to be obtained from merely shooting birds or small buck is scarcely worthy of the name. As the whist player who has been accustomed to play for a high stake scarcely feels any interest in a game on which a postage stamp only may depend, so the South African hunter does not deem it sport unless there is some risk encountered or skill required in slaying his game.

When Hans saw the buffalo killed by the lion, his old instinct came to him; and though he was alone in the desert, and had no object in running a risk, still the idea at once occurred to him of showing the lion that man was its master. Thus he determined on a no less daring feat than to approach the buffalo, and select from it a choice piece of meat for dinner.

Having made up his mind to this proceeding, Hans walked round a portion of the marsh, and then approached the buffalo, which was by this time quite dead. The lion saw Hans when about eighty yards from him, and the brute seemed quite astonished at the sight. Standing erect on the buffalo, it stared at Hans, its blood-stained paws giving it a most formidable aspect. As the animal saw Hans steadily advancing, it gave a savage warning growl; but finding that this seemed to have no effect, it then appeared much puzzled, and as Hans came steadily on, the lion turned and trotted slowly away from its freshly-slaughtered prey. Hans, having taken about four or five pounds of meat, and a great portion of the tongue, walked quietly back again, giving every attention to the lion, which had trotted about two hundred yards off, and was sitting on its haunches, watching the cool proceeding of the two-legged creature that had thus presumed to rob it. When Hans found himself at a sufficient distance from the lion to know he was safe from a charge, he turned round, and was about proceeding towards his horses, when a strange-looking object amongst the reeds attracted his attention. He had not been able to see what this was, as the object sank down among the reeds just as he turned, but it seemed to Hans like a human figure. Bringing his gun to the shoulder, Hans advanced rapidly towards the spot, in order to discover what the object was, when, to his surprise, up started three figures from among the grass, and one shouted, "That is Hans; no other man would rob a lion of his supper."

Hans lowered his gun at this remark, and, to his surprise and delight, saw that his old companions, Victor and Bernhard, were two of the figures, and Hotman, a farmer, the third.

Hans ran to his friends, who welcomed him like brothers, and to his inquiry as to how they happened to be there, they replied that they heard he was coming up the country, and so they expected him by the old waggon-track; thus they had come that way with their waggons to shoot ostriches and other game: that they had outspanned about two miles off, and were walking round to look for game before the sun set, when they saw a man standing near the vlei. Believing this might possibly be Hans, they had determined to try to stalk him. When, however, they saw that he was going single-handed at the lion, they came on quickly, and were not far behind him when the lion retreated. Whilst he was watching the lion, and cutting off the meat from the buffalo, the three hunters managed to get near him, and to conceal themselves amongst the reeds.

"We will lead the horses to the waggons, Hans. You will come there at once," said Bernhard. "All the Mensch will be glad to see you on your return. We all thought you must be dead. You must tell us all about your adventures after you shot the elephant; for we found your spoor, and came to that, though too late to rescue you."

That evening was pleasantly passed at the waggons. Hans informed his friends of all the adventures he had gone through, and of the strange scenes he had encountered, and his account was listened to with great interest. "And now, Victor, tell me the news."

"All the Mensch are well," replied Victor, "and Katrine is getting well now she knows you are alive. When she heard from us that you were lost, and were probably dead, we thought at first that it would have killed her, and she was like a body with no life in it. When your letters came, we thought you would soon come too, but then we heard you might stop in Cape Town some time."

"Did you know who had taken me?" inquired Hans.

"No; we could not find any spoor after the first day, because of the rain that had fallen; but having stopped a week near where your elephant lay, and having gone out each day in various directions firing our guns, we were compelled to believe that you must have been carried right away. We were very sad, Hans, when we were obliged to return without you; but when a month passed, and we heard nothing of you, we felt sure you must be dead. All you possess is safe, though; it has been kept for you, and it is as you left it."

"And has there been peace in the land?"

"Yes, all has been peace. Panda has kept faith with us, and will do so, I believe. We have thus been able to sow corn, and the English soldiers have left us in possession of our country; and so we shall have peace in the district, and can govern ourselves as we wish to do."

"That is good news, indeed," said Hans; "and now I am only anxious to get to the Natal district and settle down."

We must here close the history of our hero, though he afterwards passed through many adventures, and encountered dangers of various kinds. Natal was not yielded to the Dutch Boers, but was claimed by the British Government, and is even now any thing but a region of entire peace.

That portion of the history of the Dutch emigrants which we have here referred to is probably one of the most extraordinary on record, and it needs neither exaggeration nor high colouring to endow it with interest to those who study the great movements which sometimes influence society, or the singular legislation which may convert friends into foes.

The fruitful and prosperous district of Natal had for years remained unnoticed, until the Dutch emigrants rendered it famous by their battles with the Zulus. Thus England has eventually derived an advantage from those proceedings which drove away above two thousand of her colonists; and now the emigrant who desires a crop with but little trouble, a lovely climate free from disease, and a country well watered and fertile, may find these near where Hans Sterk selected his farm, and where Katrine became his bride.

Appendix

The Dutch Boer of South Africa.

The term "Boer," which in English is used to describe a man who is rough, uneducated, and illiterate, means in the Dutch language merely a farmer, or a man who gains his living by rural pursuits. It is not uncommon to hear the Boers speak of their companions as "*Mensch*" (men), a distinction which they employ especially when referring to the disputes or battles which have taken place between the English "*Roe-barges*" (red coats) and themselves.

The Boers may be divided into two classes, viz. the "Field Boer," and the "Town Boer."

The Field Boer is a man who usually resides on his farm, and breeds cattle, horses, or sheep. He is generally the owner of two or three "*spans*" of oxen, as the teams are named, of two or three waggons, and several horses for his own riding, which he is at all times ready to sell, if a chance offers. He passes his time principally in looking after his farm, but the amount of ground that he cultivates is usually very small, an acre or two being about the utmost. To hunt and shoot are the great delight of the Field Boer, and he is very expert, both in following game by their tracks, and in knowing where, even in a strange country, are the most likely spots for various kinds of game.

"I think we shall here a rietbok find," a Dutchman would remark as he rode along the side of a marshy piece of ground covered with long grass and reeds; or "Here—so look for a duikerbok," as he rides amongst a number of large loose stones near which are low thorny bushes and grass.

The Boer is commonly a large, heavy man, and disposed to become very fleshy as he advances in years. This latter characteristic probably arises from the fact that he eats very largely at his meals, and is disinclined to take walking exercise. Riding becomes to him a sort of second nature, and a man who is found walking from one place to another is considered at once to be either eccentric or very poor.

From some reason the Field Boer is rather disposed to look down upon the sporting prowess of Englishmen, but he not unusually finds himself beaten in a competition with those very men whose inefficiency he considered to be a certainty.

Within quite modern times there have been two wars between the Boers and the English; viz. when the Boers attacked the English troops in the Natal district, in 1842; and again in 1848, when the English, under Sir Harry Smith, attacked and defeated the confederate Boers at the battle of the Berea. In both these encounters the Dutchmen showed an entire inability to withstand the attacks of disciplined troops, but at the same time displayed much skill in the use of their weapons, in selecting such stations that they might be protected from the enemy's fire whilst he was exposed to theirs, and in retreating so rapidly that they escaped the usual results of a defeat As a companion in the field, the Boer, although coarse and vulgar, is still an amusing companion, and a good instructor in hunting-craft. It is from him that you may learn the habits and peculiarities of the many rare animals which inhabit South Africa. The footprints of the various creatures, the localities where they may be found at different times of the year, the best method of pursuing them, the means to adopt when encountering dangerous animals, and, lastly, the adventures, successes, and escapes that have occurred either to him or to his immediate friends, form the main subjects of his conversation; at least, after he has gained from you a full account of the height and breadth of your father and grandfather, mother and grandmother, sisters, brothers, and friends, and received also a short account of the sporting capabilities of your male relatives.

The Town Boer is usually a trader, and keeps a sort of general store, selling every thing, from a yard of linen to a pound of gunpowder, and a patent cure-every-thing pill.

The Hottentot.

The Hottentot has possessed certain peculiar characteristics ever since he was first discovered by Europeans. He is dirty, idle, drunken, and hardy. His idea of luxury is to dance to the music of a fiddle, whilst unlimited brandy is being imbibed.

The Hottentot is a small, ugly, yellow man, with very high cheek-bones, small eyes, and large pouting lips. His dress usually consists of yellow leather trousers termed crackers, skin-shoes, a ragged jacket, and a large felt hat, in which are ostrich feathers.

The Hottentots are usually waggon-drivers, grooms, domestic servants, or aids in hunting. In this latter position they excel almost all other men. They are hardy and quick-sighted, daring riders, and very fair shots, and thus are useful to the white hunter.

They can eat at one meal as much as would satisfy three hungry Englishmen, and they can go without food longer than most men. They are generous to their friends, and it is rare indeed for "Totty" to refuse to share his all with a friend.

Between the Totty and the Kaffir a deadly hatred exists, the former seeming to have a natural love for hunting the latter.

The Amakosa Kaffir.

The general term Kaffir is used for many of the tribes bordering on the colony of the Cape. These differ only in minute respects one from the other, though their connexion with the English history of the Cape is very different. The Amakosa Kaffirs are those who inhabit the district to the eastward of the Cape colony, and it is with these tribes that we have very frequently been at war.

The men of the Amakosa are fine, active, and well-made, standing not unusually six feet in height. Their clothing consists of a blanket, which is discarded when a long journey is undertaken and it is not necessary to sleep out at night. Their weapon is the light assagy, termed by them "Umkonto." This spear can be thrown to the distance of seventy or eighty yards, and it will have sufficient force to penetrate through a man's body. Lately the Kaffirs have found that an assagy is no match for a gun, and thus they have procured large numbers of guns.

The Kaffirs are very fond of horses, and many of our disputes with these tribes arose from their love of stealing both horses and cattle.

Like most of the African tribes, the Kaffirs build wicker-work huts, and thatch these with the long Tambookie grass, arrange the huts in a circle, and thus form a village, or what we term a kraal.

The Zulu tribe are those Kaffirs who inhabit the country east of Natal. They are, as a rule, shorter and stouter than the Amakosa, though they differ but slightly from them in most particulars. They use a stabbing assagy instead of the light throwing spear of the Amakosa, and are consequently in war more disposed to fight at close quarters than are the Amakosa. The English have never yet been at war with the Zulus, but before our occupation of Natal the Dutch emigrants had several encounters, the events connected with which have been detailed in the preceding pages.

The Matabili are a tribe of Kaffirs in the interior, nearly due north of Natal. They are a branch of the Zulu nation, and occupy the country situated in about 26 degrees south latitude, and about 29 degrees east longitude.

The Bushmen may be called the gipsies of Africa. They are usually wanderers, travelling from place to place according as the game travels. They are small men, but immensely hardy and strong, arrant thieves, and almost untamable. They usually live in caves among the rocks, or build rough huts in the bush. They are the only inhabitants of South Africa who use the bow and arrow, and these men poison their arrows with so deadly a composition as to produce certain death in the creature struck by an arrow.